Abendau's Legacy

The Inheritance Trilogy

Book Three

This book is a work of fiction. The characters, incidents, and dialog are products of the author's imagination, and any resemblance to actual events or persons, living or dead, is coincidental.

Copyright © 2016 Jo Zebedee

Edited by Teresa Edgerton

www.teresaedgertoneditor.com

Copy-edited by Sam Primeau

Cover Art by Gary Compton

ACKNOWLEDGEMENTS

This is the end of an era for me. My first imaginary world finishing and my first trilogy left to go out in the big world alone.

As ever, many thanks are due. My family and friends, who pull me away and keep my life in balance, as well as providing awesome fun. My kids, Becky and Holly, who cope well with being book-orphans, and Chris, my husband, for tolerating me working at weekends, and doing just-one-more-chapter. It occurs to me I should have dedicated one book to each of you, but there's time for that later.

By the time book 3 gets underway there are less beta readers than before - they need to have read the first two books, for a start, and still have time to read on. But three gallantly stuck with it! Huge thanks to Sue Jackson, John J Brady and Em Tett for reading over and beyond the call of duty.

Also, thanks to Teresa Edgerton and Sam Primeau. Teresa's touch in this book (and indeed the trilogy) may not always be visible - as a great editor's shouldn't be - but I know what she shaped and changed and how much better the book is for it. Many, many thanks. And Sam who put up with my multiple spellings of Syllte (in fact, Sam, could you check it here...) and my weird dialect moments, and kept the grammar and continuity on the straight and narrow. Also needing a mention are Gary

Compton and Tickety Boo Press for taking the chance on me as a debut novelist and allowed the world of Abendau to see the light of day. It's been a blast.

Other professionals need a mention. The unsung booksellers, for one. I've been one, I'm married to one, and I know how hard they work and how much their enthusiasm carries the booktrade. To all those who have supported – Easons, Waterstones, Blackwells and the independents who have taken it – many, many thanks. Also, conventions. I'm getting to know that circuit, and thanks to all who've given me a space at a con to talk about books. A big, big call out to Titancon in Belfast who accepted me into their fold and have given the best craic I've had when working, ever (I'd argue whether it is actually work, more of a privilege).

Finally, finally, finally, all the readers and reviewers, those who've contacted me to say you enjoyed the books, those who shared thoughts about what worked and what didn't, and helped me make the story stronger, a huge thank you. Without you, it means nothing.

Jo

Abendau's Legacy

by Jo Zebedee

Once again, for Chris, Becky and Holly. You are just amazing!

CHAPTER ONE

Early morning light filtered through rough-hewn portholes, casting sea-shimmers on the corridor's ceiling. Kare stopped at the entrance to the old Queen's chamber in the Roamer complex and stood, soaking in the warmth of the sun and the sound of waves drumming, ceaseless and rhythmic.

He touched the room's force-field, letting it tingle against his hands and play over his skin. Once, he'd thought it was a security measure – now he understood that the chamber was not just a sleeping-room, but the Roamers' museum of a culture, and the force-field prevented damp air reaching it on days when the sun was clouded and the air cold.

Get on with it. He grimaced, took a deep breath, and pushed his way into the room.

The briny air was replaced by the low musk of incense, burned in honour of the dead. The room remained as it had been when he'd last visited it, on the memorial day for his grandmother, when he'd lit the incense. Memories rushed at him: of the casket containing his grandmother's ashes, due to be released over the great ocean of Syllte; of the Roamers hoping he'd accept the room as his own, the final symbol that he was Karlyn, their King, not Kare Varnon, the cast-out; of Kerra, wide-eyed and excited at her new heritage, and Baelan, surly, standing apart from the crowd.

It had struck him, then, how like him and Karia his children were. The future they presented could have been his own if his father had not succeeded in escaping the Empress. The Empress had taken the boy, as she'd wanted to with Kare. She'd touched his young mind and tried to shape it. How did it feel for Baelan to see Kerra, so loved and secure? He and Karia had been thrust into their crazy childhood together, but had been loved by their erratic father equally. Baelan had never had any recognition of who he was. Kare wanted to give his son the chance to discover himself – and his daughter, too, so shaped by the palace and her constrained future.

He turned in a slow circle, taking in the symbols etched in the stone. Some were the earliest patterns that had come to form the complex decals of the Roamer families, others a lettering he was not familiar with, an interlinking of lines and images that made him feel certain he should understand their message, and frustrated he could not. The shelves were filled with artifacts that he'd taken the time to explore over the past days. A ship's control panel, dulled with age, taken from the first of the Roamer ships; a chart marking Syllte and its star; a book, heavy, its cover inscribed with more of the lost language. Inside, it listed the kings and queens of the Roamers. His father – once heir to the Roamers – was not listed, nor would Kare be, unless he formally accepted their kingship, here in this room.

He didn't want the anger within him, he wanted to let it go and be free. He wanted to accept what was offered on Syllte – the peace of the mesh and the power it offered, his place in a community that stood with him, watching from the mesh, collective breath held.

He zoned the Roamers out. This decision was his alone: he didn't need an audience. He wanted to accept, yes, but to do so would be to put aside their betrayal, not just of himself, but his father and sister, too.

The alcove beside him was thick with dust. He ran his finger through it, leaving a thick line, stopping at a carved wooden box. His breath caught. He hadn't seen one like it since he was seven, when his fingers had been small enough to slip into the carved runs and trace them.

Now his adult fingers didn't fit into the grooves, but ran over the top of them instead.

He lifted the box and popped it open. Inside, nestled on dark velvet, was a clear jewel.

A Seer's prism. His father had chosen to embrace the Empress' prism cell and travel the future, time and again, to find a path to free his children from her. He'd been left unable to Seer again, his mind too fragile, yet one glance at a prism had overcome him. When that had happened, nearly thirty years ago, it had been the true death of his father, his final, shocking moments merely confirmation.

Kare's mouth moistened. He remembered that day with his father, going into his first - and only - vision. He had the power to use the prism. He could discover if the path he'd walked, the path that had cost him and everyone he loved so much, had been the right one. He ran his fingers over the hard glass, tracing its angles. He'd never given in to the temptation to Seer, leaving his horror-filled dreams the only forewarning of the future. But his heritage had never shone before him like this.

He hooked the prism from the box and sat on the edge of the small bed, turning it over and over in his hand. The refracted light merged with the shimmering sea-cast. It would be easy to attach the stone to the thin silver chain hanging from the ceiling, as his ancestors had done, one after the other.

His shoulders tensed but he stayed still and straight, his promise to Karia, made curled with her in their freighter's pilot's seat, stopping him. Their father's screams - screams from Kare's future, ones he'd matched and more - had echoed through the ship. His twin's fear had radiated to him and back, a macabre dance of shifting thoughts.

His promise that night had a shared strength, carried for her and for him. He closed his hand over the prism, stopping the light. He hadn't kept his final promise -

everything hadn't been all right – but he'd kept this one for thirty years; he was damned if he was going to break it now.

A light breeze made him look up. The room was empty, but he could sense the sister who'd haunted his youth. She felt very close to him, and it was right that she did: she should be here, a princess of the Roamers, not a ghost-child left only in his mind. He tightened his hand around the prism, his once broken bones aching, until the cut-glass dug into his palm. Let it hurt; at least it was clean.

Karia's presence faded back to where she should be, leaving only a deep pain, centred on his heart. He ran his hand through his hair, pushing it back from his sweat-beaded forehead. Gods, he'd been right to resist taking this room.

Soft footsteps brought him out of his thoughts. Sonly, standing by the door, gave a hesitant smile. "I was told you were here."

He touched his head. "My posse?"

"Yes." She sat beside him. "Are you all right?"

He nodded. He held the prism tight and took a deep, shuddering breath. The sea-light shimmered, ageless, and he watched until he was calm enough to speak. He didn't need the prism to know his future path; he just needed to find it within himself to take it.

"After I dissolve the empire, I'm going back." Icy sweat broke across his shoulders. "To Abendau."

"You can't." Sonly's voice was thin and scared. "I won't let you."

"We can't live like this," he said. "My mother is in the palace, plotting against us." Sonly went to interrupt, but he held his hand up. "Not just against me and you, but the children. Lichio. She wants all of us."

"We have security. She can't get near us without you sensing her. We're safe."

He gave a tight smile; Sonly didn't believe it any

more than he did, or she wouldn't insist on centering the Free Republic in the relatively secure Ferran system, the great gas giant and satellites straddling the middle and outer zone systems. She was no fool; she knew that if the Empress regained her support in the central star systems, nowhere would be safe for him, her, or anyone they loved. She must know, too, that Syllte wasn't as secure as the Roamers insisted. His mother had a fleet of ships to throw at the planet, if she found it - if she lost some to the storm, she'd absorb it.

"We can only fly using Roamer ships," he said. "We have personal security teams everywhere we go, and outer perimeter teams. That's not what I want for you or the children. I want them to know they won't be taken to Abendau and made to face my mother."

Yet Baelan wanted to return to Abendau - and it was his place to, surely. As ever, things weren't as simple as they should be. The boy could not be sent back. Not yet. Perhaps not ever. A silence stretched, until he drew in a breath. "I need to - for what it's worth - end it."

"Then send an assassin." Her words were quick, almost desperate.

He took her hand. "She'll sense anyone else before they get close." His voice was stronger than he'd imagined it would be. "Sonly, she has taken so many lives. My father, Karia. Silom and Sam; everyone. I can't let her take any more."

The quiet stretched, broken only by the beating sea until, slowly, she nodded. He gripped the prism in his free hand and brought Ealyn and Karia to his mind. When - if - he finished this, it wasn't only for him, but for all of them.

He took a last look around the room. Until his mother was dead and he was free to choose his own path, this room and its legacy could wait. He had to know his decision was for the right reason and not driven by fear, or the need to be different from his mother - a Varnon, not a Pettina. No, more than that – Varnon was another fake name, given to his father for convenience; he needed to know whatever heritage he accepted was his own. The Roamers had cast his father out, they'd left himself and Karia to their fate; he couldn't accept what they asked of him. Not unless he was sure. Until he was, they'd have to wait.

CHAPTER TWO

The grounds of Abendau palace sweated in the hot sun, filling the air with the smell of roses and underlying loam. Shanisa wrinkled her nose. She hated the gardens, with their fake promise of life and growth; without the ice-replenished moat, the garden would die, as nature decreed it should.

Everything about Abendau was a lie. Her child, borne for the tribes, wasn't by her side as promised. He hadn't brought Varnon down and freed the tribes. Instead he'd been taken by Varnon. She couldn't bring herself to think what would happen when he realised Baelan had been created to replace him, right down to his DNA.

She crossed her arms against a sudden chill. Baelan might be his father's son in every measurable way, but he was hers in love. No matter how challenging, he'd been her son, who no one in the tribes wanted to get close to, for fear of his power. She half-smiled; even as a babe, Baelan's needs had to be met before his crib-clothes smouldered.

Later, she'd taught him discipline and patience, even as he'd screamed that it hurt to hold the power inside. She'd held him, comforted him, watched him learn and kept him firm with her love. They had been everything to each other: mother and son; teacher and pupil; playmates when the other children shunned him. Without him she was adrift and unsure of herself. She buried her nose in a flower, inhaling its fragrance, to hide her wet eyes.

"Sister? Are you all right?" Jakina's sand-reared voice, guttural and deep, cut through the still air.

She straightened. Her brother's eyes were hard and

watchful. Beside him, Ralina attempted a smile, but it was wary: since her attempt to leave the palace grounds – just for a few hours in the desert – her brothers had given her little freedom, refusing to allow attendance at the souk, or even to pray alone.

"I love the garden," she said. "Such opulence, so many smells." She walked on. Most days she came to the garden when the palace became too much for her and the walls closed in around her. Jakina and Ralina kept pace, a pair of shadows at her shoulders. She touched the prayer-coin in her pocket. "May I make an offering to our Lady Averrine?"

Ralina's eyes were soft, giving her hope, but Jakina shook his head. "Would you break our family's bond?" he asked. "The shrine is outside the palace."

"You know I will not." She touched her ankshar. Its chain might be thinner than her brothers' ankhars, its stone a quarter the size of their pendants, but it was by far the most valuable. The clutterback pearl was smooth under her fingers, rubbed and rubbed over the last fretful weeks. If she sold her ankshar, the pearl alone would bring enough to purchase a flight off world. But to give up such a precious ankshar, passed through the maternal line from her grandmother, would mean she must leave the tribe, all without knowing which planet Baelan was on, or how to get close to him. She closed her hand over the pearl, and lifted her chin. "Am I a prisoner, then?"

"Of course not," Ralina said, his voice smooth. "Our Lady fears you will be used by our enemies, and wishes only to keep you safe."

Lies. She had heard the whispered conversation between Phelps and Jakina, about how she couldn't be trusted to do the tribes' will in matters regarding Baelan, and how our Lady had asked that she be kept under guard in the palace. Ralina had spoken for her, but only to suggest a little more freedom, not that they could trust her. She glared at him: she was an elder with a child; she should be allowed to go before the tribal council and ask for her release.

She forced a deep breath. No matter how she'd stormed and pleaded, it had done no good. Indeed, Ralina had risked much to gain her access to the gardens.

"Very well, brother. I'd still like to send prayers for my son's safe return." She led the way into the sunken garden where a simple prayer-pond in the centre glittered under the sun. She knelt on the keystone of the surround and took the coin from her pocket, imagining Jakina's eyes watching her, dark and disapproving. He listened closely to the Cult, closer than he should. She zoned his presence out and bowed her head. "Blessed Lady, look after my son. Let him not be harmed, and see he is returned to his people."

She dropped the coin into the water, watching it be consumed by the dark depths, and stayed on her knees, head bowed, her focus on the ancient desert gods – a heresy, should she be discovered. She squeezed her eyes closed: let Baelan not be harmed. Let him come back to Belaudii, where she waited for him.

Soft footsteps sounded behind her. A slow dread crept up her spine, and she hastily buried the focus of her prayers and stumbled to her feet. Her Lady's face was soft, her hair styled so that it framed her face. She embraced Shanisa, her touch filled with such sympathy that it broke Shanisa's resolve, and tears fell. Minutes passed in the sultry heat, the only sound the soft trickle of water, until Shanisa broke away and ducked into a curtsey.

"My Lady," she said. She remembered her disloyal thoughts about her freedom and swallowed past a hard knot of dread in her throat. For that alone, she could be chastised and the Cult were unforgiving of those who doubted, casting them out to be found dead in the alleys of the Old City, where those who heard their screams knew not to intervene. "Forgive me."

"You miss your son." The Empress put her hand out, supporting Shanisa's elbow. Her voice dripped kindness, but behind was the terse steel of command. She leaned her head in, just a little. "The tribes tell me you are more than Baelan's mother. They tell me you are everything to him."

"My Lady, it is true."

"I wish to bring him back to where he is loved and is safe. My son will never give Baelan his proper place. He will use him for his own ends. We need to see Baelan released from such cruelty. Together we can do that." The Empress' touch carried the sense of Baelan, his tightly-wound powers, his pride. "Will you stand with me?"

"I will." Shanisa bowed her head. Resistance seemed alien, in her Lady's presence. "Thank you, my Lady."

***

The tribal family left, following the path back to the palace. The garden was silent, still as a church and fitting for the prayer-pool. Slowly, the Empress walked to it, staring into its depths until she could make out the discs dropped into the water in her name. So many; on a prayer-day this garden was open to the city's honoured.

The woman had been held by thoughts of her son. Their bond was close enough to withstand the distance away. When Baelan was returned, his mother could be the ally needed to tame him. She frowned. A subtle touch would be needed in the woman's mind. Too much, and the tribes would feel violated – never knowing, all this time, how much she had been manipulating their people since she had first been taken in by them; too little, and the woman's strength of feeling to her son would block any suggestion set.

Steady footsteps sounded behind her, and she turned. Phelps ducked his head as he entered through the bower and stood, parade-ready.

"The Roamer planet?" she asked. "You are prepared?" It had not been easy to discover the planet's location from the stolen Roamer children. Their bond with their people – even in those loyal to herself – had proven quite a barrier. To further ascertain the planet's defences – beyond the vaguest descriptions of a gas-storm – had proved impossible.

"Of course." Still arrogant, no matter how she'd reduced him since her release. Still the flare of his nose, the unflinching gaze of his eyes. It was a pity he had betrayed her – once, he had been the only person not to quail from her. Now, he was a shell of what he had been. Ruthless and efficient, yes, but needy, too.

"Flush Kare out, nothing more," she said. Even his name insulted her tongue, the hard syllables so far from the name she would have chosen for her son. "Force him to make his move."

She smiled, relishing the planning. When she'd first built her empire, each move had been planned, a step towards the future, each step another brick for her to command. She had missed that game. She rolled her shoulders, savouring the warmth of the air and the faint promise of day's end. She gave Phelps a quick nod, dismissing him. "Inform me when it is done."

He bowed. Even without her touch, he would obey. He turned, like the broken-in cur he was, and left the garden, leaving her to stare at the dark depths and glittering coins as she planned the next step in the dance towards victory.

CHAPTER THREE

Baelan hunched his legs up to his chest. It wasn't that the beach was cold so much as that everything was damp. When he burrowed his toes into the sand, it lifted in slabs, breaking and furrowing, and that was wrong - sand should be silky and hot, not clumpy and wet.

"Baelan!" Kerra teetered on a rock. Beyond her, Syllte's vast ocean stretched, lined by cliffs and coves like the one they were in.

"What?" he said.

"Come and see. There's a crab."

Big wow. On Belaudii there were lizards the length of his leg, and clutterback spiders that could bring down the lizards in one go.

"Baelan! Quick!"

He got up, brushing clods of sand off his legs. Kerra was all right - well, better than the rest of his father's entourage; he'd better see what she wanted. He crossed the rocks, damp and slimed with green algae, his arms out for balance, and made it to the rock pool. He leaned over, peering through the clear water. "I don't see a crab."

"That's because you took so long." She got into the water, ankle-deep, and prodded at a rock with a piece of driftwood. "It's under there."

"Here, let me try." He grasped the rock, and it came away with a sucking noise. The water clouded and whirled as it filled the empty space.

Something scuttled, making Kerra yelp and jump out of the pool. No wonder: the crab had serious pincers, big enough to take off a toe.

"By my Lady!" Baelan dropped the rock.

"You call her your Lady?" Kerra's look was sharp, shocked.

His face went hot. He'd called the Empress by the tribes' honorific since he'd been old enough to talk; it wasn't something he could switch off, even if a few weeks in her company had been enough to stop him worshipping her forever.

"I..." There was no easy way to explain, not without knowledge of the tribes and their focus on the Empress. "It's a habit." He pointed into the pool, glad of something to take the attention from him. "I didn't know crabs could be so large. It's nearly as big as a clutterback—"

"No, the spiders are bigger." Kerra crouched down. "He's hidden again. He's really good."

"You know about the clutterbacks?" Baelan splashed the water with his fingers, keeping his face down and hidden. He'd been looking forward to going back to Belaudii and showing Kerra the real desert. It surprised him how easy it had been to get to know her and even like her. Perhaps it was because she had powers and knew, at least a little, what it was like. Or maybe it was that she was an outsider, too. Not to her family, but to those who knew what she was destined to become - an Empress, not someone normal. Her life had been shaped by her destiny, just as much as his had. But it felt deeper than that - even when he'd first met her in the palace, he'd understood her fear and need to be safe. So often he picked up how she felt about things without trying. Even with his mother, there had been a distance between them. He could sense her presence, she was so much a part of him, and pick up her feelings, but not like he did with Kerra - as if they were, in some odd way, an extension of his own.

"Yeah. Dad said I had to learn what might hurt me. He got me a tutor - an outcast from the tribes." Her eyes still carried the sharpness from earlier. "Your necklace, do you have to wear it all the time? What about in the bath?"

"It's not a necklace. It's my ankhar." He put his hand on its pendant. He should have worn a different top, one that came up higher and hid it. He dropped the pendant, letting it swing free, astonished at the thought. A tribesman's duty was to wear his ankhar openly. Not to do so would be a betrayal of his mother, who'd chosen the green pendant to match his eyes. A wrench of loss made his stomach twist. His mother, whom he hadn't seen for weeks.

He glanced at his half-sister, half jealous. Outsider or not, she had everything to his nothing: she was the Roamer princess, next in line to inherit the mesh and their father's title, no matter how much she claimed she didn't want to be an Empress.

Baelan couldn't understand that. He'd love to inherit. No one to answer to, no one to obey, just him in Abendau Palace with the tribes forced to follow him. After years of being hidden away, of making excuses for who his father was, it would be fantastic. He'd bring his mother to live with him and help run things.

"Sorry," said Kerra, bringing his attention back to the beach. "I shouldn't have asked. I know the ankhar is special to the tribes."

"It's okay. I can't take it off. I got it the day I stopped being a child, at my naming ceremony."

"What happens then?" Kerra seemed fascinated by the tribes, and it made him feel important, to know things that no one else did.

"I drank nightfire and made an oath, and was given my quest to complete." It was nice to talk about his other life; it reminded him it was real. "If I don't complete my oath, or go against the tribe in any way, I'll be cast out and they'll take my ankhar. I bet your tutor failed in his oath."

"He wouldn't tell me. I tried to probe his thoughts - don't tell Dad, he'd go mad - but they were buried too deep. It was kind of creepy." She narrowed her eyes. "But you're not part of the tribe anymore? I mean, they gave you to the Empress."

"They didn't give me to her. My quest was about her, so I went to...." He stopped himself – he daren't tell her what he'd promised at his ceremony. He poked around the pool, trying to divert attention. "Anything else in there?"

"What was your oath?"

Damn, she was good at reading him: better than anyone he'd met.

"I can't say." He kept his head down, but the Empress' last words came flooding back, the way they'd been doing when he let his guard down. To kill his father. He gulped, trying to push the thought away, but bile rushed up, driven by her hatred. He took a deep breath, and managed to get some sort of control back. "There's a big rule that I can't tell anyone outside of the tribe."

"But I'm your sister, not just anyone."

"Yeah, I know. Even so..." The crab ran and he pointed. "Wow! There he is again." He shivered as a cold wind sprang up, whipping the rock pool into small waves. "Shall we go? My ship will be leaving soon."

"Sure." They clambered over the rocks and walked along the sandy beach away from the water's edge. A cliff rose ahead of them, its face slashed by the long, wide crevice that served as access to the port. Baelan squinted; the crevice might look huge from here, but when you were in one of the ships, streaking across the water, it seemed very, very small.

"Why are we going to Ferran?" he asked. "There haven't been any more attacks."

She bit her lip as if deciding on something, and he found his fists clenching. So much for them being brother and sister and trusting each other. She must have come to the same conclusion, because she gave a small shrug and a smile.

"Dad plans to step down. As Emperor."

Baelan blinked, trying to take that in. His father hadn't spoken to him about any of this, and he should have been told. He was his son, he had a place. He should at least have been asked his opinion.

"Really?" He kept his voice neutral. "Why Ferran?" And what did that mean for the Empress? Would it mean she could seize the title? Surely their father wouldn't be so stupid.

"He plans to centre a new republic there. It straddles the middle zone and outer zone, and its hub is the central meeting-point for intra-systems trade routes." *She* was obviously well versed. "Dad says that the Ferrans must be given their place. Mum's going to be in the governing body, she thinks. Dad says she'll be better at it than him."

Baelan zoned out. *Dad says.* It should be Kerra's nickname. Their father hadn't done anything for Baelan. He hadn't even found his mother. He claimed it was because the Empress had her in the palace, but he had agents, and networks, and he could have looked for her.

Remember your oath as a man.

Baelan gasped; it was as if the Empress was standing beside him. Kerra carried on talking, about what they'd do when they got to Ferran and what her dad had told her about the planet. He tried to focus on what she was saying and not the voice circling inside him.

He stepped through an arched entrance and started to climb the rough-hewn steps that led to the port. Their father wasn't the great hero Kerra made him out to be, but an oppressor who'd kept the tribes impoverished in the desert and launched his fighters against their settlements.

Power leaked from him, and he fought to hold it back, but it was too strong. He had to let it out, the way the Empress had been teaching him. He looked over his shoulder, towards the beach, and focused on the rock-pools until one started to hiss and fizz.

"Are you doing that?" asked Kerra.

He took a breath and found himself calmer, the power contained where it should be. "Yeah." He grinned to make it look like he'd been doing it for a joke. "Cooked crab?"

She looked horrified. "You didn't really."

He shrugged. There was no need to upset her. "No. It was a different rock pool." Although it was impossible to tell from where he was standing.

"Good." She glanced at the beach, almost wistfully. "I wish I had your sort of power."

"But you can heal. Everyone wants to be a healer." And to control the mesh: so far it had resisted every attempt he'd made to merge with it.

"Bor-ing." They'd entered the main port full of Roamer ships, their paint glistening in the lights. She leaned in a little. "Do you know what I'd love?"

"What?"

"To fly." There was a light in her eyes he'd never seen before. "You know our grandfather was Ealyn Varnon?"

"Yeah."

"He was the best Controller ever. How cool is that?"

He paused, not wanting to hurt her feelings, but when your grandmother was an Empress and your father the strongest psycher ever known, being a good pilot wasn't really up there. Her face, though, was eager, her eyes shining. It seemed, for Kerra, it was. She was the same about the mesh, going on and on about how amazing it was. He'd been in it once, and intended never to go back. All those minds, touching him and trying to know him. The thought of that, let alone the tangled circle of power that interfered with his own and fought against it, was enough to set something creeping along his skin.

"Baelan?" Kerra's voice was sharp. "Isn't that cool?"

"Yeah. Really cool."

A hush fell over the cavern. Baelan craned his neck and saw his father entering from the main cavern. Kare nodded to a couple of the Roamers, and wove his way through the ships and maintenance teams, seemingly oblivious to the awe that followed his movements. Baelan wasn't fooled. His father knew *exactly* how people were around him. He loved being the centre of attention, no matter how much he protested otherwise.

He reached Farran, hands spread, apologetic. Another delay before take-off, presumably. As if sensing Baelan's attention, he looked up and their eyes met. Baelan blocked his thoughts, hiding the compulsion that pressed on him, but it was louder than ever: *remember your oath as a man.*

He turned away from his father, and boarded the ship. Better to wait, alone, than allow his anger to build. He hurried down the narrow access-way, his steps echoing on the metal flooring, beating time with his circling thoughts, and into the cabin that had been allocated to him. Small, but functional, with a basic rest-facility provided. He pulled the door shut after him and leaned on it. He couldn't hide forever, he knew that.

He heard footsteps along the corridor, slow and measured, followed by the bang of another cabin's door, and anger surged in him again.

Forever seemed like a good option, all of a sudden.

CHAPTER FOUR

The flight underway, Kare leaned over the holo-projector the Roamers had supplied for his cabin and brought up the holo-map of Belaudii. The data was two days old, but it was in real time, and a credit to Lichio's spy network. He twisted his hand, making the holo rotate, and took in the detail of the planet's defences: too strong with too many fighters and too many soldiers, just as the intel reports had conveyed.

He zoomed in on Abendau's port and palace complex. The gardens were a startling green against the desert, their lushness obscene on such a dry planet. Without her empire, his mother must have a dent in her income – she might find it harder to afford ice for her moat. He half-smiled; Abendau would be a little less polished when he ousted her.

Ships lifted off at intervals on the display. Soldiers gathered at strongpoints along the parapets, taking a commanding view of the city and palace. He chewed his lip, mentally going over the defences, layer by layer. No easy options there, either – although, considering the number of troops, his mother wouldn't have replaced all his garrison yet. The officers, yes, but not the soldiers. That might be to his advantage.

He leaned against the wall, staring at the holo as if inspiration might strike. There had to be some chink in his mother's defences that didn't rely on him being lucky with the garrison personnel. Something the intel team hadn't thought of. Damn, he was supposed to be strategic and see things others missed. Today, no inspiration came knocking.

He needed a way into the palace. Once in, Baelan

was adamant the Empress wouldn't pick up the Roamer powers. Kare glanced at the cabin door, thinking of his son, so self-contained it was difficult to get below the surface. And not untalented at keeping his thoughts to himself. Combined with the boy's reluctance to enter the mesh – the means Kare had put in place to hold him close and know his planning – it was impossible to know what was going on in his head. Yet, the assault on the palace could end up hinging on Baelan's presumptions: he had to know the boy was sure.

He went down the corridor to Baelan's cabin and tapped on the door. There was no answer, so he tapped again, a little harder. "Baelan?"

"What?" The voice was surly.

Charming, as ever. Kare pushed the door open. "Do you mind if I ask something?"

"I'm tired." The boy lay on the narrow bunk, curled up and facing the wall.

Kare took a deep breath. It was no wonder Sonly had chosen to travel with Kerra instead of Baelan; no one wanted to spend time voluntarily with him. The argument about splitting the dynasty was a good one, and long-standing, but he'd never seen anyone select their personnel so quickly. He stepped into the room. "It will only take a minute."

The boy sat up, his face closed and unfriendly, the damnable barrier he carried all the time in place and impenetrable. "Go on, then. You will anyway."

"Thank you." Kare fought to keep his voice steady. "I wanted to ask about the way you sense psychers. What's different about me?"

"I've told you. The powers don't move with you because you take them from somewhere else. Until you pull on them, they aren't there to be sensed." Baelan lay down, arms crossed behind his head, eyes on the ceiling, clearly dismissing Kare. "Now can you go away?"

Don't react; he's the child, not me. It didn't feel that way, though. "So you can't sense me at all?"

"Provided you don't pull on the power." The boy frowned. "But you pull on them without thinking sometimes, and then you can be sensed. Like when you read another's feelings – you do that all the time."

Damn. It would be harder than he'd expected.

"Thank you." He turned to go, but something in the way the boy had closed himself off, as if seeking a place that could be his own, made his throat tighten. He wanted to pull Baelan to his feet and make him better from damage Kare had no knowledge of, nor any idea how to touch.

"You know, you don't have to lock yourself away. I'm not using the lounge. You'd have more room there."

His son lay, silent and tense. Kare shook his head. He couldn't even tell what Baelan was feeling, he was so cagey. He cleared his throat. He had to at least try. He'd taken the boy from the palace. That gave him some responsibility. "Baelan, I'm not my mother." The boy's mouth was pinched and tight. "I know what it's like to be displaced – to be the one person who doesn't fit in." He could see himself in the boy: a different self, the one he'd have been if he'd been left with his mother as a child. It made him not just uncomfortable but determined to find a way past the wall in Baelan. Not for himself – he was old enough to understand his reputation preceded him now, putting barriers in place with anyone he met – but for his son. If he could help, in any way – give something of the support he'd given Kerra, all through her life – he wanted to. "If it helps you to talk, I'm here, and I will listen."

The boy sat up, his eyes flashing anger. "You're not who I want to talk to." The lights flickered.

"Calm down." Kare put his hands out, palms up. The last thing they needed was a burst of the boy's power. Not on a space ship. He tensed, bringing the mesh to the fore, ready to close Baelan down, hoping it wouldn't come to that. "Take a deep breath and let the power up into the mesh."

"For you to use?"

Kare sighed. "For anyone who needs it to use."

Baelan closed his eyes, and the air shimmered into a quiet stasis, but he didn't enter the mesh. After a moment of quiet, Kare said, "Any better?"

Baelan shrugged. "A little."

"How bad is it?" He remembered what it was like to be out of his depth with the power. He remembered days spent at Marine's, with nothing to distract him, and the power fizzing through him – the fear of what it might do, the gnawing knowledge that it wasn't going away.

The boy bit his lip and looked about eight, not the eleven he was about to turn. He looked, for a moment, like he might answer, but gave a sharp shake of his head.

"Have you found my mother yet?" The words were mumbled. The boy knew Abendau, he must know how hard it would be to get accurate information out. "Your agents. You said they'd try to find out about her."

Kare sat on the other end of the bed and rubbed his temples. Honesty: that was the only thing here. Except he'd already been over this with Baelan, and it had made no difference – he didn't believe him.

"We think the Empress has taken your mother into the palace," Kare said, voice soft. "Where I cannot risk any of my people." Not yet, anyway. Not until he was on the planet and able to pull them out of any fire-storm.

"Not for me, anyway."

Not for anyone. Perhaps if the boy understood the wider agenda, it would help. He was many things, but he didn't appear to be stupid. "You know the Empress wants you back?"

"For my power."

"Partly. She wants you if you'll use your power for her."

"And if I don't?"

Kare rubbed his neck, along the ridged, old scar, and his throat tightened in remembered fear. *Oh, son, if you don't....*

"That's why I need to know how the power works." It wasn't even a lie. If he could find Baelan's mother and reunite them, he would. "I want to be able to return you, and for you to be safe on Belaudii." Safe and happy, not used as a pawn to be twisted and changed. "As it stands, if the tribes get you – through your mother, or any other way – they will send you back to the Empress."

"You're a liar! You don't want me to go back." The boy clutched his ankhar and power spiralled from him, so familiar it made Kare's fingers tingle from wanting that pure power, welled within him, not something to be maintained and managed, something that just was.

"Baelan." Calm, he must be calm. "You don't know what I want."

"I don't care what you want. I'm from the tribes and I want back to where I belong. Once they know what the Empress was doing, how she was hurting me, they'll understand I can't return." It was desire over knowledge, a desperate clutching at a dream. Somehow, it gave Kare hope – to have a dream, even a false one, proved Baelan was still fighting for his future. "My mother definitely will, and she's an elder."

An elder who bore a son by a man she hated, to seek revenge; who was so closely linked to the tribe there was nothing she wouldn't do for them. "Baelan..."

"Don't touch me!" Baelan got up, his face contorted and angry, his hands balled into fists.

"Calm dow—"

"Get away from me!"

A light burst, showering glass through the room. Kare raised his hands, feeling the sharp rain covering them, and forced himself to stay calm. "Stop, Baelan."

The boy's control slipped further. "You better not touch me!" His power grew, bound in wires of all-too-familiar hatred.

Kare reeled back, shocked. *His mother?* What had she primed in the boy? Whatever it was, it was consuming him, taking all sense of himself away. Kare had to end this now. He grasped the mesh and met the boy's power, looking to constrain it.

Baelan snatched his ankhar and planted his feet. His power gathered, turning darker, flowing with hatred. "You don't know what it's like to live in the tribes! To always be chased and hated. *You* were the one who sent the troops after us."

"Because the tribes were trying to kill me and mine."

Surely Baelan must know some of what he'd been taught was a lie. The time with the Empress should have proved that, if nothing else. He faced his son - if he didn't already know, it was time he learned. He had a place in the outcome - regardless what happened, Baelan carried his own blood and powers. He'd be a target, just as much as Kerra had always been. To treat him as a child and deny him the truth of that heritage - all of it, not just the Empress' lies - would be a betrayal.

"What would you have had me do?" Kare asked. "Tell the tribes to have the planet? Tell them I'd leave an empire that stretched across the systems, that was holding peace in place for billions of people, because they wanted their planet back?" He opened his hands, wide, imploring Baelan to know the truth of his words. "You think I wanted to stamp down on the tribes? They had so little - the poverty was appalling. You think Sonly wanted to stand over that, with her obsession with helping those in need?"

The boy's mouth fell open, stunned. Had he not seen the poverty? When living with it, finding pride in it as the tribes seemed to do, did it become invisible? Or was it that he was so used to being lied to that the truth hurt?

"Enough!" A line of dark anger came at Kare, focused on him. What was left of the boy's control had broken. Kare flexed the mesh, so his power scythed through Baelan's. The boy sent another blast. Kare struggled to block it, but pushed against his son, focused on closing him down. Baelan squirmed and Kare slammed into him, as hard as he was able. They stood, glaring at each other.

"Had enough?" Kare's voice was forced. Gods, let the answer be yes; he was too old for power-tag. Old and out of practice. The boy wriggled but Kare stood his ground.

Baelan stopped struggling, and the fight left him as suddenly as it had come on. "I've had enough."

Kare let go. "Good. Now what the hell was that ab—"

A wall of hate hit Kare, sending him sprawling across the cabin, into the wall.

"You know nothing about the tribes." The boy moved forwards, eyes wide and bulging. "You take people and make them do what you want. You took me."

He sent another blast, knocking Kare's hasty defence to the side. Kare yelled at the pain in his head. He couldn't think straight, let alone draw on the mesh.

"You pretend I'm the same as Kerra, and I'm not. You can't stand me. Your wife hates me. I want to be back with my tribe, and I will be when I complete my oath."

"Baelan, stop."

The boy lashed out, fast and dangerous - gods, he'd got better - and Kare braced as it hit, knocking the breath from him. Something wrapped around his throat, tightening. He reached up, dragging at his neck, but there was nothing there. His vision darkened and he barely gasped a breath. *Stop.* Nothing came out except a strangled croak. The mesh was there, beyond the blackness. He couldn't grasp it. He looked into his son's eyes; Baelan's oath shone from him, what his tribe had brainwashed him into. Kare tried to speak, to say there was another way, but slumped, clawing at his neck.

"Stop it, you little brat." Farran's voice, from the doorway, took Baelan's attention, giving Kare time to gulp in a breath. He pushed onto his knees: he had to stop Baelan. The Roamer had no hope.

"Enough," Kare croaked. He touched Baelan's mind.

One part of him wanted to smash the child's power away, to teach him a lesson he'd never forget. The rational part of him knew that would be a mistake. Baelan had spent his life being controlled. He'd never been taught to trust himself, or his own judgement. If Kare came along as another authority figure, looking to force him to his will, it would feed what Baelan was holding on to. He focused on the hatred, his touch firm and sure, but not cruel. *It's okay. Let it go, no one is going to hurt you.* Baelan met his gaze.

"Stop now," said Kare.

The darkness fell from Baelan's eyes. His shoulders slumped, and he looked at his hands as if in disbelief. "I... I..."

Farran grabbed his collar, half-choking the lad. "If he can't be controlled, he has to go."

"Leave him." Kare faced the Roamer, daring him to challenge the order. "It's between me and the boy."

Farran shook his head. "He's not safe."

"He won't do it again." Kare raised an eyebrow at the still-shocked Baelan. "Will you?"

Slowly, Baelan shook his head.

"It's not enough," said Farran. "Everyone is at risk from him. His word doesn't give safety."

Farran was right. Kare staggered to his feet. Baelan was tired now, almost slumping – it was now, or never. He'd have preferred never. *Sorry, son.* Kare whipped out, seeking the source of the hatred, knowing Baelan would hate this invasion, that he would see it as another betrayal. But he'd tried talking, and got nowhere. He could defend himself, but if the boy lost control with Sonly? Or Kerra? He couldn't take that chance.

Baelan yelled and tried to block him, but Kare was in too deep, following the pattern of images and thoughts, seeing where they led. He focused on Sonly, on Kerra, on the Roamers themselves, and found nothing but shimmering resentment. He turned his attention to the boy's thoughts about himself, and hit an explosion of hatred.

The Empress *was* at the centre of it, tight around the hatred. Kare pulled out of Baelan's mind and caught his son as he fell forwards.

"Farran, go," Kare said. "You have nothing to worry about from him. None of you do." Except himself. He had a lot to worry about. He'd add it to the list.

Farran still looked uncertain. "I'll be outside." He pointed at Baelan. "Do that once more and you never fly with me again."

The door closed, and for a moment there was silence, broken only by Baelan's breaths. He moved to the bed and lay, gasping, his chest heaving.

"I'm sorry for looking," said Kare. His own head was aching; his hands shaking. "I had to know."

His son shook his head. "You're just like her; taking what you want, even if I don't want you to. She wanted my power, so do you."

"Baelan, I don't want you because of your power." Slowly, Kare unbuttoned his shirt, displaying what he hated about himself. He tracked his finger down the scar that ran the length of his torso, felt where it merged with other scars. "This is what she did to me, and she bore me. If you don't do what she wants, what will she do to you? Why do you think she wants me out of the picture – she knows I'll never be what she wants, and she's moved on to you. What if you don't please her, either?"

Baelan's eyes skittered, taking in the scars.

"I don't want it happening to you. I'm doing my best to stop her forever." Let the boy work out what that might mean: once they were on Ferran, he wouldn't move again without a security team so tight he'd struggle to scratch his own nose. "You have to tell me exactly what she put in your mind, because I need to find a way to break it." He sat next to the boy. "I can work with you to release the compulsion."

"Do you promise?" Need shone from Baelan's eyes, sharp and driven. "Can you do it?"

He couldn't promise that, any more than he'd been able to promise Kerra she could be free of her heritage.

"I don't know." He got up, deliberately taking his time as he walked to the door, his back to Baelan. A bead of sweat ran between his shoulder blades. "But I believe you are strong enough to overcome her."

A soft sound made him turn. Tears were running down Baelan's cheeks, his shoulders shaking. To use a child like this... his mother was a bitch he'd gladly kill.

He crossed to the bed and put his arms around his son. The child might have more power than he knew what to do with, he might be surly and troubled, but he was still a kid who'd been taken from his family and forced to do things he didn't understand. Let the boy cry. Hell, he felt like joining him.

He tightened his hold on his son, and closed his eyes, adding another reason to face his mother before she destroyed Baelan entirely.

CHAPTER FIVE

Lichio looked over at Kerra, and yawned. "What do we do? Eat so much crap we're sick?"

She smirked. As a de-facto childminder, her uncle was terrible. As entertainment, however, he was always good value.

"You're a grown-up," she said. "You're not supposed to swear in front of me, Mum says."

"That's not swearing."

"It is." Although her dad said much worse, when he thought she couldn't hear him.

"When you're a bit older, I'll teach you some others." He reached down and adjusted the strapping on his ankle, the one he'd injured in Abendau. "Anyway, I've never grown up. It's boring."

That sounded good, not growing up. She looked down at her hands and said, "I'd like a place to fix sick animals. When I'm older." She couldn't imagine telling her mum. She'd never understand.

It was a moot point, anyway. Her mum had been sequestered in one of the caverns, surrounded by comms information, since early morning. Kerra was well used to being left to her own devices, but normally she had her things to keep her occupied. A tutor, at the very least, and her own room, with things to do in it. Here, unless she wandered down to the workshops – and her mum had made it clear that she didn't want Kerra getting involved with the Roamers – there was little to do. Even Baelan had left, victim to the iron-bound arrangement of the entire Varnon family never flying on one ship.

"Cool," said Lichio, not remotely fazed. "I wish I'd

done that instead of joining the army."

"Are you still in the army?"

He shrugged. "It depends. If your dad really does end the empire, I'm out of a job." A slight smile crossed his face, a hint of relief. "D'you want a helper? Although I'm not doing any mucking-out; if you're so keen, you can do that."

"Urgh." She giggled, but something niggled at the back of her mind and she stopped laughing. The mesh was throbbing, trying to get her attention, and she wasn't sure what to do. She wasn't allowed to access it on her own. Her dad had been strict about that. She looked at Lichio. "Can you hear anything?"

He cocked his head, listening. The low thunder of the waves, the constant noise of Syllte that she'd already come to love, was present. A roar built over it, the steady whine of a spacecraft coming into the port.

"You're just jumpy after Abend—" A noise, a low pulse, cut across Lichio's words.

"What was that?" she said, heart jolting.

Lichio was already on his feet, only a wince giving away any discomfort. "A ship firing." He opened the door. "Out!" He'd transformed from her easy-going uncle into the military commander he was, and his voice gave no room for disobedience.

She stepped into a corridor full of people – a mix of Roamers and soldiers from Bendau. The caves weren't designed to house so many at once, and they were bunched together in the narrow corridor. Voices came from all around, urging others forwards, calling for their family members. Lichio put his hand on her arm, ushering her ahead of him. She joined the throng, and was pulled along by it, her feet half-lifted from the ground, and she was glad of his steadiness.

A muffled boom expanded as it ripped through the caves. She brought her hands up to her ears. The rock moved under her feet, and people screamed. Something flashed, through one of the portholes, and then again: laser beams, cutting air.

She couldn't tell what sort of ships they were, or how many. There shouldn't have been any – the Roamers had been sure the base was secure. The roaring of ships grew louder as the Roamer fleet emerged from the caverns, firing back, their freighters darting. They should have known nowhere could be safe from her grandmother.

The crowd surged forwards, pulling her with them. Lichio's hand was wrenched away. She looked behind, but couldn't see him. Close-tight bodies carried her with them, frightening her. She managed to break free, muscles cramping as she fought the momentum, and pressed against the wall of the passage. Lichio appeared through the crowd.

"Get to the surface, Kerra," he told her. "Run!"

She got caught up in the crowd again. The smell of fear – sweat mixed with the salt air – shifted around her. Another boom, closer this time, caused a shower of dust to fall from the ceiling. She didn't dare look up.

A glance behind, and she saw that Lichio had fallen back, limping badly. She tried to stop, but the people around her were panicking and strong.

Shouts came from the main corridor ahead, merging with the pulse of lasers. Another explosion thudded, bringing more screams. Dust swirled from disturbed rocks, going up her nose, making it hard to breathe.

"Hurry!" she shouted, over her shoulder. "Run, Lichio!"

He swore. "Get to the main cavern. I'll follow."

An explosion hit to her left, dislodging a chunk of rock. She ducked to the side, pulse racing, and pushed herself against the wall. It missed her by inches. Forwards or back? She couldn't tell – the cracking was all around her.

"Go!" The crisp command got her moving, but the ground shook, nearly knocking her off her feet. A crack widened under her. She screamed and jumped.

"Run!" Lichio drew to a halt on the far side of the crack, his gaze running the length of it. It was too wide, she realised. At another thud, the ceiling rained small pebbles around her. They hit her bare arms, her shoulders, and she yelled out, part-fear, part-pain.

"Woods, get her out!" yelled Lichio. "Take her!"

Running footsteps sounded behind her. Hands grabbed Kerra and pulled her back, into the wider corridor. A jarring impact hit, knocking her off her feet. The corridor she had just left came down in a shower of rocks and dust that rumbled on and on.

She fought to free herself from the hands still holding her. "Lichio!" Her words echoed back. She twisted. She had to see if he was there.

A voice stopped her. "You can't."

She turned to see a female soldier, her face hard and closed. Her dark hair was cut short around her face, and she was dust-stained. She held a gun, cradled against her.

"We have to go," the soldier said.

"I have to look for him," Kerra said. Her voice broke, clogged with dust and tears.

"You can't," said the soldier. She tried to shepherd Kerra into the main cavern. "Come on."

Kerra shook her head. "He might be okay," she said. "He was close to me. He must be trapped, but he's not far back..."

Another shower of rocks fell from the ceiling, hitting off the cavern sides, adding to the rubble that blocked the corridor. It was as if they were mocking her hope.

The soldier led her to where the Roamers were evacuating. Their ships were holding the attack off, allowing others to leave in convoys. Another explosion rocked the base, and a thunderous roar filled the cavern. The last part of the corridor – the part where Lichio had been – caved in.

She bit her lip, holding back tears. The soldier squeezed her arm. She looked sad, as if she understood. Kerra took a last look at the corridor, and turned away, burying her head against the soldier's shoulder.

She stayed like that until she heard the familiar voice of her mother, calling for her. She broke away and ran across the main cavern, throwing herself into her mother's arms. From somewhere she found the strength to say what had happened, and her mother tightened her arms around Kerra, holding her close and safe.

***

Kare gasped. Voices, crying for help, cut through his cabin's quiet. A stabbing pain in his head made him put his hands up. More voices came, the sense of panic, of pain. Of death.

Farran appeared in the doorway, clutching the air-seal so tightly his knuckles were white.

"What's happening?" Kare asked, but his voice was blurred, lost in whatever was happening in his head.

"The caves are under attack." Farran tried to grab Kare as he slid down and scrunched onto his knees, head against the floor. He rocked, as if that would ease the pain. He swallowed against it, focused, and swam through the mesh, seeking the mind he needed. Panic grew, the closer he came, and he couldn't tell if it was his or Kerra's. He bit it down until, at last, he felt her. She was okay. Relief hit, and he brought his head up.

Lichio. The name was through her thoughts. He looked up at Farran, pain shifting as he moved, making him gag against bile.

"It can't be, not Lich," he said. Damn it, not like this, dead in a cavern where he should have been safe.

Kerra's panic filtered up and through him. Not dead, or at least no one knew. He took a moment, gathering his thoughts, seeking through the mesh to ascertain the extent of the attack, and the level of danger his planet still faced.

He could go back – he might be able to do something. But what? He couldn't erase time. The cave had come down. He couldn't undo this past, any more than he had Silom's death. He could only go forwards, for the people he'd already lost. Karia, his father. Silom. Lichio, perhaps. He had to break his mother's empire apart and leave nothing for her to take back, and this was the moment to do it. If he drew back now, she'd have time to consolidate herself in Abendau. He managed to get to his feet, pulling himself up on the bulkhead.

"Take us into the Ferran system, Farran," he said. The Roamer looked like he might argue, but Kare held his hand up. "What can we do if we go back? Syllte is a day's flight away – whatever has happened won't change." He sounded as callous as he felt, but this was a strategic decision. Someone had to take it. "Tell the Roamers to get Sonly and Kerra off planet. They can rendezvous with us at the hub." He rubbed a hand over his forehead. "Lichio, too." His throat closed, and he had to force the words out: "If they can find him."

CHAPTER SIX

Kare wiped his hands on his trouser seams, using the rough material to ground his thoughts and settle his nerves. A row of medals, pinned on his uniform jacket, jingled, and he fought not to straighten them. He had discarded any of the ceremonial sort, selecting only those earned in combat to give a message of authority. That was the difference between him and his mother – he was a military officer, who'd fought for his empire. His soldiers – soldiers he'd known – had died to take it. Let the families take the meaning from his uniform, let them see the message within it.

He stared ahead, bringing to the fore the Kare of the last decade. The one who looked forwards, not back, who'd endured meeting after meeting, dignitary after dignitary, to get to this point. The one who could put thoughts of Lichio out of his mind for the next few hours, if he had to: who'd learned to compartmentalise for the sake of what was left of his sanity.

The double doors opened, and he walked into the meeting room allocated by the Ferrans. It was as grand as expected – everything about the expanded hub had been designed to impress, although he preferred the older sections, constructed during constant attacks from the Empress. He liked the scarred walls and the bays that had clearly been added as need arose and not designed in a corporate office for a system finally granted the independent status it had fought so hard for, and lost so many of its people to. Rjala's home, the satellite Ferran-V had suffered particularly ferociously, its people wiped out in a devastating attack by the Empress, the survivors left to fend for themselves in the lethal fire forests.

He'd given the Ferrans their status. He'd lifted the middle zone out of servitude to the central planets. He'd given the planetary governments autonomy for their own budgets and had funded development. It had stretched even the funds of his vast empire, had been a gamble he'd faced down the families about more than once. It had been worth it - this austere, impressive room was part of his legacy. Already, the families were seeing the benefits of some of his policies - a richer middle zone was feeding money back to their central planets. It was, he supposed, appropriately ironic that he disliked it as much as any of the other trappings of power he'd inherited or built, but it still gave him a sense of pride, to know when - if: it still had to be ratified - he stepped away from his role, he'd left something to be built upon.

The delegates came to their feet. His guards kept pace with him, their own medals catching the high-ceilinged lighting: veterans of many campaigns, they'd earned their right to be here today.

He drew to a halt at the top of the table and indicated for the delegates to sit. Rilal Balandt, on his right, was first to drop into his seat. He drew his folder to him, long fingers sifting through its contents. Eva Tortdeniel sat beside him, Borlon Al-Halad another seat down, almost outshining her in his crimson formal uniform.

Kare gave a cool nod to the Menl-iar ambassador, who had the grace to look away. His family would be repaying his comms-call with Lichio, to whom he'd denied desperately needed support, for some time.

A needle of pain made his breath catch. Lichio had fought for his empire on Belaudii. He'd held the planet long enough to beat some sort of retreat, not surrender. He'd been beside Kare since he was seventeen, seeing things no one else did, offering a support that couldn't be replaced.

Later. That was for later. Kare took in the final delegate at the table, and smiled. Dimara Clorinda, the thin-stranded gold chain woven through her plaited hair glittering as if a crown. Not the family head, but a senior daughter. The message was clear: the Clorindas would support Kare, if his terms were right. Enough seniority, but deniability too. He inclined his head to her, and she did back, the cool Clorinda eyes - a colour like no other, almost amber - regarding him. For all they were snakes, he had a respect for Clorinda. They held their position at a level with the Peirets, above the other families but in thrall to the Pettina, and were not to be underestimated. They were as much sharks as any other around the table, but they were no fans of the Empress; if he could present a viable alternative, they'd go with him.

He pulled his own folder to him. Would the families see it as viable? He hoped so, but was experienced enough to know that pleasing each of them in one document was nigh-on impossible.

"I assume you have read the contents?" he said. A general murmur of assent went around the table. He flicked open the folder to its first page. "Good, then I'll open the table to discussion."

***

Kerra waited on the beach with the other survivors. The battle was over, and it had been deemed safer outside than in the caves, at least until they'd been surveyed. She shivered in the clammy air, her eyes fixed on the exit to the cavern. Survivors had been emerging over the past hour or two, first in crowds, then a trickle, many dazed and wounded.

Now, those emerging were being helped by others. Medics triaged them, racing from those able to plead for attention to the almost dead. She'd offered her help but had been waved away, treated as a child and not the healer she was. More must be lost inside - the mesh had been clamouring with Roamers seeking each other.

In the centre of it, her father's presence remained, distant and closed off. She understood why – he had work to do and needed to concentrate. But the Roamers needed him. She wanted to reach out to him, but didn't dare, recognising the coldness in him – at the moment, he was being the Emperor.

"Kerra!" Her mother's voice floated towards her, and Kerra got up. It was only her mother, though, no Lichio beside her, and the emptiness that swept through her made her breathing catch.

"They're going to try to free him," said Mum. She led Kerra back to the caverns, pushing past a Roamer who tried to challenge them, her palm raised as if she were silencing voices in the Senate.

"As far as the cordon and no further," said her mother. "I told them I wanted you here, in case—"

Kerra nodded. In case there was any hope. She went as close as she could to the line of Roamers blocking entry to the caves. Beyond the main cavern, the corridor she'd escaped along was filled to the ceiling with rockfall. She couldn't see how anyone could have survived. She found herself reaching for her mum, taking her hand and clenching her own around it.

A group of Roamers approached the corridor. One pointed at the ceiling, gesticulating with her hands, and another nodded. A joist was brought from one of the ship-building workshops and wedged into place, supporting the ceiling. Carefully, on the opposite side of the corridor, the group began to shift the rocks.

It was slow going. Dust filtered into the main cavern, making Kerra cough, and her eyes smart. She leaned forwards, watching, willing the rescuers on. At last, they'd made a narrow gap through the fall, and one scrambled in, taking a light passed by another. He emerged a few seconds later, and the squad worked with more energy, the surveyor glancing between them, the joist, and the ceiling.

The gap was widened. One rescuer stepped into the darkness beyond. Kerra let go of her mum and ducked between two Roamers in the cordon, straining her eyes to see what was happening, but the passage was too dark.

A figure emerged, moving backwards. Another of the group climbed to reach him, and they came out a few minutes later with something carried between them. Kerra's heart flared with hope. She squirmed to the front of the line of Roamers.

Lichio lay still, his face covered in a film of dust.

"Is he alive?" she asked, seeking a response in the mesh, but there was no response.

***

"Finance tariffs need more clearly ratified." Rilal Balandt leaned forwards, earnest. Nothing got a Balandt more excited than talking finance.

"There is room for each planetary government to take that forward." Dimara Clorinda - never a family to let go of a credit easily.

Kare zoned out of the ensuing conversation, his attention taken by Kerra. She was reaching for him, not consciously, but seeking comfort. Sadness was around her, and fear. For Lichio. For the Roamers. He put his hands to his temples, massaging them.

"Emperor?" Balandt's voice was insistent and Kare brought his head up.

"Yes?" Damn, he needed to concentrate.

"The tariffs outlined. *Are* they flexible?"

"Within reason." Still the insistent demand that he was needed, that Lichio wasn't moving. He blinked, dismissing it. "They are tied to the support levels outlined for the zones. Those have been agreed in principle. The planets will not be able to deny their fiscal responsibilities." Principles discussed over the past months, drawn out in various meetings with ambassadors and presidents, prime ministers and lackeys, most carried out without anyone else's knowledge. Even Sonly hadn't known what he'd appended onto meetings, burying it within committee notes in the minutes. He needed to concentrate and ensure the spirit of what he'd promised was upheld.

The mesh pulsed, demanding his focus. His people needed him, as much as those in this room did. His daughter needed him.

He got to his feet. "I have something to attend to. I'll be back very soon."

He strode to the door, allowing nothing of the circling confusion in his head to be seen. He went into an anteroom, dismissing his guards at the door. He closed it and leaned against it. His head throbbed; his brow was wet with sweat. He found Kerra, trying not to show his distraction or need for space. He could feel her doubts - that Lichio was too badly injured and she didn't know where to start. She might be a healer, but she was still young and growing into her powers. She didn't have the knack of trusting her psyche and letting it do the work.

He focused on her, allowing his power to touch her, bringing calm and control. He sensed what she did, the injuries, the broken skin, a collapsed lung that stopped the breath Lichio needed, the slow bleed deep in his stomach.

Steady, he told her. Breath first, then the bleed. The rest, the cuts and bruises, can wait. Steady but quick: he could feel how little life Lichio had left. He touched Kerra, giving her confidence, and she started to work on Lichio's lungs. Kare winced in sympathy, imagining the pain as the tissues mended. She was moving with more confidence and he drew away.

Gods, this was insane, trying to hold everything in one place. The mesh was normally held by a king or queen immersed within the Roamer culture. They had no other function but to govern the Roamers and hold the mesh. He didn't have that luxury.

He pushed the door open. At least, in a few hours, he should be free of some of his duties.

***

She'd needed him, and he'd come. Kerra dipped her head, guilt lacing her. She'd felt her father's tiredness and how much he was trying to control. But now, at last, she could feel what Lichio needed. A touch here, to meld a rib that had broken; another there, repairing his spleen and stopping the bleed. His hand gripped her forearm as she moved it, and his grip grew stronger. He had his eyes shut, and she knew the pain must be ripping through him as she healed. But it was working. Lichio would be okay.

She sent the thought to her father, felt his answering pulse of relief, and then she pulled away, giving him space to do his job. A faint wish, that he could be more focused on the Roamers, binding them as he should, washed over her.

***

Kare went back into the boardroom, his steps easier, and retook his place.

"So," he said. "The screens on your desk show your voting options. Aye for supporting a New Republic, Nay for maintaining the Empire. No abstaining." He looked around the room, taking his time. "If this is ratified, we remove my mother's power base. She cannot match the support here." He clasped his hands together, but quickly opened them, refusing to show any doubt. "If you veto it, she will be in the position to reclaim her title. I will fight that, but—" They had no idea how he planned to fight her. Dirty and deadly, as needed. "She may prevail. You could be handing her back her empire." He reached forwards and firmly pressed the aye command on his screen. "I leave it to your conscience, and good sense, to make the right choice."

Nothing to do but wait. Briefly, he checked on Kerra and she was lighter, less worried. A buzz confirmed the votes were in. He brought up a new screen and, for a moment, dizziness swept over him. The dizziness of relief, of a new path forwards. A landslide: all signataries in the room had ratified the Republic.

He called up the next screen, the document of abdication. The word seemed larger than it was: his dream for so long. With more hope than he'd felt for years, he reached forwards and scrawled his signature, waiting for a pinprick from the screen to confirm his DNA.

"Well," he said, getting to his feet. "It seems we have a new future." He met Balandt's eyes, who'd been such a stalwart, and the Tortdeniels who'd supported Sonly in the Banned's – and his – worst hour. A smile broke. "The Empire is no more."

He left the room, stopping to thank each in person. He'd done it. Once he faced his mother and finished the job, he'd be free.

CHAPTER SEVEN

Sonly set her data pad on the desk in her cabin. Soon, the ship would leave and the hiatus on Syllte would become a memory to her. She wanted to hold on to the sense of the place that had healed Kare and returned him to her. She took her time, imprinting the planet on her memory: the sandstone walls, the reflected light from the ocean, the screech of gulls and the smell of the sea. It was different in every way from Holbec, the lush planet of her youth, or the dry, hot Belaudii.

Ferran would be different again. A new apartment in the faceless government buildings of Marel, the capital. Kare would hate being hemmed in, security following his every move, more than she would. He'd prefer to stay on Syllte. He hadn't said it exactly, but he'd stood on the moonlit beach and offered her a planet in the way his arms had embraced her, loose and relaxed. She'd leaned against him, water lapping at her feet, and wished she could say yes.

Enough. Things were as they were. She slipped her hand into her pocket and touched the newly-received filche, still folded carefully, but didn't take it out. She didn't need to; the contents were memorised. President of the Free Republic. The position was hers if she accepted.

It was what she'd worked for during the last miserable decade in Abendau: a vote for everyone; the undermining of the great families' power-base; the joining-up of the disparate systems with a fairer allocation of wealth. The richest families had fought all the way, loathe to lose their power base, but the smaller families had seen the opportunities opening to them. The balancing act in bringing things to this point, where power was shifting, had taken years.

But it was the right thing to do. She'd watched kids starve in the streets of Bendau, had passed a tribesman left to die staked out in the sun, and knew that Belaudii didn't come close to how hard life was in the outer zone.

When she had finally been endorsed to the Abendauii Senate, it had been her third time of trying. She'd taken a junior portfolio, aiming to tackle poverty, rather than a more high-profile role. She'd begged Imperial funds from Kare and had thrown herself into it, going into the slums to learn how the people of the city lived, glad of a chance to escape a marriage that had started to tatter. When Kare had finally forced open elections, those same people, the poorest of all in Abendau, had carried her to the gates of the Senate. She'd been their leader, the people's president, the voice of hope.

She could be again, on a bigger scale. What she'd done on Belaudii she could do on other planets, but she couldn't do it from Syllte, a tiny planet with no influence. If she chose her father's dream, she'd have to let go of Kare's wish for personal peace.

Her desire to take the role seemed small and dirty, compared to what Kare faced in going back to Abendau. What was a job, no matter how important? She thought back to the old Queen's chamber, the sea drumming in rhythm with her fear, Kare's pale face set and determined. She left the cabin to take her launch seat, no closer to having an answer.

***

Kerra unfastened the harness on her seat, enjoying the freedom now their ship's star drive was initiated.

"So, listen." Her mum pulled the filche out of her pocket and read the last line, again. "The position of president would be endorsed by the formed council of the republic." Her eyes sparkled as she put on a posh voice and gravely bowed and thanked the council.

"I might have known," Lichio said, choking with laughter. He gave a mock bow. "So, it'll be Madame President, then?"

"If I accept." As if she wouldn't.

"What does Kare say about it?" Lichio asked.

"I haven't told him – he doesn't need distractions right now. But he has said he'll endorse the republic, stand up and deliver whatever speeches they need and lend his name to it."

"You'll have to tell him before someone else does," said Lichio. "Does this mean you'll be based on Ferran, then?"

"I suppose so. If I take it." Her mum's smile faded. "But, it's good, isn't it? Being asked?"

"Of course it is. I hope they know what they've let themselves in for."

"I just need to make sure I get it right."

Kerra frowned. It all sounded very permanent. When her dad had talked about Ferran it had been temporary, until things were established. What if he left for Syllte? Would he take Kerra back with him, or would she be expected to stay with Mum? Would her parents stay together, or separate again? She wanted to ask, but her mum had moved on to something about the great families and who was supporting who, and the moment was gone.

She wandered out of the living quarters, into the narrow access corridor that stretched the length of the ship, and followed it to the control room. The pilot – Laurena, she remembered, from when they had boarded – had the far-away look on her face that the Roamers often had when flying, and gave Kerra only a half-nod of acknowledgement. Kerra sat on one of the seat-ledges along the bulkhead, closed her eyes, and felt for the mesh.

Patterns filled the darkness. The heat of a planet and

the pull of a supernova far away were sharp in the mesh. She concentrated and the sense of space grew stronger, until she was in tandem with what was around her. She could tell where their ship was, and where the other Roamer ships in the same lane were. She bet she could fly the ship. She bet it would be easy.

"Go on, then."

Her eyes shot open. Laurena nodded at the co-pilot's seat. "Have a go?"

"Me?" Kerra winced at the stupid question; there was no one else.

"If you want to be a Roamer, you'll have to learn to Control." The pilot reached forwards and put the ship onto auto-flight. "You and the boy."

She frowned. "Why not my dad?"

The Roamer shrugged, her flying suit's thin material stretching. "His mind flexes the wrong way: iron, inflexible, willing things to his shape. Can't you feel it?"

"No." She focused on her dad and tried to understand what the pilot meant. "I can feel him in the centre." She could; his quiet presence, not paying much attention but aware of the mesh, shifting with it. "Is that what you mean? That he holds the centre."

"Not really." The Roamer smiled, almost apologetically. "You didn't know the mesh when it was held by the Queen. It was different - freer, somehow. Your father, he makes it stay in shape, he pulls the unruly strands into order. The Queen had no need to do that; she and the mesh were one, joined without thinking."

Kerra focused on the mesh again, letting it move with her, as if the beat of her heart were in tandem with it. Laurena was right - the centre *was* wrapped around her dad, but it didn't feel comfortable; each time he changed his focus, it lost some of its energy, and when he pulled it back into shape, it fought him.

It felt disloyal to be noticing it, as if there was

something wrong with what he was doing, and she pushed it from her thoughts; later, when she got the chance, she'd talk to him about it.

"A Controller doesn't change space, but only reads it. The way the old Queen did." Laurena smiled crookedly. "The boy is also rigid. It may be that in your family you'll be the only one to master space. You may be Ealyn's heir, more than any of the others."

Kerra ducked her head, embarrassed. Her dad, a couple of nights ago, had made a throwaway comment about Ealyn, and the Roamers gathered around had hushed, listening closely. He hadn't taken much convincing to tell them more about his childhood on the ship, his eyes gleaming in a way she'd never seen before, like he was... more alive, less worried. She'd liked listening to him; she'd *love* to remind him of his dad.

"Go on, then," said Laurena, taking the ship off auto. "Join the mesh again."

Kerra closed her eyes and let the darkness take her.

"The ship is under your Control now."

Amazing. She frowned, trying to keep Ferran at the front of her mind, but the ship was big and pulled against her. The Roamer convoy accommodated her, moving out to give the beginner room. Slowly, she started to bring the ship under Control, and it stayed where it should be.

It was a freedom she'd never known, as if she was flying through space herself, not constrained inside the ship. She flew on, timeless, sensing the pull of planets, the danger of a wormhole in the distance. All the time the Roamer beside her stayed close, not interfering, but supporting, her mind linked to Kerra through the shared space they flew in. It felt like they'd known each other for ages and hadn't just met on this flight. She could feel where the woman was in the mesh, which family she belonged to, her sense of self.

"I'm going to take Control back."

Kerra nodded, but when she tried to open her eyes, she couldn't. She was held in the mesh, too tightly to let go. "What do I do?" Her voice sounded like someone else's, someone far away and worried.

"You need to bring yourself back to the control room. Take your time, remember how it looked, and open your eyes."

Kerra drew in a deep breath and managed to force her eyes to a slit. The darkness faded, replaced by the soft lighting of the control room. Only a lingering sense of her flight remained, a memory to be taken out and treasured as something that had touched a core she hadn't known she had.

"You did well," said Laurena. "For a first flight, under star drive conditions, that was impressive."

"It was incredible." Kerra opened her eyes fully.

"You took to it like a natural." The Roamer woman didn't close her eyes or concentrate as hard as Kerra had, but the ship stayed on its course. Imagine, if she practised, she could do that. The woman gave another of her crooked smiles. "Few do better."

Kerra grinned; she couldn't help herself. To be good at something she wanted so much, something that felt so right, was special. All her life, she'd felt like her powers were an apology of what they should be - the great Kare Varnon's daughter who could heal and shift objects in the air, if she wanted, but none of the other things he'd been famous for. She relaxed, holding on to a lingering sense of space and freedom. Her eyes started to droop in the warm control room.

"You will make a great Queen."

She jumped, realising Laurena was talking to her. "Not for a long time, I hope. Not while Karlyn holds the mesh." She'd never called him that before, but it seemed right, when talking about the King, to use his Roamer name.

"Not yet." Laurena gave a sly smile. "But one day you will be Kerlyn, and you will be Queen."

Kerlyn. It should have felt odd, to have a new name, but it didn't. She glanced over her shoulder, down the ship to where her mother and Lichio were. In fact, the Roamer name felt like it suited her better than the one her mother had chosen. That thought brought the realisation that had been building since she'd first found the mesh and had become even stronger on Syllte. She wanted to be Kerlyn of the Roamers more than a le Payne and stateswoman, or a Pettina and Empress.

"Blood calls to blood." Laurena shrugged, and Kerra could feel how at ease she was in the knowledge that the mesh was equal to a family, that it carried more than just a blood link, but a community and a security. She said, her voice casual, "If your parents say yes, I'll teach you to Control."

"Really?" Kerra grinned, not able to stop herself, and the guilt fell away. Being a Roamer was part of who she was, or she wouldn't have this talent.

"Tell them Laurena says you can Control, and if I say so, it's true." A tug of pride filled the mesh, the sureness of a Roamer declaring something as true and the whole accepting it.

Kerra spun her seat around and raced down the ship's gangway, barging into the main cabin. Her mum was on the comms unit, and Kerra waited, shifting from leg to leg. If there was one thing she knew from being the child of the President and the Emperor, it was that you didn't interrupt calls. Lichio rolled his eyes and mimed a yawn, making her bite back a giggle.

"Balandt may be right about the tariffs." Her mum paced up and down, hands gesturing as she spoke. "We need consistency across the systems." She saw Kerra and gave a wave. "I'll talk with Kare about what has been agreed when I get there."

Her mum ended the call and Kerra burst out: "The Roamer pilot says she'll teach me to Control. Her name's Laurena and she's really good."

Her mum frowned and a faint worry settled, low in Kerra's stomach. Perhaps she should have chosen a better time to talk about this, not when her mum was distracted and might not realise how important it was.

"Do you want to learn?" asked Lichio. His voice was drawled, but it didn't fool her; he knew what the frown meant, too.

"Yes." She turned to her mum. She had to make her see this wasn't something to be refused. "It's brilliant. I was flying the ship."

"This ship?" said Mum, hand to her throat.

"Yeah. The Controller said I could fly. I could be like Ealyn."

Her mother paled, and Uncle Lichio's eyes widened. "Like Ealyn?" he said. "You know how to choose your role models..."

She shouldn't have mentioned Ealyn. She'd forgotten that everyone except the Roamers thought he was mad. Except he wasn't – she knew him now, as the Roamers did. She knew him through her father's memories of him, through the knowledge the old Queen had held of her son – knowledge mixed with guilt, raising him to some sort of mystic significance. Ealyn hadn't been mad – he'd been pushed too far, too fast, without the protection of the mesh. She bit back hot words of defence, and forced herself to relax.

"Only in the way he Controlled," she said. Except the pilot had said it was about the way Kerra used the mesh and how her mind worked, that she was different from her dad and Baelan. "I was really good at it." Her voice quavered, but she took a deep breath. If she got upset, Mum would say she'd got things out of proportion, and never agree. Better to appeal to her mum's practical nature. "It would be good to be a pilot, wouldn't it?"

"But when would you use it?" Her mum looked confused. "You're going to be on Ferran."

Kerra looked at her mum and then Lichio. "How long for?" Finally, she could ask.

Lichio cleared his throat. "It's not safe to go back as long as the Empress is running around free."

"But she's on Belaudii!" said Kerra. "It'll be ages until the republic deposes her." She grabbed her mum's arm. "You said it could take months!" Years, even - the Empress already had Belaudii under her rule, and two of the great families, including Hiactol which meant she had military support.

"I'm sorry," said her mum. "It's not just about the Empress." Her mouth twisted. "I'm not basing my decisions on what *she's* doing." She put her data pad down and took Kerra's hands in her own slender-fingered ones. "I can't run a republic from a space ship or from a planet as remote as Syllte." She squeezed Kerra's hand, as if asking for understanding. "It's too vulnerable - the attack on the caves told us that. But, also - I'm not a Roamer. I'd always be a visitor, and that's not practical. Not for someone who'll have to meet people all the time, and be the public face of the republic."

Kerra pulled her hand away. Everything was about her mum, and what she needed. It always was. It didn't matter that Kerra liked Syllte and felt at home there.

"Kerra," said her mum. "What else can I do?"

Nothing, and there was nothing she could say that would matter. Mum always put work first. Even her dad had been around more when she'd been growing up. He'd commissioned the games room so they could spend time together, and insisted the room have a comms-blackout. They'd spent hours in there, while her mum was in meetings or touring Bendau's slums talking to other kids about *their* problems. "Nothing, I suppose. Not if the job is that important to you."

She walked out, ignoring her mum's shout of "Kerra!" She wasn't going to be nice and pretend it didn't matter. Not this time. She went to her cabin, slamming the door, and curled up on the bunk. She closed her eyes. Space shifted around her, with all the same sensations as earlier. Laurena joined her in the mesh. She knew what had happened, Kerra could tell, but she was calm about it. Karlyn would feel differently, the Roamer believed; he'd understand.

Kerra sat up. Her dad *might* say yes. He'd known Ealyn, he'd understand why she couldn't deny or bury the talent. Excitement bubbled and then died; if her mum said no, Dad would too. They never went against each other. Even when they'd lived apart, there'd been a united front of parenting.

Kerra balled her hand into a fist and hit the wall. It made a bang, much louder than she expected. She held her breath, waiting for someone to ask was she okay, but they didn't. They didn't even care that she was upset. She pulled a pillow over her head. It wasn't bloody fair.

CHAPTER EIGHT

She only went to go after her daughter. "Kerra!" but Lichio took her arm.

"Give her a minute to calm down. It's hard for her, having so many changes so quickly."

"I know." And she did know - six months ago, Kerra had lived in a palace. She'd had everything she could ever need. She'd been cossetted and privileged. Now she was a space-nomad, her few friends from Abendau unable to be contacted, her whole future up in the air. "But she must see I have no option."

"I don't remember being that forgiving when I was her age," he said.

"You were a brat," she snorted. Lichio, as a child, had been their mother's golden-boy, almost a mascot for the Banned. When she died he'd changed, lashing out at anyone who tried to help him. Only Rjala, not as bent under the loss as Sonly and her father - and Eevan, who'd been nearly as broken as Lichio - had managed to reach him. She'd guided Lichio into a teenager who resembled the smart, funny child he'd been. He'd become army-mad, perhaps seeking to meet Rjala's expectations of him and exceed them, or to validate himself within a fractured family linked only by their rebellion.

"My point exactly. She could be doing more than slamming doors." He gave a rueful smile, and then sobered, and she steeled herself for a lecture. "If she's a Controller, it'll happen anyway. It's not like you can close her head down. Better that she learns to do it properly." He sat back in his seat. "Kare will agree to it, you know. He grew up with Ealyn. This won't even get filed under kooky."

Sonly fiddled with her data pad, opening and

closing its cover. Lichio was right; for Kare, the idea of becoming a Controller would be perfectly normal. He'd treat her as if she was the weird one, and that wasn't fair. She didn't make ships fly or take over people's heads.

"Lich, she's heir to the Pettina name, whether Kare likes it or not. She can't become a Space Roamer."

"She's a Roamer princess, too." He shrugged. "It's not worth fighting about at this stage. She isn't talking about running off to live in space. She's asking to learn to fly. If she's going to be around the Roamers - and I think that's a given, since they're the bulk of Kare's fleet - she's going to absorb some of what they do."

She bit her lip. "Maybe...."

"Besides," he said. "Forbidden fruit and all that; if you ban it, she'll want it. Remember what Dad used to say, you have to let them go to—"

"Keep them," she finished, nodding. Her father had let her follow the path she wanted, even though it put her at odds with Eevan. He hadn't forced Lichio to conform the way Eevan had chosen to. He'd even advised him not to join the Banned's junior reserve at thirteen, she remembered, pleading with Lichio to at least know what he wanted first, but when Lichio had gone ahead anyway, he'd supported him. She pushed her hair back. "You're right. I'll talk to her when she's calmed down."

"Of course I'm right," he said. "I'm the smart one, remember?" His voice was ironic but the humour was forced and his blue eyes were shadowed, more like those of the bereft child than the man he'd grown into.

"Lich..." There might not be another chance to talk. When they landed, it would be meeting after meeting, for both of them. "Is there anything I can do?"

"Conjure me back three months?" He quirked a half-smile. "No, I'm fine." He looked not just sad, but helpless, and she couldn't leave it at that, not knowing he had no one else he would talk to.

"It isn't your fault if Josef didn't make it out of Abendau."

"No? I risked him, asking him to put me in touch with the agents. What if that's why he was picked up?" He got up, the old reflexes coming to the fore. No one was better at deflecting concern or questions. "I can't talk about it. I need time."

"Time for what?"

"To think." It sounded like the last thing he wanted to do.

"About what?"

He looked at the ceiling, as if seeking inspiration. "Do you ever wonder...." He stopped, gave a quiet curse, and then met her eyes. "Did we do the right thing? So many have died: Rjala, Silom, Sam... maybe Josef."

What was he saying? He'd never doubted before – he'd always been so sure about what he was doing and why.

"They died for what they believed in," she said. "Just as you would have. Or me." She looked down, to where her blouse hid the scar on her side. She nearly had.

"For what we have now?" He started to pace. "Half an empire, and war looming."

She shook her head. She couldn't think that. Kare was about to risk his life – no, more than his life, his sanity, the equilibrium of who he was – for their dream.

"Not half an empire – a republic," she said. Provided Kare held as many families as he believed he did.

He took a deep breath. "Everything I thought certain has shifted. I didn't do what I did for Dad's dream. I was hardly old enough when he died to understand it."

He meant it; she'd never seen him more serious. "You were fourteen."

"I was fourteen and barely over Mother's death. I had no idea what would be expected of me. I thought I'd be a rebel soldier, and never went any further than that."

"So why did you go on? After Abendau fell?" He had to know he wasn't talking sense, that he was shaken up and worried about Josef, and had things out of perspective. "You could have walked away when Kare became Emperor. Your work as a rebel was done. With the back pay you'd gathered, you could have bought a share of a party-planet and stayed there. Why didn't you?"

He gave a strangled sound. "I..." He ran his hands through his hair, and she thought he was going to crack, but he managed to compose himself. "You know what happened in Abendau. When I saw Kare in the quarry, he didn't know me or Silom. He was broken, scarred, so thin he could barely stay on his feet." He slumped into his seat, rubbing his temples. "I knew what they'd done to take him there. I'd seen some of it, and heard more. And I'd had my share of it." He took his hands down and she wanted to flinch away at the pain-filled lines either side of his mouth, at his unflinching eyes. "I would never have come back from where he was. Never. Not just by taking the quarry, or the palace, or becoming Emperor, but in getting up every damned morning and facing himself in the mirror. In having the guts to walk out in front of everyone as if he was the sort of privileged Emperor they wanted. People knew what had been done to him, the rumours were all through Abendau, but he still faced them. He fought for people who needed him – he gave you the support you needed for reform. People he said were less lucky than him." He gave a short laugh. "To see him do that and admit I don't have the balls to overcome half of what he did..." He looked down at his hands. "I didn't even have the guts to tell you about Josef. I used my job as an excuse to hide him and stop myself committing to him."

She sat opposite, not able to take her eyes off him. Lichio had skirted around what had happened in the cells for years and avoided any questions about the past. If he was opening up now, she wouldn't stop him.

"You ask why I didn't walk away?" He rubbed the top of his arm, his fingers digging into his jacket, as if he wanted to burrow under his own skin. "I believed in Kare.

I didn't think anyone could overcome all that and not be worth following. I thought I was central to what he was doing, that only I could be the backup he needed. He trusts so few, you know?"

"You are central to it." Her voice was choked.

He shook his head, denying her comfort. "I fucked up. But Kare walked away from what we were supposed to achieve. I don't know if he was too tired to go on, or if he believes a republic is the way forward. I do know, even if he does force the agreement we need, that it will leave a half-republic-empire that could take years to sort out. If it leads to war - and it might - people will die. The little people, the ones we were supposed to be helping."

"I promise you the republic will make the difference you want." She could hear the edge of desperation in her voice. "That's why I'm going to accept the presidency: because it will deliver that dream."

"I hope you're right." He met her gaze. "But, after the raid, I'll take some time to decide..."

"Decide what?"

He took a deep breath. "Whether I'm staying or going, I guess."

Silence lengthened between them. She didn't know what to say. The idea of Lich not being at her side was alien. It was the way things worked: Lichio's intelligence; her politics; Kare, the centre - a new beginning, a way forwards beyond what his mother had offered. A three-way team who'd carried an empire for a decade and a friendship for longer. He couldn't go.

A bang broke the silence and made her jump. Lichio jerked his head at the door. "You'd better see to Kerra. I think she needs a bit of attention." He gave a strained smile. "Go on, Sonly. I've said enough."

He was right; they'd only go around in circles. She left, down the corridor to Kerra's cabin, and pushed open the door.

"I'm sorry," she said, before Kerra could speak. "Of course you should learn." She stepped in, and saw that her daughter's eyes were as red as her own. Guilt pierced her. "I just... wasn't expecting it. You psychers, I think I know all about you, and then something happens that makes me realise I don't." She smiled. "Forgive me?"

Kerra nodded. "Of course." She looked a little worried. "I didn't mean to bash the wall so hard."

Sonly had to smile at that. "Be careful, or there won't be a ship left for you to fly. We'll talk to your dad when we get to Ferran, and if he's okay about it, you can learn."

Kerra's face broke into a smile, and Sonly's breath caught. Kerra had the look of Ealyn in the way her eyes shone when she spoke of flying, the way her smile made them crinkle. She'd never noticed before, but here, on a ship like Ealyn's, it felt like she was a child again, watching him emerge from his ship, forbidding in his dark pilot's suit until he smiled and it flashed into his eyes. Kare had never had that way about him - he'd been steadier, more focused. But Kerra.... Despite the blonde hair, Sonly could see only Ealyn shining out of her, and it chilled her.

CHAPTER NINE

Averrine entered the main section of the palace, Phelps falling into step beside her. His doubts filled the air, and his regrets. Once she would have crushed those thoughts, removed them with a single joining to his mind, or the touch of their bodies together, but not now.

He was right to regret. He had betrayed her, he who had once been close to her, angular and hard, with pride enough to match her own. Sometimes, public displays were necessary, but not for Phelps; for him, the slow destruction of what he had been, the ruin of his self, was a better mirror for what he'd brought on her.

Still, he had his uses - there was no one better at doing what he did: finding people and bringing them in. He would find Kare, and le Payne. They had left her caged, to spend years pacing like an animal, unable to remove the block in her mind. She'd sat on her knees and reached into herself, the way she'd done as a girl to prove herself to her father, but it had made no difference; the block had been immovable, the tower inescapable.

She brought her hand up to her face. Age spots marred the skin, spots that hadn't been there before her incarceration, when her powers had sustained her. It wasn't just the marks: her fingers had tightened, the bones thickening until they pained her each morning when she woke. Her hips ached, bones moulded to their new shape, impossible to heal now. *Old. Kare had made her old.* The anger that had sustained her through that decade fed into her power, an endless source. He'd taken her empire, her lineage, her name, and left her to rot. That could not go unchallenged.

She needed to get out of the palace, with its high walls and silent corridors. She needed to feel air on her skin, to touch the garden and feel how it continued, timeless and strong. Already lush growth had returned, the plants thirsty for the water that now flowed through the moat, reaching the drought-stricken corners.

She left the palace by the top exit, dismissing Phelps, and stood at the start of the skywalk to the port, her guards keeping a discreet distance. Below, the gardens stretched. She breathed in the dry, scented air. It was the same air she'd breathed as a child, in Bendau, carried from the same desert.

Kare had changed so much about the palace in her absence. He'd sealed the entrance to the catacombs containing the ancient church of Abendau, its tribal heart, and flooded them to destroy Omendegon. He'd had a mosaic-tiled floor in her personal quarters removed, as if trying to eradicate her from the palace she'd created.

"My Lady." The guardsman's voice was low. "Your guests have arrived."

She smiled; her son may have changed much, but she was back, and not without allies. She walked to a small antechamber where Tom Peiret and his son, Jake, rose to their feet. Baelan's mother, Shanisa, bowed her head. Her brothers, standing behind her, clutched their ankhars with their right hands and snapped to attention. The woman's head remained bowed. Her sadness cast through the room, her thoughts singing for Baelan; everything she did was for and about the little traitor.

Averrine took her seat at the table. Tom Peiret drew in a deep breath as she touched him; he had long been hers. The boy resisted but, with a small twist of extra attention, his defiance melted. She sent a blast of reward his way, and his expression slackened. It was so easy. Easier than ever.

"I understand that the position of president of the so-called republic may fall to Sonly le Payne." She smiled at Jake, letting her eyes soften. "She wronged you, did she not?"

He tensed, and she could feel how his pride had been wounded. "She should have been honoured to become a Peiret. She claimed she and her husband had no love for each other." The hurt was clear in his eyes. Clearer than it had been when she'd first met the boy a few weeks ago, as it should be - she had set that hurt with her touch.

"And yet she stayed with him." Averrine leaned forward, enhancing his pain. "I can teach her that she was wrong." She paused, letting that sink in. "I wish for you to travel to Ferran."

"My Lady, they will know my father's loyalties are to you."

He dared speak against her. "You will travel to Ferran," she said, each word precise, each accompanied by a rap of her will. "Whilst there you will carry a message to Sonly le Payne. A very personal one."

He swallowed and she could feel how he wanted to resist; the le Payne woman still attracted him. She shot a bolt of displeasure, and his head snapped back with a small cry, but no matter - he had to be held firm. The le Payne woman was the strength behind Varnon, the hand that had guided him as Emperor. She, more than any, was a threat.

"You will do this for me," she said. He nodded and she rewarded him. He opened his mouth, drinking her presence in.

A moment later, he cleared his throat. "My Lady, I will see it is done for you." There was no hesitation in his words, no question about what she might ask him to deliver or do. The lingering thoughts of Sonly le Payne no longer moved him. It was easy, when a person was hurt and wished for revenge.

She turned her attention to Shanisa. "You will

travel with General Phelps; he will see you are reunited with your son."

Shanisa bowed her head, her face unruffled, her thoughts hard to read: a deep water, this one, able to use the depths to sustain her. Nonetheless, her desire was clear and easy to pull on. Baelan was the cord that bound his mother to her duty; to be reunited with Baelan, the mother would do all that was asked of her. Averrine increased her focus, enhancing the woman's sense of the maternal. This was what was right for her son – bringing him home to the tribes, not leaving him cast adrift with a father who was an enemy.

"Your will be done, my Lady." She met Averrine's eyes and, in that moment, Averrine had no doubt that she, too, was hers.

CHAPTER TEN

She only mimed hitting something, making Kare smile. "She thumped the wall of the ship so hard I thought she'd break it!"

Her voice was loud enough to carry through the small crowd of security staff and lackeys, which was, no doubt, intentional. Look at the normal family we are. Look at me, the president who is one of the people. As ever, she played the role well but her voice held a brittle edge he knew well - something was going on, something she was hiding with animation.

"I'll talk to Kerra later," said Kare. Although their daughter, having got her own way, had seemed mostly embarrassed and glad to stay on board. He frowned a little, sensing her, deep in the mesh. It wasn't just embarrassment. Temptation bit, to have a closer look and find out what was bothering her, but he pushed it away - that was the old Queen's way, to keep close to everyone and allow little space for private thoughts; it wasn't his. His father had taught him, from an early age, that it wasn't polite to look into people's thoughts just because he could. Having spent most of his life learning not to look closely, he didn't plan to change now.

"Kerra's lucky," he said. They moved away from the crowd, towards the Ferran hub's administration centre - it was easier to appreciate the scale of the space station now he'd been in situ for three days. "It's the one skill I wanted, and I don't have a single ounce of Control in me."

She nudged him, a little too hard. "I wouldn't complain. You're hardly a psychic slouch."

"No." But he was; all his power was stolen,

provided by others and forced to his will. It was draining, holding the mesh, and he didn't know if it was because he no longer had powers of his own, or if he'd had the wrong sort of training. Snake-wrestling would be comparable to keeping it in shape.

Farran had been working with him for the past few weeks, trying to teach him how to merge smoothly with the mesh, but it made no difference; he didn't fit and it felt like the mesh knew it. He realised Sonly was watching him with a worried face, and gave a quick smile. "Well, I'm happy for her to learn, if you are." Would that all their problems were so easy to fix: at some point, he'd have to tell her about Baelan's compulsion.

They walked in silence, their steps in tandem: in a station this size there were too many ears, ready to report everything he and Sonly said or did, right down to whether they walked close together or apart. He looked straight ahead, composed; let the news-holos read something into a face that told them nothing. They usually did.

They left the link corridor and passed straight through security. Only when the double doors closed behind them did he give Sonly's hand a quick squeeze. "I'll see you after."

She paused, as if wanting to say something, but an ambassador approached and drew her down the corridor. She'd have forgotten Kare already, immersed in work – on her deathbed Sonly would be sending one last instruction to someone, somewhere. He made his way to his own meeting room, dismissing his security team at the door, and let himself in.

"One minute." Lichio's scanner gave a buzz as he finished the surveillance checks. He okayed the readout and sealed the door. The busy nature of the hub had its advantages, but privacy wasn't one of them.

Lichio took a seat at one side of the desk. "All

clear." But for the brief hesitation in meeting Kare's eyes, and the lack of smile, it could be the Lichio of old. He had always held hard edges of secrecy, closed-off places where intrusion wasn't welcome, but there was an undercurrent that was new, a sense of caution that felt wrong. Not unlike Sonly's masked worry. What the hell had gone on in the ship on the way over?

Later. He'd get to it later. Kare tapped his data pad open and focused on the data filling the screen.

"Ops first?" asked Lichio, opening his own data pad.

Kare brought his check-lists up. It took him back years, to the first time he and Rjala had planned an assault on the palace. He wished his old general was with him now, with her sharp, analytical eyes and quiet assurance. Last time, he'd had only Sonly and Kerra to think about protecting; now he had Baelan, not to mention the planets standing behind the Free Republic whose people would bear the wrath of his mother if he failed. A memory gripped him, of a child's face strangled by poisoned air on Corun. He hadn't thought of that attack in years. *That* was what his mother was capable of: killing a whole planet without thought. This time, it could be whole systems.

"You okay?" Lichio asked.

No. But he would be. He gave a quick nod. "Before we review planning, there is something you need to know. We have an internal security issue."

"We do?" Lichio was deadpan, and seemingly relaxed. "A new one?"

Kare rapped his fingers on the desk, a quick pattern. "Yes. The boy."

"Baelan?" Lichio swiped his data pad. "From the tribes. Around ten, as near as we can estimate – possibly a little younger, depending when he was implanted. No birth records, of course. Belongs to one of the deep desert-dwelling tribes, we believe." He glanced up, frowning. "He would never have gone ten years in the city, looking like he does, and not have been picked up." His mouth twisted, not quite into a smile. "I have security-risk written all over him."

"Increase it. There was an incident on the ship." Incident: he loved military-speak, how so much could be intimated in one word. "His power slipped."

"How careless. Presumably there was a reason?"

There was no way to make it sound good. "It turns out he took a life-oath and the Empress has set a compulsion in him to carry it through. It revolves around me."

Lichio leaned back in his chair. "So he's to what – overthrow you? Report back on your movements?"

"No." Kare took a deep breath. "He's to kill me."

"I see." Lichio managed to keep his face bland, and it was hard to tell if he was absorbing the information or simply resigned to another person's being added to the list. "Where is he now?"

"On the Roamer ship with a full squad of guards. Farran is with him – if anything changes, he will inform me."

"We can arrange detention with the Ferrans," said Lichio. "The hub is designed to deal with such eventualities."

"No." He'd known it could come to that, of course, the moment the boy attacked. He laced his hands together. "We deal with it ourselves."

"You don't trust the Ferrans?" asked Lichio. "My intel wouldn't support that."

"No, I think they're genuine. But this is a big hub, with commercial transports arriving all the time. Information leaks easily." He shrugged. "If we detain him, and it gets out, the Empress would be all over it: child-napping and detention from me, the great reformer." Not that it mattered – with his resignation had come acceptance that he would become whatever history distorted him into. "Plus... what would it do to the integrity of the republic if I'm seen to be building a dynasty? It has to look like the boy is here of his own volition. He has to be seen to be so – hiding him will only give room for rumours."

"I can keep a security squad on him," said Lichio. "But I don't like it."

Nor did he, but there were no easy alternatives. Syllte wasn't safe, and he couldn't take the boy to Abendau with him - it would be handing the Empress what she wanted.

"He hasn't shown any aggression to anyone else, and I scanned him to confirm he has no intention to do so. But he's far from predictable." He gave a firm nod. "A squad. A full one. Trained to handle psychers. Our own people only."

"It will stretch us."

"Then we'll have to stretch. Unless you see an alternative?"

"No. I'll get on to it." Lichio made a note in his data pad. "Anything else?"

"Yes. I need you to stay."

Lichio raised an eyebrow. "Here? Not on the raid with you?"

"That's right." Kare cut across Lichio's attempted protest. "I can't let it be known about Baelan, but the situation needs to be managed closely. One of us has to stay." He tapped his head. "And it can't be me."

Lichio sat back, rubbing his fingers along his jaw-line. He rarely rushed into an assessment. He'd be sorting through the data about the raid, the arrangements on Ferran and the boy himself, making connections where they were relevant. After a few moments, he shook his head.

"I don't agree. I can have the situation managed without any leaks. You need me on Abendau." He leaned forwards, face earnest. "The agents are my team - I should be leading them."

"It's not ideal," admitted Kare. "It's still how I'm running things. You, here; me on the ground. You can support remotely. Besides, I have some intel I want you to run while you're here."

"Go." Lichio's voice bordered on the surly, but he was poised, ready to record the new orders.

"The Ferrans," said Kare. "I want you to explore the viability of their proposed sister-hub to increase trade to the outer zones."

"Get an economic analyst on to it."

"No. Economically, it stands up. I want to know which planets they have aligned with, and which great families have strategic alliances." Boring work, but necessary – if the new hub was agreed and turned out to favour one family over the others, it could bring down any central agreement. "Work your way in with the Ferrans, work out which person would accept any" —he paused, looking for the term— "off-piste payments, and find out what's happening under the radar."

The Ferrans had been more than helpful, offering their facilities, ensuring docking space for the Roamer ships – not a small undertaking – and extending security personnel. In his experience, helpful was not always the same as on-his-side. If anyone could find out what lay behind the facade, it was Lichio, who gave a sharp nod, accepting the orders.

"The raid, then," said Lichio. "Arrangements are finalised."

Bile rose in Kare, driven by dread. He clenched his fists, letting the pain remind him why he had to do this.

"Flight departs in the morning," said Lichio, scrolling through the details. "Space time of two days, followed by a further two days' recon on the planet before the tribal rest day and the hit on the palace."

"You're sure the Empress has reinstated the rest day?"

"Yes. Across the city, in her esteemed honour." Lichio's mouth curled into a sneer. "It works in our favour; the security numbers will be the same, but there won't be many in the way of palace staff to worry about." He projected a screen between them. "Final task force, as discussed and now confirmed with Major Hickson. The three specialist soldiers he requested are en route and will be clearing security on false docs; the rest are already in situ."

Kare scanned the familiar list of ten names. He reached the second from bottom and a familiar gnaw of worry started, deep in his stomach. He pointed at the screen. "We're sure about Sergeant Woods?"

"Hickson insists she's his best sharpshooter. She's also an infiltration expert – you need someone like that in the palace." Lichio leaned back in his seat. "We don't have many of our own people to choose from; Abendau decimated us."

"Does Hickson know she's always wanted to try her skills out on me?"

Lichio templed his fingers. "Woods has never been anything other than professional."

"She knows I killed Silom."

Lichio's right hand flexed. "You didn't."

Kare waved his protest away. A tit-for-tat would achieve nothing. What mattered was that Woods *had* always been a professional in his army. If he couldn't command her loyalty in this, he had no place in the task force. And Lichio was right, he couldn't afford anything other than the best.

"It's a good squad."

"Yes." Lichio's eyes narrowed. "You're sure about bypassing security?"

"I'm sure." Here, at least, he was on solid ground. "All your palace operative needs to do is upload a programme. It will input false data on selected DNA records." He gave a half-smile, thinking how much Lichio was going to like the little extra he'd implanted in the programme. "It will also place a new security code into the system – one only you and I will have. We will be able to move freely once it's uploaded."

"How? The palace security banks are impenetrable. You've told me that often enough."

"I corrupted the palace coding, years ago." Kare wriggled his fingers. "Given my list of enemies, it never seemed a good idea to get locked out of my own palace by them. It uploads false DNA-linked data to the security banks. It carries the same coding; there shouldn't even be a blip." He held a hand up. "I'm not confident of it surviving a full security update, however, so we hold back on uploading it until the night of the attack."

Lichio made a note. If he was offended at not having been told about the system, he didn't show it.

He brought up a map of the palace, all too familiar to Kare. "To confirm. The security team in the palace has been compromised – they will give you access to the palace. You'll join a unit within palace security and will be reallocated to the Empress' private chambers. Hickson's unit will enter the palace as a cleaning squad and will already be in situ. I don't want you going in with them – if your cover is blown, theirs won't be."

Kare swallowed, imagining going back into the palace, getting so deep into it there was no easy way out. Just thinking about it made his back itch. Once at the Empress' chamber, he'd be surrounded. He'd be lucky to make it out.

Gods, this was hard, harder than the first time he'd planned to take his mother, when he'd been young and stupid and didn't know what he faced. Now, he knew exactly what could happen within the walls of Abendau palace.

Lichio brought the screen down. His face was lit by his data pad, almost green, shadows tracing the light.

"Getting onto the planet?" he said. "You said you might have some thoughts on that."

Kare drew in a breath; when Lichio heard what he was going to suggest.... "When my father left me on Dignad, he carried out a space-to-ground landing to bypass security."

"Your father was nuts, remember?"

He bristled in defence. "Not about flying, he wasn't."

"Even so – space-to-grounds are dangerous."

"Smugglers do them all the time."

"Smugglers have pretty low life spans."

Kare drummed his fingers on the table. "The Roamers have been known to take on the odd smuggling run." Lichio opened his mouth to argue, but Kare held his hand up. "I've spoken to Farran about it. He suggests we use four ships - three decoy, one carrying us. He'll set us down in the deep Southern desert as far from Abendau as possible. I thought your agent network could pick us up there."

Lichio shook his head. "It's dangerous as hell."

"It's as safe as trying to get through the port. Safer."

"Getting down is only half the problem," said Lichio. "The desert has to be survived until pick-up. Farran's good, but I assume pinpointing a specific location whilst coming in at speed is tricky."

"He says he can get close. My desert training is up to date."

Lichio tapped his screen. "The port may be safer."

Kare shook his head. He'd had the flight from Syllte to think about this. "If I go for the port and get stopped, it's over. If I go for a space-to-ground and it isn't viable, I can pull out and retry the port." He rubbed his temples, running over both options, and brought his head up. "For that reason, we go with the Roamers. If they tell me they can do this, I have to trust them. They know more about flying than either of us."

Lichio gave a sharp nod. "Noted. For the record, I don't like it." His face softened. "You know, you don't have to do this. You can force your mother's hand politically. It will take longer, that's all."

It was tempting, but he'd been over it and over it and this was the only way. He couldn't leave her alive any longer, not knowing she would never stop. He drew in a deep breath, and it was easier, surer. That was all he had to do between now and the attack: keep breathing, keep it steady.

"If I don't...." He couldn't say what the future might hold. He couldn't make it real. "Look after them for me, Lich."

The thought of Kerra growing up without him, of Sonly finding her way alone in the future, of his son hoarding his power with no one to guide him, hurt, right in the centre of his chest. His voice turned to a croaked husk. "Promise me that."

Lichio put out his hands and cupped Kare's, holding them firmly. "Always," he said, tightening his grip. "You know that. Always."

CHAPTER ELEVEN

Sonly closed the door of her allocated suite, glad to finally be free of the Ferran ambassador and have a chance to freshen up - and review her notes - before her first planned meeting. The room was so much more suitable than Syllte, with a full range of comms equipment, access to the rolling news-holos, and a wall display confirming time and date across all key planets, proving, once again, that Syllte was wholly unsuitable for her needs, even without additional security concerns.

She keyed into the central info-banks, setting her bag on the floor. Her larger luggage had already been unpacked and its contents put away. She paged through her official messages, but stopped at the soft buzz of a new message on her personal channel. Absently, she opened it.

"For your eyes…"

She stopped, staring at the familiar opening line. What did he want? And why here, why now? He could have sent her a message any time in the past weeks. She read through the message - a request for a meeting - and the final line, the sender's name accompanied by a flourished monogram she'd have known anywhere. She leaned forwards, connecting her comms to the Ferrans' central control.

"You have a James Parnard waiting for me," she said. "Bring him up."

She scowled at the screen. What the hell did Jake want? He must know his family could play no part in these discussions - his father had firmly allied themselves with the Empress. She chewed her lip, thinking over the various ramifications. The offer of a meeting could be the opening of informal negotiations – or it could be an information-seeking exercise.

The discreet knock on the door took her back, startling her with its familiarity. She got to her feet. "Come in."

The door opened and Jake stepped through, clutching a dossier-file against him. He wasn't wearing his uniform, or any sort of regalia, but a plain black top and trousers. It made him look older, somehow. That, and the hard look in his eyes. Her stomach clenched, mostly in dread. What if he begged her to reconsider him, or decided to face Kare about the affair?

She dismissed the security guards and waited until the door closed with a soft thud. The green light over it confirmed the soundproofing was in place.

"What do you want, Jake?"

He sat, without invitation, and leaned back, his face tilted up to her. "I needed to see you."

A personal agenda, then. She took her own seat, not relieved – politics would have been easier to deal with.

"We have nothing to say to each other," she told him. She set her hands on the desk, clasped together. "It's over, Jake. I've made my decision."

"I have something to say." His eyes were fixed and earnest. "Unless you want to be blindsided, I suggest you listen." The edge in his voice brought a low worry.

"This had better be good," she said. She slid her hand under the table, unclipping the holster of her firearm. She had no reason to fear him – and had a panic button that would bring a security squad in moments – but everything in her screamed to be cautious.

"I'm sorry about this, Sonly. I want you to know this is not my doing."

"What isn't?" Her heart was thudding.

He slid the dossier across the table. "It's for you. Compliments of the Empress."

She picked it up and filches spilled from it, scattering across the table. She caught a glimpse of one and gasped. Her naked body was clearly visible, Jake's dark head bowed over her breasts. Her head was back, eyes closed. There was no doubt it was her, enjoying herself. A chill crept up her spine. It wasn't just that she was enjoying herself – that would have been bad, but able to be faced. What stunned her was the casual intimacy in the picture, the way her leg was hooked around his, the touch of her fingertip on his shoulder. How he held her, so close, one hand cupping her breast.

She picked up the next filche. This one focused on Jake's face; there was no chance of mistaking him. Behind him, she sat, naked, her eyes focused on him. She looked across the table. At least a dozen pictures, all of her, all undressed, many with Jake touching her, kissing her. Inside her. Some showed her laughing, another of a close embrace, body to body, telling the story of a relationship, not a one-off event, but something deeper.

She glared across the table. How dare he have taken these? But her anger was shrouded by fear. "Quite a collection."

His face twisted in sympathy. "For what it's worth, I'm sorry."

She pushed her chair back, putting distance between herself and the images. "Where did they come from?"

"My quarters. In Abendau."

Oh, dear lord, she was a bloody fool. She'd had his chambers vetted, of course, but only at the start. She should have known something like this was possible. She ran her gaze over the pictures again, forcing herself to face the danger. "What does the Empress want?" As if there was any doubt what the Empress would want.

"She asks that you put your considerable political weight behind her claim, that you rescind the dissolution of the empire and refute the Free Republic. If not..."

"What?" But she knew, of course she did. The value of

the pictures wasn't in what she'd been doing with Jake, it was in her relationship with Kare. It had been touted as something special and untouchable when, in truth, it had been false and used only for political advancement for years. She'd be exposed for telling lies over the years, an accusation that would leach into her reputation and leave everything she promised as empty assurances. It wouldn't matter that she and Kare were a couple again – the lies would still be out there and evidenced.

"If you haven't agreed by day-end, Ceaton-1 standard, the Empress will be placing these with one of the news-holos."

He struggled to meet her eyes, his arrogance gone as if, having done the deed, he wished he hadn't. Perhaps that was true – he, too, ran the risk of these becoming public, of his body being shown on every holo, having sex. But he was the scion of a great family – he could ride out the scandal. Ride it out, yes, but he'd never be unscathed by it. Even if his family's value went up on the basis of his actions, his never would. It might even leave him unable to lead his family – and yet he had still done this. She knew whose hand lay behind such unquestioning loyalty. Her jaw tensed – the Empress would not rely on a simple scandal to bring Sonly down.

"Along with some copies of messages forwarded to me," said Jake, confirming her fears. "Some personal in nature. Some... more political, shall we say."

She pushed her seat back. "You received no political information from me." She was a fool, yes, but not that much. Nothing left her office to uncleared sources, nothing at all.

He raised an eyebrow. "No? That's unfortunate, as I have evidence." He tapped one of the pictures. "And I don't think anyone will question it when they see the nature of our relationship."

His father was the Empress' closest ally. She scanned the table, taking in the full implications. A sexual scandal she could ride out, however unpleasant, but indications of political impropriety? That was another matter. She lifted a particularly revealing picture of her, and stared into her own eyes. They looked back, dreamy and relaxed, unthinking of this betrayal. It shimmered under tears of anger. "Why do you have them? It's over between us, why did you keep them?"

"I never wanted it to be over. I wanted to hold on to what we'd had, I suppose, in one small way." He had the grace to redden. "They were only for me."

"Porn." She stood, revulsed. "You used me for porn?" But even as she said it, she knew that hadn't been at the heart of these images. Not with the choice of pictures he'd made – of her, shadowed and half-asleep, of her arms stretched, like a cat, her fingers entwined in his.

"No." His voice carried an edge of desperation. "Memories." He reached for her. "I love you. You know that, you've always known that."

She strode to the door. "None of this is about love. It's about having something I didn't give you the right to have." She opened the door. She needed him to go now, before she became so angry she couldn't think straight. That was a luxury she couldn't afford. "You've done your dirty work. You can get out."

"Sonly..."

She jerked her head. "Leave."

He walked to the door, his back straight. He faced her. "The Empress means it, you know."

"I'm sure of it. I think you'll find I know the bitch better than you ever will." Something crossed his face, a fleeting look of anger at her reference to the Empress, and it all made sense. The poor bugger had been pulled under her spell. He had no hope now. She knew that from Eevan; her brother had grown so corrupted by the Empress' touch he'd destroyed everything he'd once believed in, the group their father had built, and betrayed everyone he loved.

The part of her that had lain with Jake, had enjoyed his company and attention, felt sorry for him, sorry enough to almost reach for him. She glanced back at the table; he'd come to ruin her, without showing any backbone of resistance. If he loved her, really loved her, he could have resisted. She knew it was possible: she'd done it. Her thoughts hardened. "Get out."

He left, and she went back to the desk. She picked up one of the photos. It wasn't blurred, or deniable, it was only her. She was ruined whatever she did. A harlot with a cuckold for a husband – a cuckold on whose name and reputation they were hanging a large part of the republic's support – or a politician who didn't believe enough in her father's dream to front the republic, who would endorse her enemy instead. Who would give her enemy what they needed to destroy the republic and embed the Empress' position. Because she had. She may not have sent the messages he claimed to have – and no doubt could produce – but she had still given them this opportunity.

Her mouth filled with a bitter taste, one she tasted rarely, and one she hated. She was beaten. Damned if she did and damned if she didn't. She could hand back the republic and hide the pictures or she could watch her career be ruined by the news-holos, who had always claimed she was hard and cold. Now they'd know: cold enough to have an affair on the husband who'd needed her, a torture victim with all the ensuing press coverage about what that had done to him. A woman so weak, she'd give her lover all the secrets he asked for.

She pulled out her communicator and stared at it. The code she needed to call and stop this becoming public was clearly written on the envelope. Her hand hovered, as she went through every option again. Decided, she stabbed the unit and waited for a response.

"Kare," she said, and her voice only wavered a little. She pushed her hair back from her face, and looked once more along the length of the table at the pictures sent to destroy her. She squeezed her eyes shut and said, "I have something to show you."

***

Kare set the final picture down, his face as impassive as when Sonly had first told him. The only sign of emotion was a tightening along his jaw; otherwise, when he met her eyes, his face was closed, a mask.

"It's my fault," she said. The words were weak. And repeated for a third time. "I - I didn't know he'd taken them." As if that made any difference. She'd known what she was doing.

"I'm sure you didn't." He stretched his arms in front of him, his fingers laced together, until he gave a slight grimace. "You're far too clever to have trusted him with these." He didn't point out she hadn't been clever enough to stop them being taken. "Your plans?"

She wanted him to tell her what he thought, to get the worst of his reaction over, but he crossed his arms, waiting, and she didn't ask, too frightened about what he might say. Scorn she could face, or anger, but anything softer, his hurt....

She bit back her questions and said, "I can't let your mother blackmail me. Otherwise, everything we try to do with the republic will be blocked by her."

"Yes." His words were flat, his face still. Etched lines traced around his mouth, ones she hadn't seen for weeks. She waited, sure he'd go on, but he just sat in silence. Damn him; he could outwait anyone.

"Kare, say something," she said, finally. Anything had to be better than this silence. She reached her hands over the table, but he didn't move to take them. "Say you hate me, that I disgust you. Say anything."

"What do you want me to say? Well done?" His eyes blazed, but she faced him, not flinching.

"Tell me what you think. How you feel." A sick feeling settled in her stomach. She wanted him to admit it hurt, so she could embrace his pain and find a way to—

What? Make it better? She looked over the photos again. There was no way to make this better. If it had been him leaning over another woman the way Jake did her, with that sort of intimacy, she'd never find a way to make it better. She looked down at her hands, blurred under tears, and couldn't find a way to face him again. She heard him get up and didn't try to stop him, heard him cross the room to the door.

"Kare," she said, finally, her voice small. He had stopped with his hand on the door, his back to her, straight and tense. "I'm sorry."

He turned and his face wasn't masked anymore, but raw with pain.

"How do you think I feel?" he husked. He paused, searching her face. "Knowing I have no right to say anything about it, that you weren't with me at the time."

"Kare...."

"It hurts." His voice sounded ripped from him. "Like you would never know." He nodded at the table. "Do what you need to. Publish and be damned. Hold your head up and ride it out. I hope the prize is worth it."

The door slammed behind him, leaving a silence more accusing than his words.

CHAPTER TWELVE

Kare strode away from the boardroom, waving his security team back. It had taken every bit of his self-control to stop himself hitting out at something, anything, but he'd seen the look on Sonly's face, how frightened she'd been, how unsure of his reaction. Hitting out wasn't going to help things.

He turned the corner, his breath tight, his throat constrained. He'd known what had happened between Sonly and Peiret, of course, but he'd told himself it hadn't meant anything. The pictures told a very different story. It hadn't been the actions that had cut through him, but the intimacy between her and Jake. Her trailing hand on his chest, in one of them, their legs entwined, casual and knowing of each other.

He had to stop and lean against the wall. That little bastard, Peiret, *would* let the pictures be used against Sonly. He must have known Kare would see them eventually – if the lad was stupid enough to believe she'd accede to such pressure, he'd never really known her. He would lie about Sonly – about what lay at the core of her, her honesty, her integrity – to bring her down. He would do that despite having known her, in the way only a lover could.

He took a deep breath, trying to steady himself. It shouldn't matter what Sonly had done. They'd been separated; he'd had no right to ask her to be faithful.

Another deep breath, but his anger still built. Peiret was going to ruin her because she didn't want him. The brat of a great family, accustomed to getting his own way in everything, was using Sonly like a toy that didn't work anymore and could be discarded and ruined.

Kare pushed off from the wall, ignoring the small voice telling him to calm down. All his life he'd done what he'd been told, and constrained his own responses. He'd spent ten years in the stuffed palace of Abendau, never admitting his true feelings. A decade before that, in the Banned, he'd jumped to the rebels' tune and made himself the heir apparent they needed. His mother had taken him and ruined him because she could. He'd paid her price with blood and pain. This time he wasn't going to do what was expected of him; instead, he'd do what he wanted.

He stormed into the guest accommodation wing and sensed where Peiret was. The mesh came alive under his mind, alert to his mood, and he left it open; an audience would be more than welcome. He pushed through the heavy door into the luxury section, past guards who didn't stop him - even now, he out-VIPed anyone on Ferran. Peiret may have used a false name to get in to see Sonly, but he obviously wasn't slumming it. He reached Peiret's door and stopped outside. One last chance to walk away. It would be the right thing to do, the political thing.

He blasted the door so hard it cracked off the wall behind. The noise reverberated through the corridor; the guards at the entrance would surely have heard it.

He strode into the room. Comfortable surroundings, the best available for the brat. He'd never known a prison cell, running with rats, so cold it was another pain amongst the rest. Or a quiet room in a rock-hewn cavern, a capsule of a heritage denied his dead family. Peiret had known only prestige all his life, the weak-boned bastard, had lived in palaces, not been chased across space in a rickety freighter.

"Captain," said Kare. "I've had the chance to look over your calling card."

Peiret got to his feet, outrage pouring from him, and just the tiniest edge of wariness. Not enough, not nearly enough. The sound of booted footsteps came from the corridor. Kare slammed the door and sealed it.

"Get out," said Peiret. "I didn't ask you to attend me."

Attend? Kare Varnon had attended no one in his life, and he wasn't starting now. "My wife tells me you're intent on blackmail."

Peiret's face changed, became weasel-like. "It's not my fault." He licked his lips. "My father gave those pictures to the Empress."

"You're a little bastard." Kare stepped forwards and Peiret flinched back.

"Unlike you, I was man enough to give her what she needed," he said.

Bastard. But finally he was straightening and facing Kare. Good, it beat kicking hell out of someone helpless.

"And she enjoyed me," said Peiret. "Couldn't you see it in her face?"

Gods, yes. Kare grabbed him by the collar. "I saw it. It was no worse than I've carried in my mind for months."

The younger man tried to wriggle free. Kare held him, grim and firm. Voices came from behind the door, orders to open up, hard knocks on the metal, growing harder.

"You can't hurt me," said Peiret. "I'm an heir to a great family, you're the Emperor, you daren't lay a finger on me."

Kare laughed. "The only thing I am is King of the Roamers, and they won't stand against me in this." A swell in the mesh confirmed they absolutely weren't standing against him. He let Peiret go, stepped back, and whipped his hand across the other man's jaw, knocking him against the wall.

Peiret brought his hand up to his chin, astonished. "You can't do that! Guards! Guards!"

The door rattled and nearly gave. Kare took Peiret by the collar of his uniform and lifted him. He let him hang for a moment, legs just off the ground, kicking, and then brought his knee up, hard, in a move worthy of Silom. In fact, he was sure he'd learned it from Silom – how to hit hard with precision. He let Peiret go, and he crumpled to the floor, groaning.

"I think you'll find I can do it," said Kare, the words squeezed past clenched teeth. He walked out, past the guards, and didn't look back. He wasn't any calmer. But he did feel better.

***

A soft knock on Kerra's door, so soft she wasn't sure it was a knock at first, made her set her book to the side. "Come in."

Her mum entered, closing the door carefully behind her. When she turned, her face was pale and eyes puffy. "Am I interrupting you?"

Kerra's stomach did a small somersault. Her mother never looked less than polished when there was a chance, even a small one, that someone might capture an image of her, let alone wander through the Ferran hub dishevelled. "No. Go ahead."

Her mum sat on the bed beside her. She crossed her arms, as if closing herself off, and hunched forward. "There's something I need to tell you."

Kerra knew that tone of voice. This wasn't going to be good. She wished she'd pretended not to hear the knock on her door rather than have to hear whatever had made her mum look so... so.... She took in her mum's stance, her turned-down mouth. So beaten.

Her mum took a deep breath. "The Empress wants me to refuse the role of leader of the republic."

That was all? "We knew that ages ago. You're too popular. Dad told me she must be trying to find a way to force you out."

"She found it." Mum leaned forwards, but she kept her arms crossed so she was all thin angles, like if she moved she might break. "Kerra, just before the coup, things weren't good between me and your father."

"I know." Things hadn't been good between her parents as far back as she could remember. It was hardly news.

Her mum went red. "I... I had a relationship with someone else."

Kerra's eyebrows went up, right into her hair line, making her forehead tighten. This, she hadn't known. She didn't know what to think, but managed to ask, "Who?"

"Jake Peiret. He was in the army, and he's one of the gr—"

"I know who he is." He'd come to the palace a couple of times, and had chatted to her once. He'd been cute, she remembered, someone she sort of fancied. To think he'd been with her mum. Her stomach churned, loud in the quiet room.

"At the time, your dad and I had agreed to split. We weren't a couple. I want you to know that." Mum finally uncrossed her arms and ran her hands through her hair. "The thing is, there are some pictures of me and Jake. Together."

"Kissing?" Kerra didn't want to know this. Mum kissing her dad was bad enough, but someone young enough to be in a holo-collection was disgusting.

"Worse than that." Her mum looked at her feet. "We are in bed together. I have nothing on."

Kerra shunted down the bed, away from her mum. She shook her head, not quite believing it.

"Those pictures have been used by the Empress." Her mum raised her head and looked straight at Kerra. The blushing had gone, replaced by a coldness Kerra knew well. It was the same coldness her mother had carried when running her campaign for the Senate in Abendau; Mum had decided she was going to get something, and nothing or no one would change her mind. "If I do not step down and put my support behind her, she will publish them."

"And will you stand down?" Kerra didn't know what answer she wanted.

Slowly, her mum shook her head. "No. I have to face this." She held her hand out. Kerra didn't move. "Tomorrow, they will be on the news-feeds. They are very clearly of me. They are very revealing." Kerra stayed silent. "I thought you should know before they were released."

Everyone would see them. She didn't know whether to feel horror for her mum or embarrassment. The only thing she was sure was that it was good not to be on Abendau. At least on the Ferran hub, no one knew her – even Baelan was in lock-down on one of the Roamer ships for some unrevealed reason. "What did Dad say?"

"He said to do what I had to. He then, apparently, visited Jake Peiret. I think Jake is just about back on his feet now."

Kerra smiled, even past her shock. Good for Dad.

Her mother stood. "Kerra, this changes nothing between us, or with your father. But you must see I can't give up the republic just because someone has something they can use against me."

Was she stupid? It changed everything. She'd betrayed Dad. She'd lied to Kerra. She was going to be on display naked. She took in her mum's cold, tight stance. It was all about her. She didn't care how Kerra felt about it, or what it would do to anyone else. She never did. "I want you to go, Mum." She turned away.

Her mother left without another word, closing the door, leaving a silence broken only by the soft hum of the heating system. Kerra stared at the door. She didn't know how she could stand to face her mum again.

She went to her small window and looked down from the space station, towards the planet beneath. She reached out to let the sense of space take her and hold her, so that she knew where she was in the world. The mesh was all around her. She closed her eyes, drinking it in as night crept on towards morning, when her dad would leave and her mother be revealed.

CHAPTER THIRTEEN

Baelan threw the ball against the wall of the ship, let it rebound into his hand, and bounced it back. Throw, thud, catch; throw, thud, catch. The repetition was soothing in its own way, a means to stop the thoughts circling his mind, careering between the compulsion and the hope his father could do what he promised and get him back to Belaudii and his mother. It was exhausting, one moment sure of his way forward, the next plunged back into confusion. He wished he could open his head and remove the Empress' voice. Perhaps then he'd know his own thoughts.

He missed a catch and the ball bounced over the floor to the closed door. Baelan stared at it. His father was leaving this morning for the palace. He thought about his scars. He remembered Taluthna's tales of a Varnon who'd been reduced to another man's dog. How, then, did his father walk back to Abendau and face that? And why? It went against everything he'd been taught about his father: that he was a coward who hid behind the walls of his compound; a fanatic who hated the tribal people and would do anything to destroy those he came across; a cold and untouchable man, with hatred driving him. Either he was the best actor Baelan had ever come across, or someone else had got things wrong. The tribes had been wrong about the Empress, after all.

The door to his cabin opened, and he got to his feet, lifted the ball out of the way, and faced it. He had no idea what would happen to him - the Roamers hadn't had any contact with him, except to give him food. He'd tried to go into the mesh, once, to reach his father and find out, but there were other minds in the way of him, blocking him. He didn't know if it had been ordered or one of the hive decisions the Roamers seemed to take.

It wasn't Farran at the door, but Lichio le Payne, who closed the door behind him.

"I hear it was an eventful trip over," he said. He regarded Baelan, making him want to squirm - the security chief had a way of looking that seemed to see more than most people.

Baelan looked at his feet. "Yeah." How to explain how things had got away on him? Or that he didn't want to end up in a cell. In the absence of anything clever, he stayed looking at his feet.

"So, what do I do about you?" asked le Payne. "I have a need for this ship, so you can't stay here." Of course, his father would have Farran for his pilot; he'd pretty much evolved into that role. "And a cell on Ferran wouldn't be ideal, would it?"

Baelan's head came up. He wasn't going to be locked up? He wasn't sure whether to be relieved or sorry. At least, in a cell, there wasn't much that could go wrong. On the other hand, quietness gave too much room for his thoughts. Better to stay busy and distracted and hope the compulsion lost its strength in his father's absence.

"So what will happen to me?" he asked.

Le Payne slid the door to the corridor open. Beyond it, a squad of soldiers waited.

"We're going to call them your personal security team," he said. "Kerra has one as well, much to her disgust." His sharp eyes hardened. "But, in your case, the security is going mostly one way."

Mostly, Baelan noticed. It gave him some hope. They didn't want him dead, anyway.

"Some information." Le Payne held a hand up, two fingers pointing at Baelan. "Your squad are trained to repel psyching. If you try anything - anything at all - you will find yourself locked up, political fallout or not. I'll take the consequences for it. The Ferrans are keen to welcome yourself and Kerra as honoured guests. There are education days lined up. I can't stop any of that. I can assure you, no matter where you go, your team will be in attendance. Understood?"

Baelan nodded, relieved. It was more than he'd expected, to be allowed any freedom, or treated as an equal to Kerra, even if the undercurrent to it seemed to be political expediency over concern for himself. He wondered what, if anything, Kerra knew.

Le Payne led the way through the ship. Baelan's squad formed around him, and the security chief hadn't been exaggerating – they gave him very little room. They left the ship by the main hatch and entered the port.

Baelan stopped at the bottom of the ramp. A few feet away, his father stood in fatigues, a squad of soldiers surrounding him. He talked in a low voice, too low to carry to Baelan, and held everyone's attention, not just the squad or the Roamers who followed his every move, but the technicians and the port staff. Everyone was watching him, either openly or surreptitiously, as they went about their work.

He didn't seem to notice, or care. His movements, as he illustrated what he wanted with his hands, were economical, confident, not flashy. He didn't look like a man who was scared, but one who was dangerous. Baelan had never seen his father as dangerous before. Powerful, yes, and surrounded by others who meted out danger. But dangerous himself, no.

His father must have sensed him, because he lifted his head and met Baelan's eyes. Baelan held his breath, and tried to read the unspoken language. His father took in the security squad, and his mouth gave a slight twist, perhaps resigned or apologetic. Determination shone from him but, almost hidden, fear showed in the set of his jaw, in the sharp lines around his mouth. Whatever he was, he wasn't the cold robot the tribes believed; his eyes were those of a man facing a battle. Baelan had seen it often enough to recognise it.

Baelan took a step forwards but paused, undecided. Should he wish his father luck and all courage, as he would a tribesman undertaking a mission? His father didn't wear the ankhar, and he didn't seek Baelan's good luck. He wished he knew what to do, that he didn't have to second-guess everything, but all his certainties had shifted under the prism of the Empress' attention.

After a moment, his father gave a thin smile and an ironic – or perhaps not ironic – half-salute, one that seemed to say he knew and understood. He'd said that on the ship, too: that he'd been an outsider and knew how it felt. He was a mix of enigmas, at once exactly what Baelan had been told – the centre of everything, a man who thought he was above any other – and nothing like it.

Baelan turned away. The compulsion niggled at him, buried at the back of his mind where he was determined to keep it. He couldn't understand how it could be there and yet he could feel such a pull to his father. Le Payne waved his squad forwards and they took Baelan from the port, down a long corridor and into the main space station, finally reaching a bedroom. Two of them took position at either side of the door. Baelan went through, and the door closed behind him, locking with a dull thud. Not a cell, then, but not freedom, either.

He sat on the edge of the bed, glad to be alone, and pulled the ball from his pocket. He bounced it across to the wall and back to his hand, the wall, and back to his hand, and still couldn't understand any of it.

***

Kerra ran into the hangar and stopped a few feet from Farran's ship. It looked odd, its decals obscured by shielding so it could be any ship, but it still felt familiar, the space-scarred hull almost clunky, built to survive the longest possible space-hauls.

"Hey." Dad approached, dressed in fatigues, hair cropped, two blasters holstered. He looked like a stranger – colder than she'd ever known him, a soldier before he was a father.

The dam broke at his familiar voice, and she flung herself against him. He put his arms around her, in the tight hold that had comforted her through her childhood and held her safe in a world more dangerous than she'd ever known. Tears streamed down her face. "I don't want you to go."

"I know." He let go and tipped her head up to his. He was smiling; it nearly reached his eyes. "I don't want to go. But it won't be long; the mission will be over in a week."

Her heart thudded. It would be over in a week, not that he'd be back in a week. "Daddy," she said. "Be careful."

"As much as I can be." His voice was soft, but serious. The mesh ebbed between them, tinged with a soft undercurrent of sadness and doubt. He took her elbow. "Did the Roamers talk to you about the mesh? I have to leave it when on Abendau?"

She nodded. She remembered him during the attack on the caves, when he'd been pulled between the mesh and his role. He couldn't do that if he was leading an assault. She understood that, but not the instructions not to touch or approach the mesh in any way while he was gone. She could barely imagine not being in it. She dreaded the loneliness of it.

"Good," said Dad. "It's important." He pushed a strand of hair away from her face. "Without a centre, the mesh will be tricky to predict." What was he saying, with his eyes that didn't waver? "One day, *you* will hold it," he said. "But, for now, we shouldn't confuse things, I'm told."

"I don't want to be Queen," she said. "It's enough

to be a princess." More than enough when all she wanted to be was a Controller, to have her own ship and be known and needed by no one.

He didn't smile or laugh. "When – if – it's handed to you, you'll be ready."

She pulled her arm away. He was talking like it was going to happen soon, and that wasn't good, not when he was about to go back to Abendau and face the Empress. He couldn't have any doubts or the witch would sense them and pounce.

"I'm not ready." She forced a smile. "So you better come back soon."

There was a flurry by the door: her mum, the last person Kerra wanted to see this morning.

"I have to go," she said. "Do what you need to and get back. Right?"

"Right. Don't be too hard on your mum, Kerra. She has a storm to ride out, and she needs your support. Right?"

His question hung in the air, but she didn't answer; she couldn't let her last word be a lie. She gave a faint smile and turned away before he could ask again, and ran from the hangar before her mother saw her.

***

Sonly stared around the hangar, her stomach jumping, partly with dread, partly anticipation. She'd grown up on a rebel base, she'd done her own basic training, and the familiar sounds of soldiers calling to one another, of ships being tested and readied, brought her childhood back to her. The hangar smelt of diesel and gas, adding to the familiarity. She wished she could take one of the ships and get away from the news-holos.

Kare stepped out from behind one of the Roamer ships. He hadn't seen her yet. She watched him move, slim and composed, saw how his eyes missed nothing about the preparations around him, and the feeling of déjà-vu to the days of the Banned was complete.

The moment passed. When he'd commanded the Banned he'd had dark hair, not white. He hadn't worn the collar of his fatigues turned up. When he stopped to check one of the ships he gave a slight wince as he ran his hand along its flank, a wince that would never have been there before Omendegon.

She wanted to tell him not to go, to stay, but forced herself to stand her ground. He needed peace and he'd never have it while his mother was alive.

He turned, saw her, and a smile made him look younger, more like the Kare she remembered. He walked towards her and she took in his fatigues, right down to the sand-boots he was wearing. Things *were* serious.

He stopped in front of her. "How bad are the holos?" His voice was light, but she wasn't fooled.

"Awful." She put her hand on his arm. "I'm sorry. I didn't want you to be leaving with this going on."

He took an audible breath, but managed a tight nod. "It is what it is. You never lied about it." He stroked her cheek, his touch gentle. "We've survived worse."

They had. And they'd survive this. "How long until you go?" she asked, her voice hoarse.

"We embark in a few minutes. Kerra came to say goodbye. And the boy – he passed, briefly."

"Lichio?"

"We spoke." He'd tell her nothing more.

"You'll be careful?"

"I'll try." There was an awkward silence, until he cracked his fingers together and gave a small shrug. "It's always the worst part. The waiting."

"Yes." He had no idea how hard it was to wait. She'd spent months not knowing if he was alive or dead, or worse. Nights, alone, trying to sleep, only to lie awake with despair circling even as she'd gritted her teeth and waited some more. "I hate waiting."

"Come here." He put his arms around her, not

seeming to care who was watching. He'd never cared how a soldier should behave, he'd only worried about doing what was right. The ever-present smell of the coffee that carried him through each day, practically on a drip, surrounded her. She leaned in to him, felt the strength in his arms, the tightness of his chest - he was doing a good job of hiding his fear, but snuggled against him there was no mistaking it. They stood, his head leaned on hers, hers against his chest. Soldiers shouted, a ship's siren sounded, but it happened outside their bubble.

Finally, he released her, only to kiss her, a long kiss, one to last an age, maybe forever. Her lips opened under his, so familiar. How could she have compared Jake to him? She put her arms around him, wanting to be closer, but it wasn't possible.

Someone shouted his name. He pulled away. A mew escaped her.

"Go," he said. His eyes were shining in the bright lights of the hangar. "Don't look back, just go. Or I can't."

He'd made her leave the night at the Banned, too, the night she'd lost him. She turned, blinded by blurred tears, and stumbled as she walked away. She had to let him go so he'd come back. Please, she thought, putting all her might into it, make sure he does. I need him to. I love him.

***

"Ready?" asked Farran.

Kare turned. The Roamer's face was twisted in sympathy, but no words were given or needed; the mesh held the shape of Kare's thoughts, his sadness, his determination to keep going forwards and not look back. He took a last look around the hangar.

At the main entrance a familiar person stood, blond hair floodlit from behind. Lichio held up his hand, and Kare nodded, acknowledging it. He climbed up the ramp and stopped at the top to run his fingers along the lip of the hatch. He selected the space-seal command. The hatch came up from the undercarriage, slowly cutting off his view of the port, first a single door, then a thicker one casting him into darkness.

His stomach lurched. This was it. He was going back to Abendau.

CHAPTER FOURTEEN

Lichio left the port, his mind racing through the tasks ahead. Baelan was taken care of – for now – with the best security team he could spare. Which left ferreting through the Ferrans and figuring out who would be happy to play, for a price.

"Lich." The voice was familiar, making his heart race. He almost didn't want to turn around in case he was wrong, but he did. Like a miracle, Josef waited just beyond the entrance to the hangar. He looked drained, his skin pale, almost sallow, his eyes hooded. Lichio wanted to run to him, to take him in his arms, but found his muscles tensing in the old reflex of professionalism.

"Josef," he said, and his voice didn't sound like his own, but strangled. "I thought...."

He didn't say what he'd thought – that Josef was dead or taken. That he was in a cell in Abendau palace, facing that hell. The dam broke and Lichio embraced Josef, a tight clinch around his shoulders. He smelled familiar: spiced tea, with an undertone of light sweat from travelling. Josef gripped him back and they stood like that until Lichio remembered where they were and how many eyes could be on him. He let go and stepped away.

"I have an office. Come with me." He led the way, his steps brisk. Josef was alive. It was what he'd been praying for.

Why, then, was he so scared?

He opened the door to the office allocated to him, dismissing his security with a flick of his wrist, and let Josef enter before him. He closed the door, and locked it.

"Still so careful?" asked Josef. His voice had an

edge Lichio wasn't familiar with. "I thought Kare had stepped down. Surely that means you're out of a job, if you want to be."

A lance of fear stabbed Lichio. They'd talked about this for years – the day when he would be no longer in such a high-profile position, and free to choose his own route. He nodded to one of two seats facing the desk and dropped into the other. Did Josef know that their relationship would not have derailed his role? He was an ambassador: did he know Kare would never have let it affect things? Lichio faced him, the lies through the years circling, and feared Josef did know. That he had always known.

"What happened to you?" asked Lichio. "Where have you been?"

Josef paused, perhaps deciding whether to pursue his own question first, but gave a slight shrug, one that said he'd play along.

"Getting out of Abendau wasn't straightforward," he said. "I had to detour to the Nova hub – and what a hell-hole that is, it needs some serious investment – and then back to Mersor. You had disappeared. I took the first flight to Ferran when I heard you were here."

"You could have contacted me first," said Lichio. "I was worried."

"I wanted to see you face to face," said Josef. "I didn't want any deflections."

Lichio ducked his head. Josef had a veneer of politeness that made him appear malleable, but he rarely gave ground on anything that mattered to him. He faced Lichio, his shoulders straight. Whatever he wanted to address – in person – wasn't going to be left unheard.

Lichio should be saying something, about his relief, about his worries, about how much Josef's return mattered, but in the face of his lover's calm assurance, the words wouldn't come.

"I have an office lined up on Mersor," said Josef.

"It includes a role for a new ambassador to the republic." His eyes didn't stray. "It's yours, if you want it."

Lichio pulled at his collar. The room was too warm. "I have a role here. Kare has not dismissed his army yet."

"But he will." Josef leaned forwards and put his hand on Lichio's knee. It was warm, and heavy. He squeezed slightly, a promise of something more. "This is what we've been waiting for, Lich. A chance to be together. A chance for you to go to your sister, to Kare, and tell them who I am."

"It's not the time."

Josef removed his hand. "When is it the time?" He ran his hand through his hair, pushing it back and revealing the dark pools of his eyes. "Is there ever going to be a time? Are my family right – that you don't care for me the way you claim to? They asked to meet you, to get to know you, and I had to tell them that I didn't know if you would." His voice caught. "I had to tell them I didn't know that you would commit – that you never had, so far." He crossed his arms. "And that's what I want. You know that. I want that commitment. I want to know that you aren't going to piss what we had away."

As he had over the past four years – pulling back at every increased intimacy, using excuses to hold Josef at bay and yet crawling back, every time, to find the solace only he gave. The room went dark, closing in.

"I..." What could he say? He'd spent his life avoiding a commitment like this. He swallowed the bile that rose in him. "I can't." He spread his hands, half-reaching over the desk, wanting what he would not give himself. He looked down at them, as if they might hold the answer.

The silence lengthened; Josef would not help him out, not this time. Lichio raised his eyes and met Josef's calm stare.

"I have spent my life avoiding what you're asking

of me," he said. "I watched families ripped apart in the Banned. The pain of the people left behind—" He'd seen it happen to his father, had felt the pain of loss himself. It never went away. "I swore I'd never allow it to happen to me again. That I would never put myself in that position."

Josef touched his outstretched hands. "Lich. You already have." His eyes softened. "Don't you see? It isn't commitment that hurts. It's love."

Love. A word so casually used, it was easy to dismiss. Love couldn't be something that could rip a life apart. He pulled his hand away, denying Josef's words.

"I can't," he said, and his voice held. He ignored the tight breaths that told him he was wrong, and that he should listen. "You should go."

"I hoped," Josef said. He looked at the ceiling, as if for inspiration. When he looked back at Lichio, his eyes were bereft, their darkness deeper than ever. "No matter who you slept with, who you so casually turned to, I hoped."

A chill settled in Lichio. "You knew?" But of course he did - Lichio had never tried to hide his lovers, even if he didn't flaunt them openly. He hadn't thought about what they might mean to Josef - he hadn't dared to, knowing the answer - but used them as a way to stay free, as another excuse not to commit.

"You weren't discreet. Presumably, you didn't want to be." Damn Josef, who'd always seen through him. Lichio remembered the first day Josef had found his scars from cutting himself. He had never believed they were anything other than what they were. How he'd insisted Lichio stop.

"Why?" said Josef. "Didn't I matter to you?" He was tense, as if ready to walk out at any moment. "Don't you see the chance you have?"

"You mattered," said Lichio. He gripped Josef's arm, his hand closing on his wrist, the familiar smooth skin over bones. *I love you*, he wanted to say. *You were - are*

– the centre of my world. He hated himself for not. "You mattered more than anyone."

"Then come with me." Josef put his other hand over Lichio's, held it tight. "We can put Abendau behind us. Start afresh." He gave a short laugh. "It might not be as terrifying as you expect."

There was no further answer, except what Lichio couldn't say – that Josef hadn't mattered more than the wall he had built to protect himself.

Josef gave a curt nod. "I'll let myself out." He stopped at the door, his hand on it for a long moment, before he turned back once more. "You can duck if you want to, Lich. But it's not going to go away. That's what love does – it arrives when you're not looking and it doesn't let go. Even if it hurts."

He left, and Lichio didn't stop him.

CHAPTER FIFTEEN

The ship dropped from space, hurtling towards Belaudii. Kare held himself in the co-pilot's seat with little more than gritted teeth and bloody-minded determination. Last time he'd been on a landing like this he'd been curled up with Karia, trying to ignore his father's worried eyes shifting from control panel to viewing window.

Beside him, Farran whistled but his eyes were intent on the planet below, his level of focus far from reassuring. Belaudii grew bigger and took on its familiar orange tinge. Kare clenched his fists as its features became clearer, much quicker than he'd have liked. The landing had to be a quick in and out, but *gods* he hoped Farran was even half the pilot his father was. Ealyn's intensity may have been alarming, but at least he'd been virtually guaranteed to get any ship down.

Three flanking ships pulled away, each focused on a section of Belaudii's great desert. An alarm sounded as the planet's space-control tried to make contact, but Farran flipped it to silent. The communicator flashed an angry red.

Kare leant forward. He could make out the green of the palace's gardens, and the port and palace, just visible as white dots. Already, ships would be mobilising in the port, to be followed by those based in his desert compound.

The ship screamed in protest at the speed of descent. Kare swallowed nausea and kept his focus on the sky, which grew lighter as they streaked through the atmosphere. New alarms sounded, altitude and speed warnings. The velocity regulator threatened to burn out for good measure. They plummeted, the ship shaking, his teeth rattling.

The first fighters emerged from Abendau's port: a small fleet, two ships targeted on each Roamer ship. Kare pointed; Farran nodded. The reverse thrusters started to slow the descent, and the freighter pulled out to streak across the blurred desert. Kare clenched his hands around the armrests and ordered himself not to scream. He was King of the Roamers, he couldn't get freaked out over a little vertical drop from space. The ship's speed, carried from space, outpaced the fighters, but it wouldn't be long until the distance closed.

"Salyn, Tarn, cover me." Farran's voice carried an edge of worry.

"Coming round."

Two of the Roamer freighters broke from their flight path, drawing behind Farran and picking up the pursuing fighters, their progress plotted on the HUD display. Laser-bolts flashed against the freighters' shields. Farran pulled away, leaving the dogfight behind.

"I'll have to set down a little off-plan," he said. "We need to do this quickly."

Kare nodded. A desert-survival would be needed, then. Damn. The ship banked and slowed; nothing for it but to get on with it. He checked his pack straps were tight and looked at his boots, his fatigues - anything other than the planet still coming at them much too fast.

"Brace." Farran's voice was calm, but Kare could feel his tension. "Touchdown in ten."

Kare pulled the brace restraints across his body and crossed his arms, letting the seat pull him against it. The ship passed over the desert, churning up the sand. Farran leaned forwards, not whistling now but watching, watching, his eyes as alert as Ealyn's had ever been.

"Nine." The countdown started from the control panel. The ship slowed, stalled, and dropped, sending Kare's stomach somewhere into orbit.

"Eight, seven, six." *Oh, gods, get this over with.* "Five."

He should have listened to Lich; this was a bad idea. Even his dad wouldn't have tried this landing. He put his head down, and went back to concentrating on his boots; they weren't much of a distraction in the midst of the alarms.

"Four. Three. Two."

Farran hit the landing command and thrust himself back, into the brace position, his brow beaded with sweat. "Hang on!"

The ship hit the ground, landing repulsors absorbing the impact with a jarring crash. More alarms sounded, lights flashed and blared; Roamer ships might be equipped for such landings, but they didn't have to like them. The ship shuddered to a halt and Kare was already unclicking his restraints, fumbling with shaking hands. "How far to the rendezvous?"

"About five miles. Best I could do." The Roamer hit the hatch command and jerked his head back. "Go. Before they pick up my position."

Kare was already on his feet and moving down the access corridor. He skimmed out as soon as the hatch lifted, and darted down the gangway, hitting the desert at a run, not stopping to check the sand-cover; if Farran didn't take off, the fighters would have him just as quickly as any clutterback.

The sky was empty of pursuit, for now. The freighter's engines were whining and the hatch closing. Kare sprinted across the sand, weaving, to the dunes. His feet slipped as he ran. He'd never get used to the desert. He sped up, feeling Farran's impatience, his need for Kare to go faster and get into the safety zone so the ship could lift off.

He jumped a scrub of grass and dived for the dunes, hitting hard with his shoulder, but it was soft sand beneath. Not clutter-nest territory, thankfully. He was as close to the ship as when his father had left him as a child, hunched against the fence of the old yard. The sky filled with a familiar roar as the ship lifted off, leaving the burnt smell of the engines in its wake.

Kare turned his head away. The roar became distant, and his teeth stopped rattling. The Roamer ship was already far in the distance, but a volley of distant specks, their pursuers, had picked Farran up. Most broke after the ship, but one – a desert-seeker, judging by the flashing along its fuselage – bore down on Kare's position.

Damn. He stayed flat, heart pounding, and crabbed his hand to the shield command, hitting it with a clumsy, clawed finger.

The air around him changed, becoming heavier. An artificial tang made his nose twitch. He stayed down, the shield doing little to reduce his sense of being exposed, his head turned just enough to track the sky above. The ship appeared, following a search trajectory, hazy through his shield's field. If he stayed quiet and still, they should not pick him up.

The sand moved in front of him. It cracked, breaking in a thin line. He barely stopped himself scrambling back. Had he read the sand wrong? If it was a clutter-nest, he was in trouble. Fuck that: he was dead, either from the ship if he ran or the spider if he stayed. Carefully, he put his hand on the sand, double-checking. It *was* soft, not compacted. This shouldn't be spider territory.

Still the sand shifted and he watched, transfixed, as a snake emerged, its tongue flicking from side to side. A baroda, and a big one, as deadly as anything in the desert. Its red stripes practically had danger stencilled on them. It whipped across the sand towards him.

He stayed still, his attention shifting from the snake to the ship, coming closer, then fading, closer, then fading. The snake drew near, tongue flicking. Under Kare's hand the sand drummed, making his fingers tingle; the shield's energy was drawing the snake. He stayed still and told himself the snake couldn't get through the force-field.

No, but it could burrow under the shield and come up within the shield's parameter. *Not good.*

"Go away, big girl," he murmured. The ship had come closer again. The snake hissed. Its tongue flicked at the shield, probing. It pulled back and started to burrow.

Oh, shit. Kare looked around, hoping for any sort of cover, but there was nothing but sand stretching in every direction.

The searching ship moved away, and he killed his shield. He'd take his chances with the ship before the snake; at least they'd ask questions before they attacked. Maybe. He scrambled back as the sand broke, inches from his right foot, and the snake emerged, fangs bared, ready to strike.

Kare slipped in the soft sand, sprawling backwards. The snake sprang at him, quicker than he'd imagined. He yelled, managing to roll to the side, and fumbled for his blaster. He pulled it from the holster in one move.

The snake lunged for another attack. Kare got a shot off, but it was wild. His boot caught the serpent and its fangs sank into the heavy material. He took aim, taking his time, even as the snake drew back again. He wouldn't get another chance, not against its speed. He squeezed off a shot.

The snake flew through the air, tail snapping. Above, the ship had turned back towards his sector. Kare hit the shield activation and flung himself flat. He didn't dare breathe, sure they'd had long enough to fix his position. The engines roared closer. A bead of sweat trickled between his shoulder blades and he waited, sure they were above him, circling, ready to take him.

After an age, the sound of the ship grew more distant. He forced himself to wait a little longer, alert for movement in the sand, or the sound of pursuit. After several minutes he sat up. The ship was gone from the sky and the snake lay dead a few feet away. His breaths were jerky and small, but still counted. He was alive.

He deactivated the shield and got to his feet, shaky as hell. Snakes were only one of the creatures to watch for. There were lizards, big and lumbering, so well camouflaged he'd be on them before he'd see them; the spiders with their buried nests, the sand above crusted and invisible, but thin as an egg. The number-one cause of death in the desert. Not a helpful thing to remember.

Stop thinking about it and get going. He unclipped his direction-finder from his belt, activated it, and set out for the team waiting for him, taking his time to check the sand-cover; being late mightn't be a disaster, but being dead would be.

CHAPTER SIXTEEN

Baelan entered the main entrance hall of Ferran-V's port, his squad practically stuck to him. Another of the Ferrans' educational days for him and Kerra, and he'd been bored by the end of the second one. It made him think he should do something, bring down a wall, perhaps, and have le Payne confine him to his room.

This trip sounded somewhat better than the others had been, however. Already, through the viewing window of his room, the port was busy with tourists and their fire forest guides, even though the sun was barely up. In one corner a kiosk sold t-shirts and holo-holders with pictures of cute fire-sprites and slogans proclaiming the purchaser had survived the fire forests. Posters showing the indigenous plants of the forest and their uses hung beneath, as well as a holo-player showing the history of the Empress' raid on the forest, and how the survivors had made it through. It was a mythology impossible not to come across on Ferran – it was in their books and their culture and in their anecdotes. Baelan half-smiled at that – they'd be better waiting until the return leg to purchase anything; at least five tourists each year didn't come back. The foolhardy ones, who didn't believe they needed a guide, or who misjudged how quickly night could fall in the forest.

He hopped from foot to foot. He'd already been waiting half an hour for Kerra. The entrance to the planetary hangars, as opposed to the sprawling annex which serviced the hub, remained closed and would do so until her security team checked in. Hence the milling tourists, some of whom must be starting to wonder why they were being delayed in joining their flights.

"Can you check where she is?" he asked the lieutenant in charge of his team.

"She's en route." The lieutenant's voice was bland, uninterested, and Baelan scowled.

Finally, a clatter of footsteps announced the arrival of Kerra, dressed in a casual sweat-top and light trousers and wearing expensive boots ideal for a forest trek. Baelan looked down at his own sneakers and short-sleeved top. He always got it wrong, damn it. On the plus side, his clothes were far from entitled. Man of the people, him.

"Are you ready?" asked Kerra.

"Yeah." He didn't point out he'd been the one kicking his heels. "I'm not missing this."

The security door slid open and they passed through. Kerra must be used to the wave-through - everywhere she went, people let her pass, knowing who she was - but he had to fight the urge to empty his pockets and hold out his arm for a DNA sample.

They reached their docking bay and the planet-hopper allocated to them - top of the range, of course. At some point he'd get used to it, surely, and stop doing a double-take to check if such luxuries were really laid on for him. He climbed aboard, and dropped into the padded seat beside Kerra before the lieutenant could make him sit in the middle of the squad. She had been the only saving grace of the last few days - if she'd been told about the incident with their father, she must have decided it didn't matter, as she blithely treated him the same as before.

Perhaps she could sense he was no danger to her - that he would, if he could, protect her. She had, after all, been helping him by pretending his guard was no different from her own and finding ways to stay beside him so he wasn't cut off by his entourage. He wished he'd known closeness like this as a child.

The door to a different future opened, just a crack.

It felt like she might teach him how to push through into it. If he did, would she come through that door, too, into her own changed future? She certainly seemed more independent than when he'd first met her, more questioning of her own path forwards. Her insistence on learning how to Control was something he couldn't have imagined the Kerra from the palace doing.

Durren, their tutor, slipped into the row behind them. "Did you read the information I filed about the forests?"

Baelan nodded. If he kept quiet, he might get away without admitting he'd missed his home-study. He started counting inwardly. One – two – three...

"It was very interesting." Kerra's voice oozed enthusiasm, and Baelan gave a half-smile; he'd known Little Miss Smart wouldn't have skipped homework. "The whole eco-system has adapted to the lava-mud." She ticked off her fingers as she covered each point. "The trees themselves have roots that stay near the surface, drawing heat from the pools by surrounding them, like a bowl. And within the roots, pockets form of warm soil – that's where you get other plants. Ferns, brambles and low bushes. That's all that grows – and each is particular to its conditions."

"And you, Baelan?" Durren touched his shoulder. "Tell me what you thought about the native species?"

Damn. Kerra flashed a "you're-in-trouble" grin. He cast his mind through what little information he had gleaned, most of it from tourist ads and not Durren's carefully presented research, and came up with the only interesting creature on Ferran.

"The fire-sprites are deadly." He'd spent an afternoon looking at pictures of the unlucky tourists who didn't make it back before nightfall. "When the Ferrans find the victims, the bodies aren't rigid. The sprites strip their heat all night and only kill them at dawn. The victim can feel their teeth ripping the skin to find the warm bits – they found one guy still alive, and he said it was the worst pain he'd ever known." He grinned at Kerra. "D'you want to know the really vile bit?" Kerra nodded, her face caught between revulsion and fascination. "They save your eyes to the en—"

"Thank you." Durren's voice was clipped. "You've obviously done extensive research of your own."

The ship's engines started and they lifted from the port, staying low over the city. The morning sun rose over the forest but even leaving this early, they'd be lucky to have four hours in the forest: Durren would err on the side of caution and leave well before the short dusk. They flew over the force-field fence separating the city from the forest, the ship swooping and graceful, its engines quiet.

That was how the Empress had taken the planet in the first war of the empire. She'd brought the fence down at night and let the sprites take the city. By morning, when she deployed her soldiers, three quarters of the population were already dead. And he had once worshipped her, not knowing – indeed, celebrating her actions as evidence of strong leadership – her cruelty. How she would hurt him and warp him. That was who his father was going up against. He was crazy, but Baelan understood why he'd had to go. Someone had to stop her. The thought of his father made his stomach flip, and he wrenched his thoughts away. He'd done well, these last days, to stay calm. He didn't want to ruin it now, especially in front of Kerra.

The ship climbed and the forest spread beneath them, its canopy tight. Occasional gaps appeared for the transport stations. Those nearest the city were busy and when he leaned his nose against the glass, nudging Kerra to make room for him, he could make out more kiosks and milling early-bird tourists who had either left the port first thing, or accessed one of the planet-hopper taxis, operating from a smaller depot in the city centre. The next of the transports left the port after theirs, spilling out over the trees.

They flew on, Durren pointing out occasional gaps where lava pools were, but Kerra had gone quiet, the way she'd been for the last couple of days. He supposed she was worried about their father. And the pictures of her mother on the nets couldn't be a lot of fun to watch. He kept his thoughts very carefully hidden; who'd have known cold Sonly could be so hot?

A tickle touched his mind, a familiar sense of someone he knew. All thoughts of Sonly left him. He reached out, sure he was wrong, but found it again. It was unmistakable: his mother was somewhere close.

She couldn't be. He dampened his excitement, but checked again. She was somewhere below in the forest. She'd come for him. She might have come to take him home. Even as he thought that, he knew it wouldn't be possible, that to go home to the tribes meant too much danger for him, let alone going back to the Empress.

Ideas formed in him, about how he could grab her and take her back to Ferran with him. Once there, le Payne would have to do something to keep her safe - he'd insist on it. The planet-hopper began its descent, and the feel of his mother got stronger. His eyes welled with tears he had to bite back. He was behaving like a child. She hadn't abandoned him. He reached out. *I'm coming, Mother, I'm coming.* Once he found her, he'd work out what to do. He'd bring the forest down around him if he had to.

CHAPTER SEVENTEEN

Kare cursed as he slipped down a dune, wrenching his ankle. He'd forgotten how hard the desert made everything. He tried to slow his descent but his boots didn't grip on the soft sand, and he hit the desert floor hard enough to jar his teeth.

Damn it, he'd had enough of the place already. He checked his bearings and started up the next dune. Not far, and if he pulled this off it would be worth the desert walk. He cast himself into the mesh, found the pilots safely in orbit, and smiled. It *had* worked. His father would have been impressed.

He crested the dune, lungs burning, and scanned the horizon. He should be able to see the pick-up by now; he was practically on top of it. Sand stretched in each direction, and the sun fell over the distant city of Abendau. Unease prickled him – once the sun went down, night descended on Belaudii with startling speed. If the transport didn't pick him up soon, he'd end up spending the night in the desert. That wouldn't be good, not with the accompanying animals and cold, no matter how up to date his desert training was. Even the tribespeople didn't spend nights alone in the desert if they could help it.

He took a deep breath, steadying himself, and activated his call-sign. He was in the right place; the pick-up was late, that was all, possibly because of the attention the space-drop had brought. He sat on the crest of the dune; no one needed him to wander off. Eventually, if he had to, he'd find a ridge, make sure it was one without clutterbacks, and wait the night out in the light shelter-pod in his pack. He'd done it once before, after becoming Emperor, when he'd realised taking the palace and port had been the easy part of mastering Belaudii. That time, though, he'd had a squad of soldiers on standby, and a tutor from the tribes. He'd never been in the desert alone so late in the day.

Baelan would have. The desert would have been his playground. He would know this view of Abendau under a huge setting sun. He'd be quite at home, no doubt, with a sleeping zone already staked out. Somehow, sitting in the desert, Kare felt closer to his son, as if by sharing the same expanse he could see how the boy must feel. It must be alien to be taken from the freedom of the desert and shoved into the entourage that was the family Varnon's life. The sense of the desert followed Baelan, the low thoughts of loss that Kare hadn't managed to pinpoint until now, imbued with this sense of place. The boy needed space to grow into his powers, and to do that he needed to be in touch with the land that had grown him, more than Kare's genes ever had.

The sand shifted in front of him, scattering his thoughts. He scrambled to his feet, mouth and throat dry. If it was a lizard, his best hope was to run before it emerged; if a clutterback, staying still was key. The sand shifted again – the creature, whether spider or lizard, was huge.

The sand raised into a dome. He backed away. Even for a lizard it was giant, but not impossible.

It formed past any lizard's size, taking on the shape of a desert transporter, one of the dual-function types, used on the desert sand or in the air. It had been waiting most of the day, judging by the amount of sand it displaced. This wasn't what had been planned.

He inched his hand to his blaster – not that a blaster would make much impact on a transporter designed to withstand the fierce storms of the central plateau. But if his team had been infiltrated, he'd take out the first soldiers and buy time to run. Where to, he didn't know.

The emerald V-symbol of his empire, etched into both flanks, had been replaced with his mother's stylised P. Shit. He brought his blaster up. Night was falling, fast, the shadows stretching. If he had to run, he'd have no way of knowing what sort of sand he was on. He backed away, to the crest of the dune, and stood, poised to run.

The hatch opened with a grinding noise, shifting sand to the ground. A familiar figure, dusky-skinned, soft-eyed, technically too old to be undertaking active missions, appeared, and his breath left him in a whoosh. Simone.

He skidded down to the transporter. It had actually worked. He was on Belaudii, about to go to Abendau. If he'd got this far, suddenly the rest didn't seem impossible.

Abendau. He glanced at the distant city, its lights stark against the darkness. Abendau, where he'd have to remain undiscovered for two days, despite having the most recognisable face in the galaxy. The cropped hair wouldn't make any difference, not after a decade of being on holos every day, on flags and credit chits. And his face was only half his problem.

He took the mesh and found Farran. *It's time.* The answering pulse was wary, resigned. Kare found the centre of the mesh, centred somewhere in that part of him his power had once inhabited. He stopped at the bottom of the dune and squeezed his eyes shut. To go back to the powerless darkness unsettled him, almost as much as the thought of the task ahead in Abendau palace did.

Get on with it; you have no choice. He concentrated on the shape of the mesh, how it joined with him, and he closed the link, squeezing it to nothing more than a pinprick. It fought him, a thing alive the way his own power had never been. He gritted his teeth, focusing on what was needed, but it took a few attempts before the mesh vanished to something small, almost hidden.

He stumbled forwards. Every other time he'd lost his powers, he hadn't been fully aware of them departing: the first time he'd been facing the horror that was Beck; the second he'd been falling into a breakdown. This time he knew and felt half of himself: bereft.

He fought the urge to find the little core he'd left. Farran had said when he rejoined the mesh it would still be there, and that he would be able to hold and shape it again. He had to trust the Roamer – he knew more than Kare.

He reached the bottom of the gangplank, his steps oddly dislocated. Simone joined him, and her wide smile was enough to push away the doubts. "Sir. It's good to see you made it."

"It's good to see you, too." He reached out and took her elbows, squeezing them in a quick embrace. "Let's get on board."

He followed her up the ramp, pulled his pack and shield-belt off and rolled his shoulders. It was good to be free of the weight. He leaned over and ran his hands through his hair, sprinkling sand onto the transport's floor. That, more than anything, brought home the realisation he was back on Belaudii where sand seeped into every building and carpeted every floor.

"Why come in advance?" he asked.

"We left before the landing, in case it caused an alert and the city was closed. That being the case, Major Hickson decided we were at risk in the open."

He nodded. Lichio's people had always had a wide remit in their operations; it wasn't his place to second-guess decisions taken on the ground. Especially when they worked. He took one of two empty seats in the second row back.

From the row opposite, a hard pair of eyes met his, dark and unfriendly. Kym Woods, here to welcome him. He met her glare and didn't look away; he had held those eyes in his mind for ten years since Silom had died under their stare. They could deliver no censure he hadn't given himself. Besides, Silom was one of the people he was going into the palace to repay; it was good to be reminded how much he'd mattered, however unpleasant.

Kym looked away first and he took a deep breath in. Her grief was different from his own. He missed Silom, every day, and blamed himself for his death, but he hadn't lost his future. She and Silom were to be married. They'd talked about a child. Instead, Kym was a veteran soldier in his army, pledged to fight for a dream Silom had died believing in. She was one of the finest soldiers in his army, earning commendation after commendation.

He'd rarely had the chance to study her over the intervening years, as happy to have her positioned away from him as she was to apply for off-world missions. She seemed the same taut, focused soldier, nothing other than lines around her eyes to show she'd aged.

Sand swirled around the transport as they gained height. He wished he'd found a way to reach her over the years. But that was his need, not hers - to push for it would have been a selfishness too far. She was a specialist with years of experience behind her: he could ask nothing of her but that she did her job, just as she'd always done.

CHAPTER EIGHTEEN

The planet-hopper landed with a soft thud. Kerra pressed her nose against the viewing port. Dark woods surrounded the clearing, creating an eerie look even on a bright morning, giving her a feeling of unease. She tried to quell it. They were going in with a native Ferran, a tour-guide who knew the forest well. Not to mention two security squads. And this sector, the Green Zone, had been cleared for her and Baelan. It was perfectly safe, like everywhere she visited. Even the busy souks of Abendau city had been cleared of tribes-people so she could visit. It was also, she admitted in a small thought, boring.

The hatch opened with a low hum, and her security team moved out first. Durren gestured for her to follow, and she headed down the gangway, but Baelan was surrounded by his team even before he left the ship. She gave him a sharp glance - at some point, she'd have to find out what had happened to change his security pattern; on Syllte he'd been treated the same as her, here he was akin to Ferran's most wanted. She bet the mesh knew, if she was allowed to access it.

Her team had fanned out, checking the clearing. Durren beckoned her and Baelan to the edge of the clearing, near the tree-line. The air grew musty, akin to wood that had been stored damp, but there was a sharpness too, ozone-like. It made her want to sneeze.

"Amazing," said Baelan peering deeper into the forest. His voice was laid-back, but his eyes were sharp as he stared forwards, and he was tense. Between that and the closeness of his team, something felt wrong, almost claustrophobic.

She tried to tell herself it was the heaviness of the

air, but it was more than that. Was it Baelan? She liked him, partly because he was hard to predict. Her whole life had been full of a long line of predictable tutors and governesses, and safe friends; he made a refreshing change, if not a relaxing one. Or was it the absence of the mesh that was putting her on edge? It was incredible that she'd managed all her life without something that was so much a part of her now.

Baelan walked farther into the woods, his squad with him. She wished she knew what he was thinking, but he was closed off, unreadable. In the mesh, he was easy to sense, a jarring wrongness that shone as brightly as a laser in space. It was as if his power didn't match, the way hers did, that it had the same jagged edges Dad's had—

She squashed that thought, shocked. Dad was the King: he wasn't just part of the mesh, he was it. Of course he felt different, he was the centre, the focus of everything. Without his control, the mesh had collapsed and lost its shape.

Durren nudged her. "Come on, I don't want to get split up."

She stepped under the canopy and coughed as the acrid air grew stronger. One of the soldiers glanced sharply at her. "Face mask?"

She shook her head. The orientation-holo on the forests had said the discomfort usually passed. She followed Baelan and Durren through the forest. It was so quiet, as if the dense air held secrets. Her unease deepened, tickling the back of her mind. She wanted to go back to the transport and take off.

"All right?" asked Durren.

She nodded. The forest was spooking her, nothing more. "Where's the guide?"

"At the tourist station." He pointed to an arrow-marked path cleared through the forest. "About five minutes' walk."

"Wow." Baelan's voice carried from ahead, the

sand-harsh tones of a native Belaudiian odd in the forest. He was standing at the base of one of the trees, his head tilted back. "You can't even see the top." He pointed up, and he seemed perfectly normal. She *had* just been spooked. "Seriously. Look."

She did. The canopy was far, far above them. She squinted into the forest. A few metres away, the glow of a lava pond softened the darkness. She pulled Baelan's sleeve and he followed her glance.

"I didn't know they were *that* big," he said.

Durren joined them. "No going near the pools before we've met the guide. Come on." He led the way, picking his way to the giant holo-station, and shook hands with the man standing by it, a young man with blond hair and pale eyes. They started to talk about what information would be covered during the visit.

Kerra touched the holo-command and brought up a map which showed the location of the biggest pools.

Baelan moved closer to her. "I'm fed up being babysat," he muttered. "I'm going to lose the team. Cover for me."

She looked at him, shocked. "You can't."

He rolled his eyes. "Kerra, I can do anything I want. Who's going to stop me?" He touched his head. "Who can?"

"You'd get into trouble."

"So?" His voice took on a dismissive edge. "What's a bit of trouble? Anyway, I'm not asking you to do anything – just cover for me, eh?"

She had to take a deep breath, thinking of the trouble that would come from her doing that. "What if you get lost?"

He tapped his head, harder this time. "I'll just concentrate on where Durren is and come back." He grinned and his excitement leached across to her, a sense of freedom she'd never had. She wanted to see something real, not the sterile front put on show for her. Baelan had spent his whole life free – it wasn't fair that she never had. He gave a wave of his hand and dodged to the side, off the path and into the trees.

"Hey!" One of the soldiers grabbed for Baelan but he dodged, laughing, and sped away, into the deeper forest.

Kerra looked between the way-marked path and Baelan disappearing into the trees. He was right. This sterile trip wasn't the way to see the real forest. Without thinking any more – and certainly without thinking about the trouble she'd be in – she ducked under a branch and followed Baelan, speeding up to keep him in sight.

She started to run, jumping over tree roots, getting faster and faster until she'd almost caught Baelan. Booted footsteps sounded from behind and voices shouted her name. She slowed. "Nice try, Baelan!"

He glanced over his shoulder, grinning, and she felt the power as it passed by her. A crash sounded from behind, followed by yells. They went farther and farther into the forest, which grew darker around them. Each lava pool was a red eye in the gloom. Finally, all sounds of pursuit fell away and she slowed, bending so that her hands were on her knees to get her breath. She coughed to clear her throat.

"Kerra, you should go back," said Baelan. He glanced over his shoulder, his face worried. "I have something I need to do first."

What could he need to do in the forest? She started to ask him but something touched the back of her mind, a prickle of warning from the past. She looked up, startled, her hair swinging long and damp in the moist air. Dread settled in her stomach. There was someone in the forest, someone she'd met before.

It sparked the memory of a line of ships against the night sky, and Sam, the doctor who'd made her run. Suddenly, she knew who was waiting for her. She wrenched her arm free. "Baelan, we have to go."

"You go," he said. "Tell the security teams I'm lost, and send them the wrong way. It will buy me some time." He paused, his eyes searching hers. "Please, Kerra. It's my mother."

How could it be his mother? She was on Abendau, with the Empress. Kerra backed away. Figures approached from the forest's shadows. She was about to cast out, but Baelan ran to them.

"Mother!" he yelled, and flung himself at one of the figures. He turned back to Kerra, and she could feel his power focused on her, ready to stop anything she tried. With his power, he'd do it, too.

Her hands clenched. *Let him go.* She turned to leave. In front of her stood a soldier, tall and lean, with hard eyes and a thin face and nose. Phelps.

His mouth broke into something that might have been a smile. "How nice to see you again, Miss Varnon. Your grandmother will be pleased." He reached forwards, fast and sharp, and a high smell replaced the forest's stench as he slammed something up to her nose, his other hand on the back of her head, holding her in place.

Everything faded.

CHAPTER NINETEEN

Lichio left the holo-studio, nodding a terse acknowledgement to his security team. Rent-a-quote, that was him today, yesterday, and the day before. It was getting old, defending Sonly and her record, not to say desperate. Too many voices were speaking up, prepared to go on record against her – it didn't bode well, especially with the first talk of leaked information. It was also taking up too much of his time and had slowed his progress with the Ferrans' chief finance officer, who seemed open to his approaches regarding extending their interests in the hub.

He shook off the doubts and reached his desk before opening his data pad. He should be reviewing Simone's latest report from the city and checking for an update on Kare's flight. He drew a picture of a dark-eyed man in the corner of the screen with his finger. Or he could draw pictures of Josef and muse on that confusion. He might be right – that their relationship had gone beyond Lichio's denials and insistence on distance. It certainly hurt enough.

He erased the picture, and stared out the window as the transport passed through the streets of Marel. The port, with its regular hops to the space-station hub, dominated his view.

His comms unit buzzed and he pulled it out of his pocket, hands responding automatically. A message scrolled across, marching to its end, then started again. High priority, from one of the security teams on Ferran-V. He read it, blinked, read it again.

"Shit." He tapped the screen and opened access to

the port and his pilot. Damn, he should have vetoed the trip to the forest, or nailed the boy down tighter before it, not got distracted.

"Set us as a priority," said Lichio. "I need to get to Ferran-V now. Clear anything in our path."

***

Sonly stared at the holo-screen over her desk, not sure if its size was a good or a bad thing. It gave her no place to hide from the accusations coming fast on this, the third day since the pictures had been released. Anyhow, she wasn't sure she wanted to hide. At least she knew the detail of her downfall, could see and pore over every image of herself, could hear everyone who cast her down. It had to be better than hiding in fear – imagination could always do more than reality.

The screen changed to the earlier news-feed, an interview with Harald from the Abendauii Senate, and Lichio, standing in for one of the republic's ambassadors at the last minute.

"Utterly ruthless," Harald said. His sun-lined face added gravitas to his words. "She used the poor of the planet to gain votes and when she got into the Senate she carried out half of what she promised."

"Twice as much as you opposed her on." Lichio leaned back in his seat, a slight smile on his face. "Perhaps you had a funding aversion, Senator? Or will we see you putting the reforms in place under the Empress?" His face hardened. "The fact is, Bendau was in ruins when the New Empire took over. At least its kids have clothes now."

Harald bristled, and picked up a data-filche. "General, I can give you figures if you want."

"No need." Lichio's smile widened, guileless, and he waved the offer away. "But if you do want some spending tips, I can put you in touch with the president." There was a light ripple of laughter and he let it play out for a moment, then leaned forwards, his eyes sharp. "Or better yet, we can let the republic complete the reforms. Then we'll see what Sonly le Payne can put in place when properly supported."

There was a ripple of applause from the audience, making Sonly smile, just a little. Lichio was wasted in the military. He was so at ease in public, turning barbs into light comments that were more effective than her cold-seeming responses. Her smile faded. Lich might be good, but it wasn't enough - everyone knew using her brother, a military specialist, to defend her was a last resort, borne out of the fact no one else was prepared to.

As if to prove the point, Harald drew himself straighter. "Or we can ask how much of the republic's data she will hand to her political opponents. After all, security doesn't seem her strong point." He tapped the dossier in front of him, the first of the supposed leaks from her. "The reforms for Bendau were shared months - many months - before they were implemented. What else will she share?"

Damn. The original reforms hadn't even been hers to share - it had been Kare who had first signed them off, shortly before he handed the Department for Planetary Improvement to the Senate. She could protest, but to argue, to bluster it was a lie, only made the allegations more accusatory. She switched to a different studio, but with the same dimmed lights and serious atmosphere.

"—the sort of damage done to a person who has faced a regime of torture isn't easily overcome."

The name of the speaker flashed up: a doctor she was unfamiliar with. Where did they dredge these people up from? She wanted to throw something heavy and hard at the holo-deck, but the damage would be found at some stage and give the whisperers more ammunition.

"So you believe it would be hard for her husband to meet her demands?" asked the presenter.

What demands? She'd told Kare, early on, that she'd support him no matter what. And she'd tried - no one knew how hard she'd tried except her and Kare: through night after night of nightmares and years of rejection. He'd been left with more damage than either of the spoiled, ignorant men on the screen could ever imagine.

"Given the sort of treatment he endured..." The pause was just long enough for the watchers to imagine what wasn't being said. "...I think that's entirely possible."

"That's an interesting perspective, thank you." The interviewer faced the recorder. "The failure of the erstwhile Emperor to show public support for his wife is, commentators believe, the most telling factor. Despite the statement issued by him, there's clear reticence on his behalf to speak publicly."

Damn it, they were insidious, using rumour and insinuation that she couldn't stand up and refute. It wasn't like she could announce why Kare wasn't available to the media.

She snapped the display off, leaving a single line of silver for reactivation when she next needed to torment herself. She didn't care what the commentators said about her, or even Kare, who'd heard worse over the years. But Kerra... there'd been a whole morning of commentary on her, the child supposedly from a broken home, damaged by her mother's political greed. It mattered more than any political mistake they'd accused her of. Only the thought of the bitch in Abendau being handed a win had kept Sonly smiling through every interview, and left her ready to face the council of the New Republic and beg for the presidency.

Speaking of the council: she had a speech to carry off, or she *would* be forced out. She started pacing, practicing sotto voce, her hands moving in time with the words. It looked like she was pleading. She put her arms down by her sides, hating the idea of any sign of weakness.

Hating the thought of going in front of the council, but the campaign had been masterful in its timing. With the republic barely founded, it couldn't ride out much negative publicity. A day or two, maybe, but there was no sign of the momentum easing.

She glanced at the time – the council would be well through its first review of the footage. In an hour she'd have her only chance to convince them she could keep their ambitions intact, and she'd been losing ground today. She knew that from the missing delegates at her lunchtime meeting. A knock sounded on the door, much earlier than she'd expected, sending a shiver of anxiety through her. Being called early wasn't a good sign.

"Come in!" She ran her hand through her hair and put her shoulders back. Whatever was decided, she'd face it with dignity. Well, as much as she could muster.

A soldier entered, not an attaché from the council. Her heart missed a beat. Kare would be landing on Belaudii today, but confirmation of that would surely be no more than a communication from Lichio. Only if something had gone wrong would a nervous-looking captain come to her office.

"What is it?" she managed to ask, but her voice was too thin. She took a breath and calmed a little – better to know.

The captain stood to attention, not quite meeting her eyes. "Ma'am, General le Payne sent me."

Surely, if something awful had happened, Lichio would have come himself? He wouldn't want her receiving bad news from someone else. "Go on."

The soldier cleared his throat. "The general says there is no cause for panic."

She'd have pointed out she wasn't panicking, but didn't think she could squeeze the words out.

"Ma'am, the children have gone missing in the fire forests."

His words sank in, and then panic did hit. Ferran-V

had the shortest days in the system. Night would fall soon. She had to put her hands on her desk to steady herself. She forced herself to swallow the cold dread that would solve nothing. The children had an experienced guide and two security teams – they couldn't stay missing.

"What do you mean – missing?" she asked. Her voice was thin. "Is there a mechanical problem with their transport?"

"No, ma'am." The man looked like he'd rather be anywhere other than in this office with her. "The security teams report that the children ran into the forest. When the squad tried to follow, some sort of force-field knocked them out."

Only one thing could have caused something like that. "The boy?" she asked. Damn, she'd known he was trouble; she should never have allowed him anywhere near Kerra. Except that Kare was right – any difference made between his children would have been pounced on by the opposition and if they'd tried to hide Baelan, and news of who he was had leaked, that would have been even more fodder.

"General le Payne is en route to Ferran-V and will oversee the search," the soldier said, deftly avoiding answering. "He asks that you wait for him to contact you with more information." His face softened. "Ma'am, I'm sure they'll be found."

Why was he? The fire forests claimed lives every year. It was why Lichio had insisted on the local guide and the double security team. If the boy *had* done something – and she remembered Kare when he'd first come to the Banned, power radiating from him, barely constrained – who knew why? And Kerra was with him, with nowhere near what she needed to defend herself from him, even with Kare's training.

"Ask the Roamers," said Sonly. "Tell them to find Kerra."

"They say they can't."

Sonly sank to her seat. Of course; Kare had said he'd have to leave the mesh when he reached Abendau. With him gone, the mesh wouldn't connect the Roamers as it should. The image of Kerra lying in the forest, still and hurt – maybe worse, who knew what the little sod had done to her – flashed before her. She pushed it away; she had to, or she'd never manage to think, and she needed to focus and work out what to do.

"Perhaps the children just don't want to be found, ma'am. They definitely left under their own steam." He tried a smile. "It may be a chance to explore the forest without their tutor. Or perhaps their idea of a trick."

Sonly swallowed the panic that clawed at her throat and insides, and pushed off from the desk. "I'm going..."

"The general asks that you stay here and he will report in. There are search parties combing the forests. The Ferrans are helping – they have specialist heat-seeking ships for forest-searches when tourists go missing."

Tourists who went missing, only to be found dead the next day. Sonly had seen footage of the bodies, what remained of their eyes, wide and staring. The forests were huge; searching even a tiny section would take hours, and heat-seeking was not an exact science, not with the ground giving off heat through the lava pools, let alone the other tourists in the forests. Until dark fell, heat-seekers would be of limited use. And once it was dark....

She remembered Rjala's tales of the sprites who stole heat from people; the sucking noises, the screams. How it had taken an older man, with knowledge of the forests, to show her how to survive the forests. It had been a gory, terrifying fun when she was a child, safe on the Banned base. Not now.

The captain backed away. "Ma'am, if I hear anything, I'll let you know."

She gave a slow nod. Lichio was right; there was nothing she could do on Ferran-V to help. In fact, she'd be a hindrance: another person to report in to and delay the search for. "Tell the general I'll be in my office and to call me the minute he knows anything."

"Yes, ma'am." The captain left. She stood in a silence which gave no comfort, ignoring the flashing light on her data pad calling her to defend her position, and could do nothing to dismiss the image of her daughter lying cold on the forest floor.

CHAPTER TWENTY

Michio stepped into the docking bay on Ferran-V, his squad falling into place behind him. The military-grade planet-transport allocated was already primed. He got on quickly, refusing to go down the line of guesswork about what the boy had done and why. Find the children, that was the priority – after that, he could find out just what the hell had gone on.

The ship took off from the dock, banking over the city and out to the forest. The last of the late-afternoon sun broke through clouds. The day was falling quicker than he needed it to. Below, search teams had spread out to fan through the forest on hover-bikes and personal speeders. The air was filled with transporters, all military; tourists had been ordered to leave the forest within half an hour of the kids' security teams checking in, although some more intrepid parties were still emerging from the deeper forest. Beyond the security perimeter, media-ships hovered, making him frown. If any of this leaked, he'd take the Ferran headquarters apart by hand and teach them something about running a secure mission.

Except the Ferrans hadn't been running the children's security. All their personnel had been hand-picked from Kare's forces. The lad should not have been able to blind-side two security squads, both of whom had training in handling psychers. Even Kare, back at the Banned, had struggled to take out a five-man Star-ops team.

Which left the unsettling fact that the boy was more powerful than any of them – even Kare – had realised. That thought was a sobering one. He'd been with Kare on Corun when he'd lifted four men off the planet under the fire power of a full troop of the Empress' soldiers.

"How far out are we going?" asked Lichio.

"Not much further," said the pilot. "We'll be joining the main search in the forest. We have an hour before we pull out."

"That's not a lot of time. The Ferrans won't search overnight?"

"They'll search from the air. Nothing goes into the forest at night."

"Damn." He didn't argue, though; becoming sprite-bait didn't appeal. Perhaps, as night fell, the kids would come out, having had their afternoon of freedom. After all, neither was helpless; it was that knowledge that had kept him calm since the news had come in.

The ship dived through the tree canopy, aiming for a small clearing. Down and down it went, slowing as it did, until it sank vertically into place. Lichio went to the hatch, using his shoulder to speed its lifting. Beyond, the forest was utterly silent. He shivered at the dank air, but got out, and his team followed, spreading out into a search pattern. The lead sergeant's eyes flitted across the forest.

"Pretty eerie," said Lichio, coughing when the air caught in his throat.

"Yes, sir."

Lichio ducked into the deeper forest, being careful with his footing. It didn't do to be careless - there were tree roots everywhere and the lava pools were not all the red of the younger pools; some were a deeper shade and hard to see in the dark. Some of the older trees had plants growing at their base.

Within a few feet he had to stop and pull his collar up against the dropping temperature. He was well under the canopy, and the sun no longer penetrated to ground level. His breath turned to frosted white. He stopped, listening for the sound of feet or the kids talking, but there was nothing. He strained his eyes, watching for any movement, but it was impossible to see through the greying light and the steam rising to wreathe the trunks in white mist.

There was no birdsong, no animals moving, nothing but steady hissing, the spit of mud bubbles bursting and the rustle of the undergrowth, water dripping as the cold air met the warm. It was stunningly beautiful, everything Rjala had described, but the strangest place he'd ever been.

He crossed to the nearest mud-pool, skirting the fire-spruce's encircling roots, and crouched. There were no footprints in the mud. He turned on his scanner, tracing the path ahead, but there was no sign of any life.

A noise from above made him scramble to his feet and wait, listening, until the pounding in his chest settled and he calmed. Just the rustle of leaves in the damp air and nothing to worry about; the sprites would be high in the trees until night fell.

His direction unit beeped, taking his attention. Movement, up ahead, and not his search-team. He brought his wrist-comm to his mouth. "We have something. Follow my nav-code and stay close."

His team appeared from the darkness and he led them to the edge of a small clearing. The pod gave a single beep. He turned to his team. "Fan out and search."

He stepped forwards. A shape appeared between the trees, then another. Relief came, and he started to jog towards them, but another shape appeared, and then another. He took a step back as more shapes emerged from between the trees.

"Ambush!" he yelled. A laser blast came at him, making him dive to the side. One of his team gave a cut-off warning.

Lichio rolled to his knees. The ground was hot under him – a lava pool bubbled not two feet away. A blast echoed, this time from his team, followed by one from the other side of the clearing. He was surrounded. He cursed. Stupid, stupid. He should have brought a proper assault team, not a hastily scrambled search and rescue, but he'd had no intelligence to suggest a trap.

He pulled his blaster out. The light had faded, making the lava pools glow in the darkness. He waited. Another blast, another shout, and then silence. Figures separated from the trees ahead, coming forwards, rifles cradled in their arms.

"On your feet, General." One separated from the others. "We were advised you might come along."

Lichio stood, his blaster by his side, eyes darting. Useless. There was nowhere to run, even if he could see well enough to know where to go.

"Drop your weapon, and put your hands up."

Lichio took in the soldier's insignia: a sergeant. A familiar twisted star glinted in the dim light, and his stomach fell.

"Drop your weapon, le Payne."

Lichio cast his gaze through the forest, weighing up his chances. Phelps - assuming he was behind this - wouldn't want to hang around any more than he did; the sprites didn't care what side anyone was on. Besides, if he had the kids, he'd got what he came for. He glanced at the soldiers in front of him, took in their focus, and amended that thought: Phelps had got most of what he wanted, damn him. The soldiers moved forwards, trapping him.

To hell with that. Lichio brought his blaster up, aiming from the hip, and took the sergeant on his shoulder, sending him spinning away. He dived to the side, just evading a bolt that hit the tree next to him, close enough to make him flinch. He ducked behind the tree and stood where its roots twisted around the lava pool. Steps approached and he waited, hand on his blaster. If nothing else, he'd take some of the bastards with him.

"Pull out." The soldier's voice was strained. "We can't stay any longer. Besides..." He pitched his voice high enough to carry. "He'll be drained by morning. We'll inform General Phelps."

"He wanted him alive."

Lichio barely breathed.

"He'll have to take him dead."

Their footsteps left, crunching away. A few minutes later, somewhere in the distance, a transporter lifted off, flying low enough for him to feel the heat from its engines.

Something moved in the canopy above him, and he tensed. There was a rustling of leaves, the clicking of claws on wood. He snapped his head up and tightened his hand around his blaster, listening, and knew exactly what was stirring.

CHAPTER TWENTY-ONE

Darkness had fallen over Abendau, the familiar quick change from day to night. The abandoned chapel he was in was little more than a ruin. The climb to its parapets had entailed the remnants of a stone staircase, its supports long gone so that it reached up to the sky. The reward, however, was a view over the city and even towards the palace. In fact, with the scopers he had with him, it was possible to make out the palace and port, and the long skywalk stretching between them.

Palace Boulevard was easier to pick up, lit up and gaudy, but farther out the old city's warrens of entries were dim. Darker still was the massive tribal enclave in the midst of the old city, hidden behind such high walls that the glow from its great church was barely visible.

Kare stuck his head out of the shattered bay window and took a deep breath. The desert air was fresher in the evening and as cold as the day was hot, bringing with it a wave of... not nostalgia, exactly - he hated the city and its palace as much as when he'd first been taken to it - a sense of wasted time, perhaps.

He'd spent ten years moulding the city so it was no longer his mother's. That the alleys in the old city were lit was down to him; when he'd come to power the sector had been poverty-stricken, its residents left to fester in dark houses, hidden from the rich residents of the central boulevards. Now she was back and the lights were already going out, the hope of a decade snuffed and dead.

"What do you think?" Simone hunkered beside him, and he was glad of the distraction.

"Not good." He lifted his scope and focused on the

central streets close to the palace. They adjusted quickly, picking out details in the darkness, controlling the light input from the busier areas.

The main streets were bustling, the blazing lights of the strip of bars and restaurants standing out against the embassies' dark gardens. The palace loomed over the city, its white walls stark against the night sky: unchanged, unchanging, eternal. He hated the place. "They've upped the garrison."

"It's been doubled." She pointed at the port. "See the new defence turrets? Your compound has them too."

"Damn." He adjusted the scope and picked out the turrets. Even Roamer ships would struggle to withstand the new firepower. "How many agents managed to infiltrate the garrison?"

"Eight."

"Eight? That's all? What did the rest do, forget to lick their officers' boots?"

She grimaced, her teeth white in the darkness. "Security proved tighter than anticipated. But they're well placed to do what you need."

He lowered the scope and stared over the city. "And when I'm in?"

"There will be a small protest rally. We've been holding them periodically, so it won't rouse suspicion. Once Hickson's squad is in, the protest will turn somewhat nastier than usual and draw some security from the palace."

He nodded, but kept his focus on the palace. What he needed was a full-scale attack on the city to give him a proper run. He didn't say it; Simone already knew.

"Sounds good." He put the scope into its pouch on his belt. "We can go; I've seen what I needed."

His legs protested as he straightened and stretched before bringing his hood up. Simone led the way from the chapel, consecrated before the Empress' church had spread, and left to fall to ruin ever since. She passed through the graveyard and ducked out of a low gateway into a side street.

He put his head down and walked beside her in silence. He'd be unlucky for anyone to recognise him in the darkness, but his voice didn't have the rich tones of a native Abendauii, nor the guttural edge of one desert-bred, and, on a still night like this, a voice easily carried.

Ahead, the palace stood, reaching into the sky. He could trace every part of the building, from the private quarters on the top floors, through the administration section, to the now-flooded basement that had housed Omendegon. His scars itched at the memory of the torture chambers, but he pushed the thought away and hurried after Simone. He had an assault plan to finalise.

They slipped through the streets, stopping at the head of each entry to check it was clear, and used their cover to slip past the busier streets. He skidded in dregs of rubbish that had rotted in the sun. During the day, this place must stink; it was barely tolerable at night. The streets became busier as they reached a residential zone.

He ducked his head, pulling the hood closer around him. "How much further?"

"A few streets." Her eyes darted, taking in the alley they were in, and the entrance to another.

They hurried through the last streets. Here, the city had lost its genteel air, and any semblance of policing. People spilled from bars onto rough benches in the street, saving themselves additional credits for drinking inside. Voices reached him, rumours of a curfew and extra security checks. Fear ran in an undertone – whenever there were changes in Abendau, these streets felt it first and hardest. It made him want to hurry before he was picked out as a stranger who might bring more trouble to the city, but he forced himself to match Simone's careful pace.

Finally, they reached the safe house. His shoulders relaxed, telling him how tense he'd been, as they were let in by one of two soldiers maintaining a watch. The street the house was in was quiet. There were no pubs, nothing but darkened houses. Yet the stillness didn't comfort him; instead, it seemed to shroud secrets.

The soldier pulled the outer door shut and activated its sensors, and Kare made his way to the small room designated for planning.

"Secure," he said. A sound-wall hummed into place and a holo-projector - a full-scale, military-grade one - rose from the centre of the table. Beside it, a command console blinked. Normally Lichio would be on the other end of it, a real-time Lichio. Damn, he wanted him here.

The squad crowded in and Kare moved his focus to them. There was nothing he could do about Lich, he had to make the best of what he had. He checked them off as they came, bringing to mind what he knew from their personnel files. It was a good team, with all the disciplines covered.

He gave a nod to Major Hickson, making a mental reminder to praise his selection later. Hickson nodded back, and shifted to the side, allowing room for Kare to join him at the top of the table. He stayed slightly behind the major, however - he wasn't the specialist they needed. Hell, if he ran an active raid, it would be the first time in a decade.

"To confirm the planning." Hickson brought a holo-map up. "Turn your attention to the red areas specifically. Those are the Empress' personal quarters, where we're the allocated cleaning-crew." He nodded to Kare. "You will already be in situ. I plan to split us into four teams."

The soldiers gathered around the desk, the outline planning document already held by many. Hickson changed the screen and there were a few murmurs as the squad read over their final allocation. Kare glanced at Kym Woods, waiting for her reaction, but her face was impassive, hard to read.

"Team one." Hickson pointed at four soldiers, each in turn, and they gave a firm nod. "Standard room-clearance through the quarters. Three zones have security posts." The holo changed, highlighting three entranceways in orange. "There will also be roaming patrols."

"Do we have a fix on how many?" asked one of the soldiers, a lean man. Rix, Kare recalled. Tactical-ops specialist.

"We have an assessment of current levels of patrol and predicted patterns." Hickson tapped a command on his data pad and handed it over. "I'll share those details with you - but be aware, they are predictions only."

Rix nodded, jotted something on his own plan, and Hickson pointed to four more soldiers, already bunched together; this team were tight, evidently. "You control the security entrance to the private sector - no one gets through. Any non-military palace staff in situ will be placed under your care. If all goes to plan, we'll be accounting for our actions to the republic - I don't want to have to explain any innocent deaths."

The holo zoomed in on the Empress' personal chambers, taking a moment to sharpen. Kare's breath caught. He knew the rooms well. Her living-area - his for a decade, when he could bear to stay there - with its huge window overlooking the city; her sleeping quarters, big enough for the average family to fit into.

He could imagine her spreading out from the chambers, a spider in the centre of the palace, sensitive to every movement within. If he could get his team as far as her quarters, she'd know something was wrong in the palace, something focused on her, even if she didn't pick up his presence. Without the protection of the mesh, his team's minds were vulnerable to her - she'd soon find out they were there. The timing of his use of the Roamer power would be vital: too soon and she'd have security in place waiting for him; too late and he'd be useless against her.

"Myself and Sergeant Ta'riq will take her sleeping quarters," said Hickson. He drew in a deep breath. "If the Empress is awake, then it falls to the commander in chief and Sergeant Woods."

Kare met Kym's hard eyes, and stepped forwards. "Once I join the Roamer mesh, every security team in the palace will be targeted on us." He glanced around the squad, their eyes on him. "We have one chance. I believe we can do it. Questions?"

Voices broke out, confirming lay-out plans, weaponry, timing. Kare stood back, letting Hickson answer, and closed the holo down. The team began to file out, their questions answered. Hickson left with a quick nod, Ta'riq beside him, heads together.

For the first time, Kare became aware of how tired he was after the trek in the desert and recon. Time to find a bunk or bedroll. He turned to leave, and found Sergeant Woods waiting in the doorway, dark eyes fixed on him.

All thoughts of sleep left him. "Sergeant Woods. Have you a question about the mission?"

She raised an eyebrow. "Me, sir? No, sir." Irony dripped from her clipped voice, but there was nothing overt he could pull her on.

He paused. This was his chance to put things on a better footing between them.

"Sergeant, I know how you feel about me." It was too dark to see her face; he'd have to play this on instinct.

"Do you, sir?"

Perhaps. He knew how he'd feel - that he'd used Silom, kept him too close and brought him into danger time and time again. That, sooner or later, it would have ended as it did. Kym didn't know - if that was indeed how she felt - that it went further back, to when Silom had been a boy. She didn't know that Silom had been a pawn for the Roamers, who should never have known Kare outside the face on the credits in his pocket. She just knew the end.

"Sergeant, Silom was where he wanted to be that day," he said. "But I was slow. I should have predicted my mother. There isn't a day I don't think about what happened and blame myself."

A silence lengthened between them.

"I was told you were the best," he said, trying a different tactic. He lowered his voice to little more than a whisper. "Is that much true?"

"It is." Her eyes glittered in the dark.

"When I take the bitch down, I'm doing it for Silom," he murmured. "I need someone who won't miss."

"I never miss," she said. She pitched her voice even lower than his. "Perhaps you should keep that in mind, sir."

"Oh, I do." He turned away, frustrated. His usual empathy was no use here – the barrier between them too great.

He stopped at the sound of her voice. "You won't back down this time? You'll kill her, no matter what?"

He turned back to her. "No matter what."

She gave a firm nod and left, back straight, her walk the same swagger it had always been. Let it be enough.

CHAPTER TWENTY-TWO

The feel of movement; the drowsy knowledge of being on a ship. Kerra forced her eyes open. She was on a narrow, hard cot, nothing like the comfortable bunks on a Roamer ship. She turned her head, ignoring a dull thud of protest, and saw a row of cots crammed on top of each other, lining the wall opposite. The walls were grey metal, unadorned, the sheets on the bunks a deep green. A military transporter, she assumed.

Cautiously, she propped herself up on one elbow and the memory of the fire forest came crashing back. She was in trouble; Phelps taking her could mean only one thing. She shivered at the thought of the Empress, and looked around the room, slower, checking for anything that might be of use. She had to do something, not just wait to land in Abendau, but there was nothing useful, not even a pole she could bash someone on the head with.

She couldn't believe she'd been so stupid. She'd known something was up with Baelan - she should have been on her guard. Everyone would be worried. Her mum and Uncle Lichio would be looking for her.

Uncle Lichio... something came to her, like a dream. Something someone had said as she'd been taken to this cabin. She sat straight, ignoring the dizziness the movement brought. The soldiers had said he was in the forest and not to worry about going back for him. Baelan's descriptions of the bodies found in the forests rushed at her. They were cold, sucked of their heat. Fed on all night long. She doubled over as a cramp raced across her stomach, sickening her. Lichio, her fun uncle, who'd always treated her as an equal, not a kid. Who understood what it was like to be expected to fill a role because the rest of the family had. She might have got him killed. The thought circled, the idea almost too big to grasp, and there was nothing she could do to make things right. She'd promised her dad that she'd help Mum and not make things worse, and she'd ended up causing this chaos.

Something pulled at her thoughts, something insistent and impossible to ignore. The mesh: tiny, compared to what she was used to, but still there. She bit her lip, knowing she should pull away from it. Dad, and the Roamers, had been adamant that no one should access it until her father took it back. But when she tried to flex her own powers, there was nothing there. They'd drugged her again, like last time. All she had was the mesh, and it had to be better than nothing, even broken and small as it was.

She started to prod at it, trying to work out what was so different about the feel of it. It wasn't just that her father was missing, although without him the mesh wasn't circular and whole but a confusing mess of individual minds. It was that the mesh was demanding her attention in a way it never had before, insistent, drumming with intent. She scrunched her eyes, concentrating, and the mesh expanded and took on something of its old shape. Her headache faded. It felt like the mesh wanted her to do this, to take hold of it and make it whole again. It needed someone to.

She reached within herself. If she fixed it into the right shape, she could sort through the jumble of Roamer minds and tell about Lichio in the forest, and get them to raise the alarm. She could tell them where she was, too – if their ships could reach her before she reached Belaudii, she'd be safe. Guilt warred with need. The Roamers had been adamant she must not. She tried to put it out of her head and think of something that didn't involve messing with things she should leave well enough alone.

A click at the door made her jump. The handle

turned. She held her breath, sure it would be Phelps with his thin face and cruel eyes, and didn't know whether she wanted it to be him or not. Yes, he frightened her, but he might tell her something. Since he was, presumably, taking her back to the palace, he wouldn't do anything to hurt her.

The door opened, and when a soldier came in with a tray she drew in a proper breath. No, she didn't want it to be Phelps, it seemed. Not ever.

A doctor followed, the long needle in his hands catching the light and glinting. She backed herself close to the wall, but when he lifted her arm she didn't pull away. He jabbed her, and she didn't let out a whimper, but glared at him instead. Her dad had been brave in the palace, and her mum. That was how a Varnon behaved, and she wasn't going to do anything less.

She pulled her sleeve down and waited as they left the room. The door closed, leaving her in silence. Phelps wouldn't allow her powers to come back. He'd hold her in this cell and when she got to Abendau her grandmother would be waiting, and all the time Lichio would be lost. Cold washed through her, remembering the touch of the Empress' mind, how she'd known Kerra with just one glance and dismissed her as a nothing. How chilling she'd been.

She rubbed the needle mark on her arm. Phelps didn't know about the mesh; he expected her to be powerless. Why should she stay that way? If her dad was here, he'd tell her to do what she needed to get away. And she knew he'd tell her to do what she could to help Lichio - he would never have left him if there was any way to change things.

Yes, yes, the mesh pounded. She broke out in a sweat, her hands sticky and warm. She tried to tell herself not to, that things weren't the way they should be, but even as she thought it a part of her was diving into the broken mesh of minds, seeking the right shape, for the way to make the mesh work. She told herself it was because she had to and not because everything in her cried out to take the mesh and shape it the way it should be, the way her father never could. The way she'd been wanting to for weeks.

***

Sonly read, once again, the report about Lichio's squad, her focus coming back to the final lines, the only ones that mattered: missing, presumed dead. In Ferran-V's fire forests, the presumed was a formality. Both he and Kerra had been swallowed by the forest.

She set the report down, hands shaking. Lichio had heard Rjala's tales, hanging on to every word just as she had. He'd know what lay ahead for him in vivid detail.

She wished Kare had stayed. He'd take the forests apart, blasting the sprites if he needed to. He'd have troops to do it with, unlike her who only had useless political allies. How had she moved so far away from who she'd been in the Banned? Then, she'd led a task force to Abendau in support of Kare's slave rebellion. Now, she couldn't even leave for Ferran-V; the airspace was closed to anything other than the search ships, and without her political privilege she was just another person seeking permission to land. She couldn't even commandeer a ship for herself, not when she might not have a political position any more.

She stood and paced up and down her small office. She tried to forget Rjala's cold voice telling of the screams, and the silence, of the bodies left to be found in the morning, but wasn't able to think of anything else.

CHAPTER TWENTY-THREE

Lichio gripped his blaster, scanning above him, but it was useless: he couldn't see the sprites, let alone shoot the little bastards. The sound of claws drew closer, moving from the top canopy, and he tightened his grip, ready. Anything had to be better than waiting, knowing those claws were meant for him.

Anything? He brought his blaster up, holding it below his chin. It'd be quick. He'd thought that many times over the last decade, usually around the anniversary of his escape; thought of Silom dying and how quick it had been. He raised the barrel to his temple, his hand surprisingly steady, his thoughts both sharp and removed from him, as if in the most vivid dream, one he'd wake from, yelling. Maybe he'd wake in the morning and tell Kerra he'd dreamt about her running off in the forests. Hell, he might even wake in time to veto the trip.

Leaves rustled above his head. This was no dream. He tightened his finger on the trigger. One quick depress and it would be over. If he was going to do it, now was the moment. He squeezed his eyes closed and pressed the barrel tight against his skin.

Damn, it shouldn't be like this; he was Lichio, his mother's clever son. He used his brains to solve things. Those brains wouldn't do much good splattered on the tree trunk behind.

The claws drew closer. He might be smart but he was outnumbered, and knew nothing about the forests. He tightened his finger on the trigger. A moment of bravery, that's all it would take. Then he'd know nothing more.

His breath caught. He knew some things about the

forest. Rjala had told him about the Empress' attack many times: when he'd been about seven, it had been his favourite tale, the one to relive in games and scare himself shitless with. He lowered his hand. Rjala hadn't known the forest; she'd lived in the city. The knowledge that had saved her had been the folklore of the forests – the same folklore the Ferrans bigged up when selling their merchandise these days.

He spun, seeking through the dark. Thornberries, that's what he needed. He wracked his brains, trying to remember what she'd said, but he'd been a kid, more interested in the gore than the salvation. They'd cut her hands to shreds, he remembered that.

All the plants in the forest grew near the trees. The lava ponds were too hostile – the plants needed the protection of the trees to survive. He sought, all around. The thornberries were parasitic, he dredged from somewhere, and grew on the older trees.

Older trees. Older pools, surely. He ran, using the sound of gentle plopping to guide him. If he could hear a pool and not see it, it was dark – and they were the older pools, slowly losing their heat to the chill air.

He forced himself to zone out the clicking of the sprites. One made a smacking noise. At any moment they'd be in his hair, on his clothes, seeking his flesh.

There. Just the smallest bubble of red gave the old pool away, muted, not angry like the livelier pools. He ran towards it, staying away from the tree trunks, going as fast as he could. The sprites were tree-dwellers; across open ground he might outpace them. He reached the pool. A thicket of thornberry bushes twisted around a fallen tree, low to the ground.

He fell to his knees beside them. Thank you, oh lord of the forest, or whoever was looking out for him. Rjala, perhaps? She'd been here, terrified as he was now, and had found a way to survive. He reached into the thorns, ignoring them raking his skin, and pulled the sharp berries, wincing. A handful, two. He brought his hands back to his chest, and they were shaking. Now what?

Rjala had squeezed them all over her skin. He pressed the first one. Its thorns dug into his skin. He bit down a yell; the sprites almost certainly knew where he was, but he was damned if he was going to make things easier for them.

The berry burst and juice drenched his cut skin. He bit his lip against the sharp pain, and the taste of blood filled his mouth. The smell of the berries reached him, heavy and sour, making him gag. He brought his hand up and juice trickled down his arm, a thin thread of red, more than he'd imagined the hardened, dry exterior could hold. He ran his hand over his face, covering it with the juice.

He needed more. Rjala had stripped, sure the sprites would find a way up her clothes until they burrowed against her skin. He pulled off his jacket, letting it fall to the ground. His trousers followed, his shirt and underwear. He squeezed the next berry, eyes half-closed against the sharp pain.

Shapes, in the darkness, scuttled over the forest floor. The next berry popped. He spread the juice, picked up another and another, each squeeze an agony more than the last, until his body was red and glistening.

The sprites stopped, just beyond the pool. One drew its mouth back, revealing a line of sharp teeth, white against the darkness. It hissed, but didn't come closer, and the relief flooded him – that Rjala had been right, and the juice repelled them.

She'd also told him the juice had to stay moist to work. Already he could feel his skin stiffening as it dried, his face stretched and pulled. He crouched and reached into the very centre of the thicket, past long, raking thorns, to fill his hands with berries. Once again, he squeezed.

CHAPTER TWENTY-FOUR

Baelan lay, his eyes heavy and closed. For now, it was peaceful, a peace he rarely knew, and he didn't want to move. The doctor had given him something, he remembered, when he'd fought against the second injection and kicked out at the doctor. It had made no difference. Phelps and Jakina - his uncle, who'd never liked him - had held him down.

A hand touched his brow, warm and dry, smelling of musk perfume. His mother: she'd been allowed back to him, then.

"How long will he sleep?" she asked.

"Another hour, perhaps." The voice wasn't sand-harsh like his uncles', but flat, unemotional and clipped. Phelps.

"Why does he need his powers subdued? I'm here now - I can control him."

"I can't take that chance." Phelps' voice was low and close. "Our Lady is determined he be returned to her, and that's what I'll ensure happens." His steps clicked back and forth. "He rejected her. She won't forget it."

Baelan tried to open his mouth to explain it hadn't been like that, that the Empress had been hurting him and he hadn't known what else to do, but his lips were too heavy and the words got lost in the blackness within him.

"Why did he do such a thing?" his mother asked. "He was raised to be true to our Lady."

Baelan would have cringed if he could. Without knowing the circumstances, it was unthinkable that he'd sided with Varnon. Already, back amongst his own people, he couldn't quite believe he had.

The bunk shifted a little as someone, presumably Phelps, sat on the end of it.

"Shanisa," he said. "The Empress had much to teach Baelan and little time to do it. I believe he found her a hard teacher."

A bitch, more like.

"Did she hurt him?" His mother's voice carried an edge Baelan knew well, one that most of the tribe knew not to cross. Hope rose in him; perhaps his mother could be a source of help after all. She just needed to know the truth, that he'd done nothing wrong and yet the Empress had hurt him.

"Her time in captivity reminded our Lady her time is short. It hardened her."

Another gentle stroke of his forehead; his hair smoothed back. "I will not let her hurt my son."

"You will be crushed if you stand against her." Phelps' voice was firm, like iron. "You think Baelan is her only option? She's created three heirs; she can create another. With Baelan, she has the DNA template she needs."

"Then we must not return him," said his mother. "If it isn't for him to take her place, why do we?"

"The Empress is aware of her age," said Phelps. "While a baby grows to maturity, there will be others waiting in line to take its place."

"So, she may still have use for Baelan?"

"I believe so." There was a long pause, during which Baelan almost forgot to breathe, and then the General continued. "I've known her long enough to tell you she will not stand for the sort of betrayal Baelan showed. Especially not when that betrayal concerns Varnon. She won't forgive easily. If Baelan wishes to regain his privilege, there will be a price to pay."

His mother's hand faltered on his forehead, before resuming. "He cannot go back to the tribes. They will not let him live."

Fear caught, making Baelan's chest tighten. He'd known that risk, when he'd turned against the Empress. How could he have been such a fool?

"The Empress promised me his place in the palace," she went on. "She swore, on oath to an Elder, that she would not harm Baelan. I would never have allowed him to return if his place was not assured."

"She lied," said Phelps. "She does that."

A chill crept up his spine. If he could, he'd shiver. He thought of his father's scarred chest, of the ring of ruined skin encircling his throat, his crabbed fingers, and panic welled. Instinctively, he reached within, seeking his powers. He'd deal with Phelps and get the ship turned back to Ferran.

There was nothing there, except the stupid mesh he didn't understand and that hated him. He touched it, even so – some power would be better than none – but it was broken, the power normally held within it fragmentary and useless.

"What about the girl?" asked his mother. "Could she be chosen instead?"

"The girl is not Baelan," Phelps said. "She has nothing like his power. She carries Sonly le Payne's genes, and the Empress hates the le Paynes second only to her son. Baelan can still be the future, but only if he can restore her trust. Make no mistake: if he does not, the Empress will keep your son only as long as she needs him." Another pause. "I fear, while she keeps him, she will not be merciful."

"I cannot let this happen." His mother got up from the bed; he could hear her skirts moving as she walked, a rhythmic swish-swish. "I will speak with the tribes. I will seek forgiveness for his action. He will do whatever penance requested of him."

He wanted to sit up and say no. A tribal penance

could be worse than the Empress'. He could be cast out, into the desert, and left to survive alone. For what he had done, turning on his Lady, that penance could be weeks, or even months. Every day, seeking water and food. Seeking not to become food. On his own, allowed no shelter from the sun or the night's cold. If he met a tribesman, he would not be allowed to speak, or ask for help. He would not be permitted to return before they came to retrieve him; few were ever retrieved in time.

He remembered, when he was a boy, a man who had been sentenced to a four-week penance. When he returned, they'd stripped and burned his penance garb. He'd been thin, his ribs like sticks. He'd muttered to himself, making no sense to anyone, his skin aged and parched like an elder's, and not the strong man who'd left.

Yet, once over, the penance would wipe his slate clean. He would be returned to who he had been on his naming day. Baelan was young, and strong. He knew the desert. He could survive it.

"Baelan *must* be returned to the tribes," his mother said, her voice stronger than previously. She had made her decision. "I will demand it."

"The council will overrule you." Phelps stood, the bed shifting as his weight lifted. "She will see to that."

"I am his parent; I have the right to keep him with me."

"You are one parent. You need both to make it binding."

"The tribes are hardly going to ask Varnon's permission." The sound of her skirt stopped. "You're his tribal father," she said, after a moment. "You stood for him."

"I did." There was an edge of something in Phelps' voice, not pride so much as resignation.

"You must have some regard for Baelan, to do so."

Baelan held his breath, ears straining for the answer. It shouldn't matter: Phelps was nothing to him except the stranger who'd visited through his childhood to keep tabs on his development.

It *did* matter. No one else had stood for Baelan. He'd celebrated his naming ceremony and had shared nightfire. If he didn't matter to Phelps, who could he matter to?

"I like the boy," said Phelps. "He's smart. A survivor." Baelan filled with pride. "He was also necessary for our plans."

The pride vanished, quicker than it had come. He had been used, nothing more. A pain filled his chest, the pain of disappointment; of hurt. He wanted to lash out, to hurt Phelps, but couldn't. Even if he'd been strong enough, he couldn't admit to having heard this conversation.

"You could speak for him," said Mother, her voice pleading, and anger curled in Baelan. She shouldn't need to plead for anything from Phelps, who wasn't even of the tribes. "You said he was a survivor – give him that opportunity. If we both demand his freedom, the Elders will have to agree."

Baelan's breath barely came. He had a chance here, one he'd never thought of having. Phelps had said he had some regard for him; let it be enough.

"I can't." The words were choked. "Even if I gave my promise – and part of me wants to – when I came back under my Lady's attention, I wouldn't see it through."

"You're weak," said Mother. "You don't hold your own mind."

"I can do nothing to escape my Lady." His voice seemed to come from a distance. "She has held me for years; she will hold me until I die."

"You could leave."

A harsh laugh escaped. "I can no more leave than a mouse escapes a cat. I – she touches my mind. I know her as no one else does."

"You were lovers." It was a statement.

"Once. Long ago." A bitten-off curse. "Now – I... I cannot go against her."

Baelan lay, his muscles tight and tense. A chance to live: that was all he wanted. To know he mattered enough for Phelps to keep his oath as a father. But he didn't. Everything he'd done, everything he'd carried out for the Empress had been for nothing, and his real father wouldn't come for him again. He'd said when he'd rescued Baelan that he could only do it once. To want his father to come for him again, after years of hating him, felt unreal – and yet he did.

Besides, when he learned that Baelan had left, and had taken Kerra with him, he'd disown him for sure. Assuming he was still alive and free. Baelan tightened his eyelids against a hot wash of tears. The deeper he was pulled into things, the harder it was to know his mind the way he had when he'd lived in the desert and everything had been simple.

CHAPTER TWENTY-FIVE

The sprites had gathered, more than Lichio could count. When he'd been a boy, he'd thought Rjala's description of them more gruesome than possible. He'd grossed out on it, adding details of slobbering jaws and wicked eyes. If she were in front of him, he'd tell her she hadn't done them justice.

Small, with teeth that glinted. As his eyes adjusted to the dark he made out suckers attached to their skin, barely covered by thin fur. They pulsated in the faint glow from the lava pool. He stared at the suckers, imagining what they would do once attached to his skin, as his hands worked at the berries. He shivered and shuffled closer to the lava pool, its warmth the only thing cutting through the freezing air.

The night wore on, the hours stretching longer than they should. More sprites gathered, coming through the forest in troops, easily in their hundreds, coming and going, replenished incessantly.

At last, as he'd known it would, the store of berries by the pool ran out. He had to crawl to seek more, feeling the juice dry on his body, praying he'd make it in time. His skin tightened. His shivering turned to shuddering. The sprites came closer, braver, waiting their moment. He crawled forwards, not looking back, seeking, seeking.

The slightest heat on the ground made him stop. An old trunk stretched in front of him, reaching to the canopy, wreathed in the thornberry bush. He forced himself to his feet and ran forwards, reaching for it. His right hand closed around a bunch of berries. He pulled them, desperate. The rustling grew louder behind him; the sprites knew they had to act now. Something touched his leg, gripping his ankle, and he wrenched it away. Another touch, this one with sharp pain – the suckers attaching to his skin.

He burst one of the berries, ripping his fingers. He spun, spraying the juice behind him with a yell.

The sprite drew back, spitting. The juice spattered through the air, but the sprite stayed only a few feet back, waiting. Lichio popped another berry and smeared its juice on him, ignoring the stench, worse as each layer mixed with his cold sweat. The sprite drew back and watched him, its teeth bared.

Lichio drew his legs up close to his body, hunching over his stash of berries, a golem protecting its treasure. Even as one hand worked at the berries, the other reached through the bushes until he found another bunch. His fingers fumbled, too cold to work fast, and he barely kept hold of each bunch he pulled. He drew them into his pile; it was pitifully small, and each was taking longer to open. He wasn't going to reach morning. Not at this speed. He tried using his mouth to pop one, but the thorns ripped his lips, and he had to stop.

At a rustling, he glanced up. The forest was still dark. He tried to guess how long he'd been here. Hours, anyway; the shivering told him that. How long did night last on Ferran? The long dusks and sunrises took up part of the day, the pure dark Sprites'-vigil, as the Ferrans called it, less. He squinted at the canopy, but there was no sign of lightening in the gloom. Too bloody long, that was how long it lasted.

A distant cry made him jump, a keening that brought the patter of more feet through the forest. They knew he was almost out of berries. They were surrounding him, ready to pounce. He scrunched into the bush, yelping as it cut into him. Another cry echoed and he burst a berry, not daring to check how many remained. At least he'd survived this long; when they took him, it wouldn't be long until daybreak. It would be quick.

He kept his head down, concentrating on the berries, not letting himself think of what lay ahead. He could make out their colour, a deep red, not the black they'd appeared all night. He looked up, hardly daring to hope. The tree above him hung thick with sprites, but beyond them, in the upper canopy, the forest was lighter, he was sure of it.

A third cry came, different this time – more of a warning. The sprites retreated, hissing, their mouths drawn back, revealing rows of sharp teeth. With a rustle of closing branches they vanished, into the canopy, as quickly as they'd appeared the night before.

Lichio slumped forwards, dropped the last of his berries, and gave in to the scream he'd been holding back all night, muffled against his knee.

It was morning.

***

Sonly looked at the clock: four o'clock in the morning, Ferran-standard time. Ten minutes after she'd last looked and at least another hour before the search teams would go back into the forest.

The night had stretched, unbearably slow, filled with fear that she'd lost Kerra and Lichio, that Kare was driving himself to his death on Abendau for a dream that didn't matter, not at the cost of everyone she loved. Grief surged, again, pushing past the coldness she'd tried to hold in place – *had* to hold in place, or she'd be no use to anyone. Grief and the knowledge, sickening her, that everything anchoring her life – their lives – had gone.

The sun rose over Marel City, glinting off the high towers. It was a sight on a million holo-vids, the great purple-tinged sky, the sleek transports that ferried between the Ferran planets. At the edge of the atmosphere the hub, lit up though the night so it was visible on the edge of planetary space, began to fade from view. Later, when it was full daylight, it would appear again, a dim grey moon in the daytime sky.

Surely, by now, the sprites would have returned to their trees and ended their night's torture. For once, she wished she followed a religion but the Banned had been made up of people so diverse that religions had merged with each other during her childhood, and she'd never fallen under the spell of any. It had left her a lingering sense of something out there, but no clear idea of who or what. She envied those with faith. Sam had faced hell and found a way past it, not least because of his belief.

There had to be something; too many believed for there not to be. She dropped to her knees, surprising herself, but it felt right. She closed her eyes and prayed, her thoughts formless and raw. She prayed for her daughter and brother in the dark forest, for her husband in the desert facing his nightmares. She prayed until she ran out of thoughts, and then she tried again, this time murmuring the word please over and over again. That was all she wanted: that please, something, somewhere, listened to her. Finally, drained, she opened her eyes and got to her feet. She had no idea if the prayer had made any difference but she felt lighter somehow, as if she had actually done something useful.

A freighter descended from the hub to the planetary port, the first in hours. She should have already been out of Marel and on Ferran-V, ready for the daylight. She was no use to anyone. She couldn't even get off the planet without a ship and a pilot. The freighter swooped towards the port, heavy and graceless, the opposite of the Roamer freighters she'd grown used to.

The Roamers. She could have pounded her hand off the glassine at missing something so obvious. They might not care who she was outside of her connection with Kare, but they cared about Kerra. She was a Roamer princess. They'd understand why she shouldn't be left cold in the forest, waiting for a stranger to claim the body. She gathered her jacket and left the room, ignoring the guards standing at either side of the door. She made her way to the transport stands and climbed into a planet-hopper.

"The port, please." She smiled. The port, where the Roamers waited their King's return. She wanted to contact him and beg him not to face his mother, to come back to Syllte and leave the fight for someone else. She'd tell him she was done, that she could risk nothing more. The transport flew over the streets of Marel, already filling with early commuters. She gave a thin smile at herself in the window. She could tell him whatever she liked – whether he'd listen was another matter altogether.

***

Get up, Lichio ordered himself. He had to get help: Kare needed to know that Phelps had the kids before the assault. And Sonly needed to know; she'd be out of her mind with worry. And Josef needed him to come out of this alive, and do whatever deal was needed.

He managed to stand, and yelled, properly yelled, as the thorns scraped his skin. The noise felt good in a perverse way, as if he was reclaiming the forest for himself.

He stumbled to the clearing. Last night, crawling, it had felt like a mile; today it took moments to reach. He found his clothes and pulled on his shirt, but even its soft fabric made him cry out. His trousers, dragged over ripped skin, brought a sharp hiss. Reaching with swollen fingers, he checked his belt. His equipment-cache was gone, including his comms unit and emergency supplies. Damn, he needed it. A quick search confirmed it wasn't lying anywhere obvious, and he didn't have time to spread out further. For all he knew, it was in the canopy with the little sprite bastards. He'd have to manage without.

A wave of dizziness passed over him. His shirt was already stained red, and he didn't know how much of it was blood and how much juice. If it was blood, he'd lost more than he'd thought – and certainly more than was ideal.

He pushed his hair back from his forehead and took a deep breath. The dizziness eased, letting him think straight. There was nothing else for it, he'd have to walk. The thought of pulling his boots on was beyond him, so he stepped barefoot into the centre of the forest clearing and paused, trying to get his bearings. He could be anywhere. He started to walk in the direction he thought he'd come from yesterday, but there was no noise around him or sign of a search. He needed to find a path, any path. If he did, he'd be on the tourist trail, and someone would pick him up. Either that, or he'd reach a station and raise the alarm from there.

The sun reached its zenith and started to crawl towards evening. Thoughts moved lazily across his mind as he walked, plans to get to the palace and the cells, plans to use his agents to break Josef out, memories of what happened in the hidden depths of Abendau, quickly quashed only to return a moment later, circling for chinks to attack through. Transports droned overhead; searchers, he supposed. He stopped, too tired to go on. He wouldn't survive another night, he knew that. And this time he didn't have the option of his blaster; it had been lost long ago, buried somewhere in the thickets of thorns.

He sank to his knees. The ground whirled beneath him and he fell forwards, pitching onto the earth. He closed his eyes, not caring if he ever moved again or if the sprites did come for him.

Faces swam in front of him, from his past. His father, Eevan, Rjala, all gone. His mother, who he thought of rarely – he'd been so young when she died, it seemed a different life to the one he led. Her hand reached for him, but he didn't reach back: he hadn't been clever enough to get out of the forest, or to get her to safety during the raid that had killed her.

Think of others – think of the living. Of Kerra, on her way to Abendau; Kare already there. Sonly, who must know he and Kerra were missing. Josef. He focused on Josef, imagining the kink of his hair, the determined curl on the nape of his neck, just big enough to twist around his little finger. He'd never get the chance to find the words he should have said. He'd never be able to admit he'd been an idiot who hadn't taken the chance to put his past behind him, to open up to the risk of love. If he could go back to his office, and face Josef again, would he still stay silent? He didn't believe he would.

How many sprites were in the canopy, waiting for him? Would they track him from above and know where he was as soon as darkness fell? Of course they would; they'd want to keep their prey close. Just like the Empress. He licked his dry lips. He hoped Kare didn't find out about Kerra and the boy. He shouldn't be distracted by them, or anything. He wished he could get a message to him. He'd tell Kare to take his mother out, however he could. Once the head of the snake was dead he could get to the others.

Useless thoughts, nothing more. Lichio closed his eyes and lay, exhausted, waiting for the night to fall and the sprites to finish their business with him.

CHAPTER TWENTY-SIX

Kare stepped into the living area of the safe house, which had been turned into a makeshift dorm, with sleeping rolls laid out in neat rows. He claimed an empty one a little away from the door, glad he hadn't been offered the single bedroom which had been turned into an impromptu armoury. Sleeping in the midst of an arsenal didn't appeal but, more importantly, it would be good for the squad to see he was equal and no more in this raid - not even that, the most junior of this squad had more experience than he had. If the raid went wrong he'd be just as dead, after all. He'd see to that, if nothing else.

He dropped onto the mat and pulled off his boots. His toes relaxed, and he stretched before lying on the surprisingly soft mat. Things had improved since he'd been a squaddie, it seemed. He pulled the blanket - standard issue, thin but warm - over his fatigues.

The sound of quiet breathing surrounded him, broken by the occasional rustle of people turning over to get comfortable. It took him back to his early days at the Banned, sharing a barracks with fifteen other recruits. He'd been so scared then, not knowing what the future held and if it would be as horrific as his father's visions. At least he knew *that* answer now.

He closed his eyes. Sleep played with the corners of his mind, not quite taking him. Images flickered, of Sonly, of the kids, of Syllte - familiar images that should soothe, but added a trickle of worry instead. He took a deep breath and tightened and relaxed his muscles one by one. It was no wonder he was stressed: coming back to

Abendau was enough to make anyone tense. Sleep finally embraced his tired body as it drew him under.

The floor became harder and colder; the quiet breaths were replaced by silence, broken only by the drip of water, a drip he'd listened to for months, counting pain by it. It wasn't going to be a good dream. He tried to rouse himself but was too deeply under.

Footsteps echoed. He had to get out; they'd hurt him again. His hands throbbed; his stomach ached, empty and hungry. He whimpered. The steps became clearer: sharp steps, not the heavy boots of Beck. Sweat broke as fear washed through him. He tried to sit up, pushing his hands against the cold ground.

He stared at his hands. They weren't his. They were too young, no more than a child's.

The cold deepened. The steps were close now, and he knew whose they were. He wanted his power back. The thought came to him, raw with anger, immature in its simplicity. If he had his power, he'd hurt the Empress like she'd never been hurt before. She couldn't do this to someone from the tribes. It wasn't right.

The cell door opened. He tried to back away but was too weak. It wasn't just the Empress silhouetted in the doorway: there were others with her, soldiers on either side. If they were going to take him, she was finished with him.

The first soldier took hold of his arm, but he kicked out, ignoring a jarring pain in his leg. "Get away from me!"

"Sir, are you all right?"

Who was the sir? He kicked out again, but the Empress turned her attention to him, making him yell at the familiar pain wrenching through him. He pulled at his manacles, not caring that it hurt his wrists.

"Kare, wake up!"

The voice was insistent, and it made no sense; Kare was his father.

"Kare! You're dreaming, sir."

The chill lifted and the drip of water receded. He managed to sit up, and pushed his sweat-laden hair back from his face. His hands were shaking, and he brought them to his chest, trying for some sort of control. Others in the squad were sitting up, watching him; obviously, he'd made quite a spectacle.

"Are you all right?" Simone's voice carried an edge of concern. What had he shouted, from the depths of his cell?

He managed a nod, but it felt unreal, as if he was only half in the room. "Yeah." A nightmare, nothing more. He mussed his hair, trying to bring some semblance of normality back, but it felt wrong, damn it, too brittle. Like him.

"Sir." Her words were unusually hesitant. "We have an urgent message from your wife."

A chill settled in him. Sonly would not contact him – anything military would come from Lichio – about anything other than the family. He followed Simone to the single bedroom full of weaponry, and leant against the small sink unit, his stomach twisting.

"What is it?" he asked, his voice somehow steady.

"There have been some problems on Ferran." She indicated the bed. "Sit down."

To hell with that; it didn't matter if he was sitting or standing, just that he knew. "Tell me."

"The children are missing in the fire forests, as is General le Payne. The Ferrans don't believe any of them will survive the night."

Kerra hadn't been in his dream, or Lichio, only the boy. It hadn't been a vision, just bad timing. And yet it felt like it presaged something. He gripped the sink harder, using its cold to anchor him in this room, this moment, and not let his mind run away with fear and possibilities. This was his fault. He had let the boy stay free after the attack on the ship, when he could have taken the political hit and had him locked up. It had been his call, and he'd made the wrong one.

What had Baelan done with his freedom? He thought of the cold cell, the drip-drip marking time, and fear clawed its way to its familiar place at his centre.

CHAPTER TWENTY-SEVEN

The Ferran freighter banked over the forest far below, displaying its mile-upon-mile of green. She finally understood why the Ferrans had told her the search wouldn't be a quick one. Even with a fix on the last known location, the dense forest would take time to search. She pressed her nose to the viewing panel and tried to decide how to play things on the ground. Losing her cool and demanding the searchers look harder wasn't going to help anyone.

The Roamer pilot, keeping to the height the Ferrans had grudgingly given permission for when Sonly had made it clear she wasn't leaving, banked the ship back towards the city. Below, smaller search ships tracked over the canopy, concentrated in the area where Kerra and Lichio had gone missing.

She clutched her comms unit. It flashed, but all the traffic was on her personal channel and held no interest for her. She was out of a job, either forced out or by her own intent. It didn't matter – she was sick of her and hers being targets, sick of this life she led. Let someone else carry the flame. The military channel was the only thing she was interested in. She stared at the unit and willed it to do its job and let her know what was happening, but it stayed stubbornly quiet.

***

A transport droned over Lichio's head. He hadn't escaped. He was going to be taken to the quarry. Silom was quiet. He might be dead. That felt true in an odd, buried, way. A thin thread of pain and tiredness held him to the ground, as the beat-beat of the transport sounded far in the distance. He was happy to lie and let it pass over.

Water dripped nearby, a sound distinct from the distant engines. He turned his head, thirsty, sure it was a trick; there shouldn't be any water on Belaudii. And the sun should be warm on his face. He opened his eyes, expecting bright light to stab him, and looked up at a sky of muted greys and greens. He blinked and it came back to him: he was in the fire forests with the sprites. It must be getting later if the trees were dripping condensation back to the ground.

He groaned and rolled over, making it first to his knees, and then to his feet. He had things to do – things that had become clear to him over the last night. There was nothing like facing your death to work out what really mattered, and it wasn't protecting himself. Not anymore.

The tree-cover around him was thin; he must be near a clearing. He paused, tired enough to give up, but shook his head to clear it. He hadn't survived last night for it to end here. He limped to where the trees were thinnest, and stepped into a clearing. Wincing, he pulled his shirt off, flapped it over his head and shouted in a rasping voice.

***

The ship banked, hard, and headed over the forest again.

"They've found something," the pilot said. His voice was terse, his face unreadable in the typical Roamer fashion; she might be Kare's wife, but she'd never be one of them. "See? Ahead – the search ships are being pulled back." He swooped towards a decent-sized clearing. A military transport and two specialist forest-search transports had already landed. A medical-copter also landed, its team disembarking to duck into the forest.

"Pilot, return to your prescribed flight path," the control panel blared.

The pilot glanced at her. "What do you want to do?"

"Can you land?"

The pilot shot a look of disdain. "I can land in half that space."

"Then do it." She stared out of the viewing window. Two military fighters approached from the city. "If they shoot me out of the air, they'll have a publicity nightmare on their hands." She glanced at him. "I will *not* tell Karlyn his daughter lay cold in strangers' hands."

He gave a sharp nod and took the ship down. She sat forwards, watching the fighters approach, but they only took up a flanking position. The Ferran authorities knew who she was, it seemed. The pilot settled the freighter in the clearing.

Sonly unstrapped and was on her feet before the engines had shut down. She opened the hatch and jumped to the ground, rather than waiting for the gangway to lower. She shivered despite the late-afternoon sun – the air was cold already. How much colder must it be at night? Her thin boots were more suited to the boardroom than a forest, and she was glad of the warmth in the soil.

A flurry of activity at the edge of the clearing took her attention. The medics emerged from the forest and between them, a foil blanket around his shoulders, stood Lichio, his face gaunt, his eyes shadowed. His skin was streaked with blood and dirt.

"Lich!" She darted across the clearing, ignoring the soldiers' shouts for her to stop. One grabbed her arm, but she threw him off. She reached Lichio and embraced him, careful not to hurt him. He clung to her like she was holding him up.

"You're alive," she said. "How?"

"Later," he slurred. He pushed her away. "Kerra's not in the forest; she's been taken."

Her heart skipped a beat. Kerra was alive. Both of them were alive. It was the miracle she'd been praying for all night.

Lichio's words sank in. "Taken? Who by?"

"Phelps," said Lichio, but she'd already known it had to be him, the carrion crow who hunted people and found his way to them however he had to. Lichio swayed and one of the medics took his arm and started to lead him towards their transport. He shook the man off. "She's being taken to Abendau."

"General, come over to the transport," said the medic. "We need to attend to you."

Lichio let himself be pulled away, or was too tired to stop them, but looked over his shoulder again. "Don't tell Kare! He mustn't change the mission."

She watched him go, trying to make sense of his words? Not tell Kare? He was on Belaudii - he could do something, where she couldn't.

"The Empress has to be stopped!" said Lichio, wrenching his arm away from the frustrated medic. "It's the only way to end things."

He might be right. She paused one moment more, deciding, and then ran for the Roamer ship, her comms unit already in her hand and activated. He might also be wrong - and she would never be able to face herself in the mirror if Kare could have done something and she never gave him the chance. He was Kerra's father, and Baelan's, too - it was up to him to decide what mattered most.

CHAPTER TWENTY-EIGHT

Kare stared at the command-comms unit, as if hoping it would take the decision for him. When he finally lifted his head, Hickson and Simone were looking at him with something like sympathy. Behind them, Kym Woods, having delivered the order for the assault squad to stand down from their preparations for the raid, kept her face in closed blankness.

Sonly's message had been stark, delivered in a cold, computerised voice that must have been nothing like the way she had recorded it. The kids were on their way to Belaudii and his mother. They'd arrive close to the time of his planned raid.

"Any thoughts?" he asked, his voice steady now that he knew the worst.

Hickson cleared his throat. "Any data on the type of ship they were on?"

"Nothing yet." Hickson was right: focusing on the practical, not the what-ifs, was the thing to do. Kare tapped his fingers on the table, thinking. Phelps, the bastard, would've planned the snatch well. "Phelps must know if he's discovered close to the main Roamer fleet, they would take steps to recover the children." Well, Kerra anyway – the Roamers were no more enamoured by Baelan than anyone else.

"A cruiser, then?" said Simone. "He'll want something quick, with firepower."

"And a mid-range fighter squad," said Woods. Hers wasn't a question, but a statement of fact. "He'll run if he can and let the fighters do the work."

That made sense. Kare nodded his thanks and

started to tap the command console. "Let's work within those parameters." He glanced at Simone. "You have access to the port records?"

"Limited."

He winced. In the compound he would have been able to run sim after sim, of all possible fleet parameters. He'd have the planet on full alert, picking up any incoming space traffic from the edge of the system, and would have hours to decide his strategy. This... this *toy* of a console, slowly building the first sim rather than running it in real time, wasn't what he needed. He wanted to thump the console and see if it would speed up, but he didn't dare damage it. The safe house had been set up to run an assault force, not interstellar attack parameters, and it was all he had. It had taken all his skill to work the programming up to this level.

"Limited records are better than nothing," he said, but didn't sound convinced. "Check for any fleets leaving—" He did a quick calculation; Phelps wouldn't have stayed on Ferran long before the snatch. "In the last three days. Stretch it to four, if we don't find anything. Then see if they've listed a return." He got up and stretched; he needed a break. "Call me when" *—if—* "the sim's finished and I'll review the data." He left, heading for the kitchen-area and a strong coffee.

"Sir?"

He stopped at the voice. "Sergeant."

Kym faced him. "You said you'd take the bitch down." Her eyes blazed, the message clear: he'd promised. "That's what we should be doing, and the rest day is the logical time for it. Your concerns about the children shouldn't govern your thinking."

Her words nagged at his own doubts. He forced himself to meet her eyes. If he was going to take the action to delay the attack - and it was a big if, dependent on what he discovered - he'd stand over it, even to her.

"I appreciate how this appears," he said. "But I don't believe a delay will jeopardise the attack."

"But any attempt to take the children will," she pointed out, her words clipped. "If you do that, you'll be allowing the Empress to dictate your actions. The way to free your children is to take the bitch out."

Militarily she was right, but not every decision was about what was right. If the cost of his children's lives was to retreat, he'd pay it.

"I know what I'm risking," he said. She stared at him, not moving. "Sergeant, stand down." He softened his voice. "I will take your concerns into account. I don't intend to jeopardise anything, if I don't have to."

She paused, before giving a sharp nod.

"Sir," she said, but it was clipped and formal, a person paying lip service and nothing more. She turned on her heel and he watched her go. He'd taken her future. Now he might break the promise he'd made in Silom's name; he deserved nothing more than her contempt.

***

Kerra sat on the edge of the bunk, hands knuckled against her temples, and tried to get the mesh to form into something useful. It was full of unconnected thoughts, with none of the hive-consciousness she was used to. She'd tried up to the lights dimming in her cabin yesterday evening, through the night, and all today, but nothing had worked, and she needed it to.

She took a few deep breaths. Psyching was never effective if she was upset. She tried to remember how she'd flown the Roamer ship, the sense of space all around her, the peace it had brought. That was the closest she'd ever felt to the mesh. Groping, clutching a strand of power, she reached out and was rewarded by just a touch of Control.

Their ship was one of a small fleet, coming up to the Belaudii space-zone. Which meant she was almost out of time. If she wanted to turn the ship back to Ferran it would take more power than the mesh currently held, and, she feared, a lot more skill than she had.

She bet the pilot with the crooked grin could do it. She groped for her name. Laurena, that was it. A soft pulse responded to her thoughts, making Kerra jump. She concentrated on the shattered mesh, searching for the pulse, but it had gone.

She squeezed her eyes closed and felt the pulse again. This time, she almost pinpointed where it was. She thought of the pilot and how it had felt to fly beside her, and again the pulse came. This time she could see which segment of strands it came from, and she dove past the fragments, teeth gritted.

Laurena? The pulse of the Roamer came again, stronger, and she homed in on it, herself and the mesh a circling of knowledge and power, growing all the time. It was so right, so perfect. She'd be as strong as Baelan with this, as strong as their father. She opened herself to it, calling the Roamer minds to hers, putting them where they'd always been. It was a cycle, one that generation after generation of kings and queens had maintained, a perfect blend of mind and power, and it was what she'd been born to. It was what her father had never been able to do - give himself to the mesh - but it was what the Roamers needed from him. And, if he could not do it... then the mesh would claim what it needed: a true heir to Ealyn. He could not make a difference to what had happened on Ferran-V. He couldn't stop Phelps taking her. But she could.

She turned her focus on the hive-mind, delivering a single instruction for the Roamers. It responded, heaving, in immediate obedience: this close, so near the centre, it was more vivid than she'd imagined. She delivered a second pulse, warning them about Lichio, and receiving a reassuring one back. It was working again. She held on to the mesh, and felt it embrace her back: it had chosen its new Queen.

CHAPTER TWENTY-NINE

Josef put his travel bag down. "You asked for me?" He must have been ready to leave when Lichio's request reached him.

"Yes." Lichio pushed himself up on his elbow, ignoring the draining tiredness. Josef took his other elbow, helping him to sit, and Lichio had to let him - it was either that or have the conversation while looking at the roof.

"They tell me you're lucky to be alive." Josef sat on the edge of the bed, his eyes raking Lichio. There was little of the calm assurance from their previous meeting. "What happened?"

"It was a rough night." Lichio cleared his throat; despite the fluids he'd been given, the forest air had left it dry and sore. "Josef - when we talked, in my office?"

Josef stiffened, but didn't move away. "Yes?"

"I was wrong." Saying the words felt good, as if he was coming back to the person he should have been. He forced himself to meet Josef's eyes - even if it was too late, he'd say what had to be said. If it was over between them - if he'd broken things - at least let it end on an honest note. "You were right."

On more than one level. He thought of Shadeen, so flattered by his interest in her, not knowing what he'd used her for. Not the sex, which had been mutual, but the implicit promises that he'd given - that she meant more to him than she had. That he was something he had not been: free and available. He felt shoddy. "I should have been open about you."

Josef gave a curt nod, but said nothing. Lichio was on his own here, as he should be. He swallowed, wincing at the sharp pain, and forced himself to go on. To make this about actions taken and not the deeper feelings – the feelings that had been tearing through him, hurting him as he'd sworn he would never be again – would be as much a lie as his avoidance had ever been.

"I want to be with you. No more hiding." No more pretending things were different than they were. It felt freeing. He took a deep breath – better to know, than to wish he had asked. "I will not hide again, if you will give me the chance."

Did Josef remember the long nights in his embassy, sitting, feet entwined, talking out their hopes and dreams? Did he know that Lichio had never done that with anyone? That he wined and dined and entertained, but had never trusted?

"You asked for a commitment. I barely know what that feels like." He'd never wanted to. "I'd like to." He wanted to run, to dodge, to avoid as he always had, but he fought the reflex. "I love you. I should have thought of you. I have not been the person you deserved."

He waited, prepared for the rebuffal, his breath tight. God, it hurt, to be so raw, to open himself to this. And yet, amongst the hurt, there was something else, something freeing.

Josef bent towards him, a slight smile on his face. He brushed Lichio's lips with his own, light stubble rasping.

"You're not being fair, Lich," he said. "I didn't ask you to stop." He held up a hand, cutting off Lichio's protests. "I told myself you'd come round, eventually, and let things go on."

"But you never had anyone else?" It was important to know, and he understood how Josef had been feeling, the breath-stopping fear that he hadn't been enough, that what they'd had wasn't real.

"Never."

Relief flooded Lichio, lifting the draining tiredness. He'd been right to ask Josef to come back. "So, do you still want an ambassador?" His heart gave an extra thud, dull in his chest. "Is it still possible, do you think?"

"I think so." Josef smiled, his face relaxing, crinkled laughter lines framing his eyes. "I want you to come with me. You know that. I think you need to come with me - Abendau will suck you back down. Staying here, tempted by all your duties, will too."

Cautiously, Lichio nodded. This was his chance to do so, perhaps his only chance before he took the next opportunity offered to him, and the next. A chance to be happy - to have that wrapped up in something he'd been so terrified of was an irony hard to miss.

"I agree. But first..." If he'd been afraid of his last words, what of this? "Kare is taking the palace. I need to support him." He met Josef's eyes, desperate for understanding. It wasn't just Josef he had committed to, even if he'd never wanted to recognise it. Kare had been his leader for ten years - longer, from right back at the Banned. No matter how much he wanted to seize this chance and go to Mersor, he could not walk away. It wasn't about being someone's number two and supporting them in practical ways. It was about loyalty - about being prepared to lay his life down, if demanded of him, and lose whatever future he had gained.

"Do you understand? I can't let him go in alone, not if I can help. He ordered me to watch over the boy - and I failed. The children will arrive in Abendau soon - Kare will be facing a firestorm there, well beyond what we hoped he would. I can't walk away now."

"Of course I understand." And he did; he always had. Josef stood. "Do what you must, Lichio. Mersor can wait. For now."

***

Sonly pushed open the door to the med-bay. Lichio was sitting up, at least, and his skin-tone was better. From hearing who his visitor had been, she thought she might know why.

He raised an eyebrow at her, waited for a medic to finish a scan, and said, "I'm making a habit of hospital stays."

The medic made a note on the records-screen, and gave a sharp nod before leaving. If he knew who Sonly was, he gave no indication, and she was grateful for that: everywhere she went, it felt like she was running the gauntlet of public opinion.

She sat at the edge of Lichio's bed. "How are you?"

"Rjala didn't exaggerate." He shuddered. "Unbelievably foul creatures." He lowered his voice. "Perrault told me you contacted Kare. I asked you not to."

"I know." She manoeuvred to face him more directly. It wouldn't be the first time the military had tried to force her actions, and it presumably wouldn't be the last. Just because it was Lichio made no difference. "I wasn't prepared to take his decision for him. I gave him the facts - it's up to Kare how he runs it in Abendau."

"Very noble of you." Lichio's voice was frosty. "It's a hell of a decision to be handed in the middle of a mission."

"It would have been a hell of decision not to tell him." She glared at him; surely Lichio understood that Kare had a right to know. "How would you have me tell him his children are dead if we did nothing? That his daughter was in the torture chambers?"

He nodded, a terse nod. "None of it is straightforward. I would have preferred to run some intelligence for him in advance of the information."

He had a point. She inclined her head, acknowledging it. "We have analysts supporting his requests at the moment." She gave a small shrug. "I couldn't have withheld it from him, Lich. That would have been worse."

"For you, maybe. Not for the mission." He gave a resigned sigh. "So, what has he decided?"

"I don't know," she said. Nothing had come out of Abendau other than terse requests for information. But she knew Kare. He'd do the right thing, and that was to get Kerra out. And the boy: even if she didn't like him, he was still a child and she knew, as Kare would, that the Empress would use the children in whatever way she could. She would wish that on no one. She hunched forwards. "Will he get her out, Lich? Is it even possible?"

His face softened. "It'll be tough. But Kare has the best record of anyone for getting in and out of the palace." He stretched, and grimaced. "I hear the vote went against you?"

"Yes." The betrayal welled in her, sharp and bitter-tasting. "The republic's council voted me off." While she was on Ferran-V and they didn't have to tell her in person, the weasels. His look of sympathy made her throat catch, and her voice was choked when she went on. "It doesn't matter, though – it's only a small thing compared to everything else—"

"The hell it is." Lichio sat straighter, his eyes shining, more life in him than there'd been for months. "It's the most important thing of all. You, more than anyone, spoke for the people. You were the one who made it possible to remove her empire; without the strength of the Abendauii Senate, Kare would never have forced his abdication through. They have not ceded the city's chamber to her yet – and without it, she does not hold the city." He took her arm, circling it with his hand. "Damn it, Sonly, in removing you, she's taken the first step to retaking her empire. If Kare doesn't succeed in Abendau – and if he does go for the kids, he won't – it comes down to a political fight. No one else has the position – and the backbone – to take on that fight."

She wanted to tell him her backbone was gone, that she didn't have the answers anymore, but he had turned from her to point out the window, at the hub's distant lights.

"All the people in the outer zone, barely scraping a living... she'll turn on them, like never before. They supported you. The Ferrans—" He shuddered, his face bleak. "You have no idea what it was like in that forest. She killed a planet that way – kids, old people, everyone. She'll do it again if she has to."

She didn't need a lecture in politics. She'd spent all day – between fretting about him, Kerra and Kare – worrying about what the Empress would do if the republic didn't have the strength to oppose her. "I know what she did, Lich." She also knew that she wasn't the person to take the fight to her. With her dirty exposé, delivered with devastating timing, the Empress had seen to that.

"But have you seen it? I was on Corun, remember? You didn't believe me about the sort of planet it was. You said nowhere could be that bad, but it was. They had nothing: it was grey from the sky to the ground. The most miserable place you could imagine."

His eyes looked far away, as he relived his first mission as an officer. What age had he been? Seventeen at most. Far, far too young to be in command, but that had been the way of it in the Banned – childhoods lost to the knowledge the base could be attacked at any moment, and if you were caught and a rebel, it didn't matter what age you were.

"The Empress ordered the dome broken to get what she wanted," he said. "Children died choking on the air. Children I'd known. Local soldiers I'd trained." His face twisted as he tried to get his point across. "How many more Coruns are there in the outer rim? How many more Ferran-Vs? She will spread across the galaxy, taking everything Kare has built in the last ten years." He tapped her arm. "Everything *you* built. You can't let her."

"I can't stop her." He had to know that; he wasn't stupid. "Without the republic's backing, I'm nothing but a failed politician."

"The republic didn't get you to where you are. The people of Abendau did that. You did it - not Kare, not me, but you."

She pulled her arm away and rubbed it absently. *Not Kare.* Something sparked in her mind, but she couldn't quite grasp it.

"That's all history," she said. "No one comes back from where I am. I'm not just shamed by it, I'm being implicated as a security risk. Someone who'd share secrets to a lover. And not just me - the longer I hang in there trying to ride it out, the more dirt gets slung at others."

"Kare, you mean?"

She nodded. Yes, Kare, facing a new ream of questions about his past. And Kerra, how must she have felt?

Lichio snorted. "Kare doesn't give a damn what the news-holos say about him. They've said much worse over the years. And you? You think the people who voted for you care about a few naked pictures? They cared about being given a voice, about being listened to, about educating their kids."

He didn't understand. It was about her daughter being in the position to be hurt again, because of who she and Kare were. It was about finding a different life than this madness, and if that meant letting the Empress win and walking away, so be it. Let it be someone else's fight - she and Kare had done enough, surely?

"Lich, she has Kerra." She had to pause as memories rushed at her, bleak times when she'd lost Kerra. "You said I hadn't seen what the Empress has done in the past. I've had so many people I love in her claws. You don't know how frightening that is."

"I know you've always fought to get them back." He swung his legs out of bed. Scratches ran the length of them, red and angry, from the cuffs of his shorts to his ankles. "And you've always won."

"What are you doing?" she said. "Get back into bed. You're not well."

"I've been worse." He pushed to his feet and put his hand out to steady himself on the bedside cabinet. "She's taken too much, Sonly." He lifted a shirt, folded on the top of the cabinet, and pulled it on with a hiss. "I'm going to Abendau. So should you."

"We wouldn't even clear the port." Kare hadn't come up with any way to get through its security.

"Maybe not, but we'd make headlines while they eject us. And those headlines might spread. That's where the Banned started, after all: headlines and passion and nothing more." He grinned. "Don't you remember Dad's collection of holos? The early ones, of him and Ealyn - how they courted the publicity? The lightning raids by the daring pilot and the trusted statesman? The audacity of them? That's what Dad built everything on - publicity and passion. Nothing more." He held his hand out to her.

Hope fizzed in her, driven not by his words but by the belief in his eyes and the strength of his voice.

"You're the politician; you work out how best to play it." He shrugged. "I remember you coming to power. No one can manipulate the media better than you."

She, too, remembered the crowds in Abendau cheering her on, as if their shouts would be enough to carry her to the palace. Hands had reached for her, thanking her, as she made her way down the Grand Boulevard. People had held up children who would attend the schools she'd pledged to create.

That time was past – her political career was lost. But she could still make a noise. She could be the thorn in the Empress' side she'd always been. She could remind the bitch that she could scheme and blackmail and still wouldn't get rid of Sonly le Payne. Her smile widened. The Empress hadn't taken what drove her: her belief, her father's trust. Her strength. She'd only dented it.

"I'll go," she said.

"Good," Lichio said. "I'm sure Kare will try for his

mother, even if he breaks cover with the kids. He knows he won't get onto the planet again. If he does, he'll be attacking a palace ready for him, with his mother waiting for him." He glanced at his comms unit. "If we leave now, we might get there before he launches that second attack. He'll want to get the children to safety first." He gave a quick grin, a flash of the old Lichio. "While you're doing your singing and dancing, I'm going to slip into the city and join my agents. I'll see what I can do to support him and see if we can't get him out, and the kids."

CHAPTER THIRTY

Kare's eyes strained against the darkness falling over the city. The port was lit up and busy, especially for the rest day, confirming the data he'd spent the afternoon working on was right and the ship with the children had to be due. Already his original plan had gone awry – he should have been in situ by now – but that was tomorrow's problem. Tiredness tightened the skin on his forehead, making his head ache, but he leaned forwards and scanned the sky, pushing it back.

Come on, come on; where was the ship? He shifted, but stayed crouched in the bay window of the church, awkwardly tucked into the corner. From here, whilst at a distance, he could make out the skywalk.

Closer to the palace, Hickson and his squad waited. Soon, Kare would have to decide whether to carry out the planned attack on the Empress, abort until he had more information, or, if it looked viable, order an attack on the port.

"Sir." Simone pointed to the sky just beyond the palace. He nodded, taking in the lights of an approaching ship, and brought his scope up, zooming in as close as he could. A military-grade cruiser, just breaking through the outer atmosphere.

"That's our boy," he murmured. He tried to get up, but the roof was too low, so he stayed in his crouched hunch. "I hope."

"You need to be sure."

He nodded. He had to wait until he saw the children. Otherwise he was risking the mission on a hunch. He zoomed in further. A good hunch: the ship was big and the squad of fighters flanking it a good size. The Empress wouldn't send such a fleet for no reason.

"They're opening the palace doors on the skywalk, sir."

He turned his scope onto the raised path linking the port and palace and watched as a squad of soldiers emerged and marched across, toys in the distance. "That's it," he said, decided. "They don't send a troop across for import duty." He watched them move across. "Damn her. She knows the skywalk is hard to take from the ground."

"Wait." Simone exuded calm. "Be sure. They'll be landing soon enough."

The sound of the cruiser's thrusters reached them, so familiar over Abendau it was unlikely any of the citizens would stop to notice. As the flotilla reached the port, the fighters broke off, but the bigger ship carried into the main docking bay. Kare shifted position, trying for a better angle, until he could make out the port-side exit onto the skywalk.

That was how he'd been brought into Abendau as a prisoner. He'd been forced across the path high over the gardens, Beck's bindings on his arms tighter than they'd needed to be, the sadistic bastard already turning the screws. Were his kids feeling the same fear, knowing they'd be taken to the Empress? They certainly knew enough to imagine what lay ahead.

He licked his lips, grainy with the sand that made its way into every building, and waited for the doors to open. Simone stood at the next window, silent and still in the darkness. He envied her calm

"If she only sends one squad, an attack is still viable," she said.

He nodded, but wasn't convinced. The skywalk was vulnerable, but only with air support. He wished he'd kept the Roamers close enough to call down. Two or three of their ships could carry off an attack on the skywalk easily, but he had expected to return - assuming he did return - with the rest of the squad to the military transport waiting in orbit.

His shoulders itched, tense with holding their position. He wanted to give an order - any action had to be better than this waiting - but he held his breathing steady and waited. If he got this wrong, Hickson's team would be exposed.

The squad of the Empress' soldiers flanked the low parapets. He scanned the length of the walk, across to the palace. More soldiers were at the palace entrance to the skywalk, and no doubt more were spread through the grounds. He thought about where Hickson would need to attack from - the bowels of the palace, practically - and straightened, his decision made: no attack on the skywalk. Not tonight. He might want his children back, the crawling pain from his vision as Baelan might be fresh and terrifying, but he couldn't risk the soldiers he'd been living amongst for days. Not on a mission they'd so little hope of achieving.

"Order the squad to stand down," he said. "If it is the kids, we can get the palace agents to confirm where they're held tomorrow. Once we're sure, we'll lift them from the palace."

He was making it sound easy, but the Empress must know he'd go after the children; she'd be banking on it. His only real hope had been a swift in-and-out, a snatch and grab before she expected it. Now, he might have to enter with Hickson's squad. It had been one thing to risk his computer adaptations on himself, but now a whole squad would be dependent on his having got that right.

He ran his hand through his hair, reviewing every option for a rescue tonight, each more desperate than the last, but the outcome remained the same; he didn't have enough personnel, no matter how good they were. He lifted the scope again, waiting to see who emerged. "The woman must have about a hundred lives. She's luckier than a sand-lizard."

"They're probably related," said Simone, her voice sweet. Despite his nerves, Kare snorted and had to hide a grin. Unfair to the lizards, that.

***

Kerra stumbled forwards at a hard push from Phelps, barely catching herself from falling into the docking port. Her thoughts were fuzzy, only half on where she was and what was happening, the rest of her focus on the mesh. She could sense the Roamer thoughts but hadn't enough ability, or power, or focus, to catch and know them. How had her father dealt with this? He'd been able to connect with anyone in the mesh, just by thinking about them. Her own powers were of no help - another of the injections had been given to her just before landing. She didn't know how long, exactly, they lasted, but from her time in the palace, she could put a guess at half a day at least.

The port's doors ground open. In a moment, once the technicians had finished, the doors would open onto the skywalk. From there, she'd be taken to the Empress. If there was any hope of stopping that happening, it had to be now. She wanted to find the Roamers and discover where they were and if they *were* coming for her, but catching something so specific was like chasing smoke.

So, if not the Roamers, could she do anything? She pictured the skywalk. It was broad where she'd step out to it, but then it narrowed, funnelling walkers across the middle section. There were bound to be soldiers lining the way across, so that there would be nowhere to go except the palace.

Baelan joined her, his mother beside him, and met Kerra's eyes briefly, his cheeks flushing a little. That gave her hope - if he was embarrassed that he'd got her into this mess, he mustn't have realised she'd accessed the Roamer mesh. She was tempted to reach out and see if he had his own powers, and was ignoring the mesh as always, or if he was drugged and didn't know he had another option. She didn't, though, too scared that if she touched him, he'd learn about the mesh for sure. If he did, he might try to take some of the power. Greedily, she drew it towards herself, hoarding it.

Baelan hunched against his mother, like a child half his age. His arms were tracked with needle-marks, the same as her own. Her anger vanished, replaced by an odd pity. He had no one other than his mother; it was no wonder he'd gone to her on Ferran-V. The mesh shifted, aware of her change in focus, accepting her feelings as if they were a new command.

The cargo doors raised enough for her to see the white stone of the skywalk stretching beyond. Nerves jumped in her, and the mesh throbbed, picking up her fear. The Roamers were coming, she was sure of it. In fact, they might even be here already, ready to lift her. She pictured stepping onto the walkway and finding a line of Roamer freighters waiting for her. Their plasma-bolts would strafe the palace. Phelps would run for cover as the ships swooped down to rescue her, the way Farran and Lichio had only a few weeks ago. Excitement bubbled, low in her stomach; the images of her rescue were so vivid, they had to mean something. She fought to keep a smile off her face; the Roamers would soon teach Phelps a lesson.

The cargo doors shuddered to a halt, and a wash of cold air came through them. Baelan's mother stepped forwards, her hand on his shoulder. He was shivering; he knew their grandmother better than Kerra, and seemed even more frightened.

"Go," said Phelps. He gestured her to the skywalk, almost a gentleman. She stuck her nose in the air, the way her mother did when she wanted to show disdain, and stepped through.

It was dark outside. Somehow that seemed worse than stepping out into the familiar blue of a Belaudii sky and feeling the heat of the sun on her face. She wrapped her bare arms around herself, fighting the chill in the air.

There were no ships waiting above the skywalk, just a line of soldiers on each parapet, grim-faced, holding rifles. She stumbled forwards, listening for the low sound of ships' engines, and scanned the sky for any lights. Nothing.

"Get moving." Phelps' words were terse, and she could feel the caution radiating off him. He wanted them over to the palace as much as she wanted to fight against going. Baelan huddled against his mother, no use to anyone.

She took one last look at the sky and then across the walkway to the palace, and her stomach churned with a low fear. The Roamers hadn't come. She was on her own.

CHAPTER THIRTY-ONE

Lights flared, cascading all around her. Sonly ducked her head, shielding her eyes, but a holo-recorder was shoved in front of her, accompanied by a barrage of questions from behind the recorder.

"Keep going." Lichio grabbed her elbow, holding it tight, and with his free hand gave a quick signal to his team. "Clear that reporter."

The security squad pushed the recorder away, and Lichio hurried Sonly along the short walk to their transporter. Questions were shouted from each side but, through long-standing custom, she didn't answer. Her mouth was so dry, she didn't think she'd be able to get out much more than a croak anyway. She'd expected some media, yes, but not this amount – they stretched beyond the transporter stand, surrounding it on every side.

Lights continued to flash; voices continued to shout. She reached the transporter. Its gangway was already down and ready for her, but she tried not to rush at the first glimpse of the ship's interior and safety. It was imperative she didn't seem rattled – when she reached Abendau, she would need every vestige of control left to her.

She reached the top of the gangway, Lichio just behind her. His squad formed up at the bottom, keeping the press back. Slowly, the gangway retracted into the ship's belly, and the hatch sealed with a short hiss.

She leaned against the heavy hatchway, relishing the silence. The entire day had been hectic, pulling in favours, preparing in advance of the flight, while all the time the gnawing panic about what might be happening in Abendau grew.

"We need to strap in," said Lichio. He seemed unflustered by their rush through the media, barely a hair out of place.

She pushed off and went down the narrow access corridor towards the passenger space. The ship, a small corvette, was designed primarily for in-system flights, rather than deep-space, and lacked the luxury of a bigger ship. She'd have requested a Roamer ship to bring her into close orbit of Belaudii before switching ships, but the Roamer fleet had left, informing no one and filing no flight plan. That, more than anything, had started her panicking about Abendau – the whole fleet would only commit if there was a danger to their precious mesh. And if that was the case, it meant Kare – and Kerra – were at risk.

She slid the door to the passenger space open. She had no idea who Lichio had requisitioned the ship from – all he'd told her was he'd had an educating week learning who to ask for what on Ferran. Which was good because, given the accusations surrounding her actions, none of the great families would openly support her by providing a ship. Not even Tortdeniel, who'd supported as far back as the Banned, could be called on. She remembered begging for their help when Kare had been taken, how gently it had been broken to her what had been done to him, how they had given money for the children in the Banned when no one else would. They, of all the families, knew what she'd achieved for the poor, those whom Tortdeniel had long ago taken as their own, giving humanitarian aid to planets in need. If even they did not support her now, her career was ruined, unless she found a way to disprove the allegations – and they'd chosen their attack well, linking it to some of her best-known reforms.

The door slid closed behind her, locking in preparation for liftoff.

"Well, this is cosy." Lichio sat in one of four bucket seats bolted to the floor. He still looked pale, his face drawn, and the wounds on his hands had only healed to long gashes before he'd discharged himself, but he seemed something like his old self in mood.

He was right about the ship. It was basic – a server-unit provided ship's rations, the seats and a small workstation were all that adorned the room – but it appeared well-maintained. A hatch at the front of the room led to the control room and pilot's quarters but it was closed and, she assumed, locked. They wouldn't see the crew during the flight; their employer would not want them to know who had procured their services.

A second hatch led to a tiny passenger cabin. She went over and stuck her head through, ducking to clear the hatch. At least it had two bunks, even if they were so narrow she'd certainly have to raise the side-bars. They wouldn't have to sleep in shifts. After the roominess of the Roamer ships, it was hard to remember only the rich could afford even a small personal ship such as this; most citizens relied on the passenger cruisers which shuttled between the more populous planets.

She sat in the second bucket seat and gently nudged Lichio's long, stretched-out legs out of the way.

"We'd have had more room on a military transport," she said. Not necessarily more comfort, mind.

"We have to get into Abendau port somehow. I doubt they plan on a red carpet." He grimaced. "Well, they might if I call ahead and offer my head on a platter. Presumably that'd get me down." He started to unravel the strapping for his seat. "Ominous amount of this." He finally got the lap belt sorted and started on the shoulder restraints. "If we could use our own ships to get into Abendau, Kare would have." He cursed, spun round and sorted the strapping behind him. "And I certainly wouldn't be spending two days in a tub."

"It will be worth it. If it works..."

"If it does, I'll happily take back my room in the

palace and make myself comfy." His mouth twisted a little at the statement, but she fussed with her own straps rather than responding to his lie – he hated the palace almost as much as Kare did, preferring the military accommodation in the compound, or, as she knew now, the comforts of the Mersor embassy. She finished with her straps, tightened them, and wriggled in the hard seat.

She brought her folio onto her knee and started to sort through the contents: contact details for members of the press and what remained of the Senate of Abendau. Despite the Empress' dominance in the city, the senators were influential people who still carried support through the city.

She paused; influential people who may have aligned themselves with the new regime, either because there was no other way to influence policy or because of old loyalties.

She read through the names, making a mental note of whom she could trust. She reached Harald's name. Three months ago, he'd have been top of the list of those to be contacted, but... she remembered the day the photos had been released, and his censure of her. It had been impossible to know for sure, watching him on a screen, if he'd been sincere or coerced. Was she such a bad judge of character? She was risking much on those she made contact with – she had to be sure.

"Lich," she said. "Harald? What do you think?"

He looked up from his own data pad – the austerity of the ship didn't seem to be bothering him, despite his words. "I don't think he betrayed you when the city fell. Certainly, there is no evidence to support any of the Senate being involved with the coup." His words were slow, though, and careful. "But since..." He shrugged. "I do think he put Abendau before you. Once the pictures were released, he knew what it meant, and that he had to place some space between you and the Senate."

That, at least, rang true of the Harald she knew – and it would be hard to argue that he hadn't been right to.

"But I didn't find much warmth in him," said Lichio. "Not that he ever had a lot of time for us military types." He grinned. "I think he reckons we're all stupid."

"I was his president; he should have supported me."

"The Empress may have influenced him." Lichio looked at the ceiling and pursed his lips. He'd be recalling everything he knew about the senator, she knew, sifting through the information before making a judgement. Finally he looked back at her. "I don't think you can be sure enough to trust him."

"His support would make a difference." Lights over the pilot's hatch started, racing across, indicating the pre-flight checks were underway. It made it easy to pretend the churning in her stomach was to do with the flight ahead and not the thought of the Empress going through the Senate, turning them against her and making her an outcast from what had been, once, the centre of her life.

Lichio shook his head. "It's too much of a chance. I'll get him checked out, though, if it helps. If he is on our side, I'll let you know."

"Preparing for launch." The faceless pilot's voice came over the ship-comms system.

The engines began to thrum. This time, when her stomach did a somersault, there was no doubting why: she hated launches as much now as when she'd been eighteen and taking her first diplomatic visits for the Banned. Lichio turned his focus to his data pad, annoyingly unconcerned. She pressed back in her seat, her hands gripping the armrests tightly, her lips moving in a silent plea to get the next few minutes over with.

Lichio glanced up. "You'll be all right." He tapped his pad. "Once we land, I'm going to make contact with Simone. Kare will have no contingency for getting out of the palace if his mother knows he's there – the current plan is a quick in-out. It won't work if he walks into a trap." He frowned. "Even in the best scenario, the chance of getting out was slim."

She blinked, more at his bluntness than his words. She knew their truth, from the sadness shrouding Kare before he left, but they hadn't spoken of it. Lichio's frank admission, his open allowance of what was to happen, hit harder than it should. "Lichio, I need him out."

"I'm going to see if I can't find a way to use your diversion to do just that." His hands moved independently, flicking across the screen. "I'd like to get the palace under our control, which means Kare needs to be there to claim it back."

She cleared her throat, coughing past the tightness in it. "So, Lichio, who gets you out?"

He drew in a breath. He looked eighteen, his face pale and shadowed. Whatever answer he might have had was lost as the engines' noise ripped through the cabin, stopping all conversation. The ship launched, the g-forces strong enough to push her into her seat. The ship wasn't big enough to cushion any of the launch pressures.

It was some minutes before the familiar lurch in her stomach told her the anti-grav had kicked in, and the ship settled into smoother flight, allowing her to sit straighter. The noise of the engines died away and she turned to Lichio, ready to ask the question again.

"I don't know," he said, so quietly she had to strain to hear him. "But I'm going in anyway. What Kare's doing is right." He took another deep breath. "If it means I go down beside him, so be it."

Shadows chased the lines of his face. He was right, this was the moment where they – all of them – had to play their part in the dance. She had to return to Abendau, knowing if she didn't win through, her daughter could die to pave the way for the Empress' chosen heir. Kare had to face the demons of his past and free himself from his mother. It stood to reason that Lichio, too, had a part; he'd been in it from the beginning, born to it as she'd been. They stared across at each other, the last le Paynes, and gave twin nods. Let what would be, be.

CHAPTER THIRTY-TWO

Kerra stumbled forwards. When she'd been little, she'd loved visiting the skywalk with her nurse. She'd watch the sudden surges of the fountains in the formal garden, the water reaching above the height of the skywalk, and listen to the chinkle of the waterfall in the wild garden. She used to lean over the parapet, as far as she was allowed, and drop credits into the moat that wound underneath.

All that was gone, lost under the reality of the soldiers forcing her forwards. She tried to listen for the waterfall, to do anything other than think about her grandmother waiting. She bet she'd be sitting on the throne Dad used to make the most awful comments about, sending her into giggles until Mum made her leave a function one evening. It would be obscene to see her grandmother where he should be, her cold eyes casting judgement.

She strained, listening for the sound of engines, still not quite believing the Roamers weren't coming – she was sure they had sensed her and knew where she was. She gave a small sound, not quite of panic so much as loss, and something soft touched her hand; Baelan, his eyes lowered, walked beside her. He took her hand in his, but she pulled it away. It was no use trying to make things right now.

Phelps pushed past them, his steps steady and back straight. Baelan's mother put one hand on her son's shoulder, her sad eyes telling Kerra something awful was planned, making her shiver in the chill air.

A soldier prodded her forwards and she kept her head up, looking straight ahead. She might be terrified, but she wasn't going to show it. She reached the narrowed centre of the walkway, almost halfway across – in moments she'd be passing into the entrance hall of the palace. She focused on each step, each single one, keeping her fears hidden. The last time she'd met her grandmother, she'd been so scared she'd cried. Well, not this time.

"Form up!" The sound of soldiers coming to attention cut through her concentration. They crushed against her, all hard bodies and stern faces. The Empress' soldiers, remorseless, sworn to do her bidding. Kerra's bravery faltered. Her steps slowed. She found herself reaching for Baelan's hand, seeking the warm comfort he'd offered. She caught it and tightened her grip around it. He squeezed back, twice, making her look at him and something in his face – the set of his jaw, maybe, or the look in his eye – was so like her father it hurt. She wished he was here, beside her, knowing what to do, but the still night stretched on and he wasn't coming for her. No one was.

The mesh pulsed, reminding her she wasn't alone, that she never would be again. She scanned the walkway and began to look for possibilities.

***

"Damn," said Kare. "It is them." He put the scope down, his hands shaking. Knowing the children had been taken was one thing, seeing it another. He hadn't been able to make out the detail of their faces, but there'd been no mistaking their size compared to their escort, and he'd recognised the dark-uniformed figure striding down the skywalk ahead of them. If hate alone could kill a man, surely Phelps would be dead right now. His hands tingled, wanting to have the general under them, and it was all he could do not to pick up his comms unit and order Hickson to take the kids and destroy Phelps, no matter what it cost.

Slowly he unclenched his fists. It had been a good

decision to base himself away from the palace: it gave a distance he needed. Even so, the part of him that wanted to lash out and hurt wished he'd been bold enough to try the assault.

Simone touched his arm, her touch stronger than it should be. "There's nothing you can do now."

He nodded, glad he'd brought her. Her calm presence had been a blessing. "I know." He lifted the scope again, tormenting himself by watching, and tried to force himself to calm; he'd serve no one if he didn't think things through. There was information to be had in how this played out. He sharpened the focus of his scope. The children were approaching the palace. Floodlights came on, making it easier for him to make out their details. Kerra had her head up, not cowed, every inch Sonly's daughter. He bet she was glaring at the soldiers as she walked. Baelan looked tiny and beaten, but he was walking steadily forwards, a tribal woman at his shoulder, presumably his mother.

He zoomed in on the woman, scanning over her, the mother of his child. What had it asked of her to carry Baelan? He caught the gleam of her ankshar in the lights. She was truly of the tribes, which meant she must hate him, as all her people did. Had she been glad to carry the baby created to bring him down? Or had she felt tainted? Had she even had a choice? Nothing in her stance gave any indication, except the hand she kept on Baelan's shoulders. Regardless how she felt about Kare, she obviously loved the boy.

He watched, silent and useless, Simone's soft breathing his only distraction, as his children came to the middle point of the skywalk. They'd be at the palace soon. Still, they didn't falter. His ears drummed with the force of his fear and he didn't know which was stronger, his fear for them, or his pride.

***

Kerra took everything in, a tight line of clarity that pulled on more than just her knowledge, but that of the Roamer fighters who might be able to see a way past the soldiers, the planners who assessed where she was and what might be available to her. It didn't like what it saw – too many soldiers, and she wasn't practiced enough in what she needed to do. She kept walking forwards, the distance to the palace growing smaller.

"Kerra?" Baelan's hand tightened on hers. She glared at him. He was why she was at the palace, caught and in danger.

"The moat," he breathed.

She kept her eyes forwards, not even glancing at the parapet. The moat wasn't a possibility. The jump alone could kill them. She felt the first touch of her grandmother's presence. It would only get stronger.

Baelan squeezed her hand again, insistent, and he might be right; the jump could be better than facing the Empress. She squeezed his hand back.

"One," he said, under his breath.

"Two," she mouthed. She sped up a little, pulling away from the guards.

"Three!" they said together.

They ran to the side of the skywalk, darting between two of the guards. One grabbed her t-shirt and tugged her back, but she put her head down and the momentum pulled her free.

She jumped onto the parapet and, without thinking or looking down, leapt at the same time as Baelan, their twin yells breaking the air as they soared high over the gardens.

***

Kare swore. "They jumped!" He turned to Simone. "Gods, it's at least thirty feet down!"

Simone lifted her scope and leaned forwards. "They're over the moat."

She was right. He couldn't see the moat from here – anywhere with that clear a view of the palace would have been pulled down long ago – but he could imagine its thin ribbon of dark water threading the grounds.

"It will make no difference." He took in the soldiers along the parapet, the urgency in their movements. "The grounds will be searched; they'll be picked up." He shook his head, partly in admiration. "They don't lack courage."

"Indeed." She gave a sly smile. "They carry more than just a name."

He ducked his head, embarrassed; any courage he had was hard-earned through self-preservation. There was no way he'd have jumped at twelve. Hell, he'd struggle to do it now.

"We need to find them. Before the Empress." He cursed: his operatives in the palace had key roles in the assault; he couldn't risk their cover. At best, he had a squad at his disposal. The Empress had an army. He scrambled to his feet, wanting to run to the gardens and start looking himself, but stopped. Light from the palace spilled over the gardens. Many, many lights. The search was underway.

***

Kerra sank under the water, her chest narrowing at the cold. Baelan's hand pulled from her, his fingers flailing. Her breath left her, forced out by the shock of hitting the surface and barreling under. She kicked at weeds that tried to wrap around her legs, and fought for the surface. Her lungs burned, needing air. She kicked harder – she should be near the surface.

She broke through, spitting water. Baelan was nowhere to be seen. She swept her hands under the water but couldn't feel him. She didn't even know if he could swim; he'd been brought up in the desert, after all.

She ducked her head under. She shook with cold – at this time of the night, the ice-replenished water stayed near freezing – and scrabbled her hands. She came up for air and would have shouted for him but didn't dare give a sign of where she was. The soldiers would be here in a minute and she could still feel her grandmother in the distance. She'd be looking, too, and she'd find them for sure.

Baelan; I need to get Baelan. She couldn't leave him – he was her brother. They'd jumped together; they needed to stay together. She took a frantic breath and ducked her head under again, and saw something pale in the water. Surging forwards, she snagged it and pulled it to the surface. Baelan broke free of the water, propelling himself up for a huge gasp, and then sank under again. She grabbed him with both hands and pushed him towards the bank. He managed to grab the grass overhanging the moat, and she pushed him until he slithered up the side. It took ages, he kept slipping back down, and she could hear yells from the skywalk, but finally he reached the bank. Lights swept over the garden and she was able to work out that they'd emerged well beyond the skywalk. Good. They had time.

Baelan grabbed her wrist and pulled her out easily. They crouched, shaking, on the bank. A light swept towards them. She grabbed his hand, pulling him towards the waterfall and the wild garden. There'd be more cover there.

"We have to get away from the palace," gasped Baelan as they ran. "Can't you feel her?"

She could. Growing more insistent, angry at being taken by surprise, at not locating them easily. They'd been lucky that the moat had carried them so far. She remembered why her father had left the mesh – he'd been worried it would bring the Empress to him. She didn't dare use the power when she was here. She ducked as a light swept close to them. "Where to?"

"The desert."

The desert had lizards and snakes. And clutterbacks. She hated the desert. She hated Belaudii. She wanted to be back on Syllte. A yell carried through the air, not that far away – the searchers were coming. She groped through the darkness and found Baelan's hand. He was right, they couldn't stay here.

"Come on," she said. If anyone could find a way out of the gardens, it was a kid who'd spent half her childhood crawling through them. If she could get them out, maybe a desert child could take them even further. "Let's go."

CHAPTER THIRTY-THREE

Chelps fell to his knees before the Empress, at the foot of the great staircase. The entrance hall was silent around him. "My Lady, I have the children."

She smiled and he inhaled, ready. Heat spread from his stomach, and he put his head back, his breath coming in quick gasps. This was what he waited for, why he obeyed. He stirred under her touch, growing hard. Later, alone, he'd come back to this moment, replay it while he still had the lingering sense of her. For now, he drank the power in, glad to be its focus. How had he survived without it for a decade? Barely; like a withered stump, deprived of what it needed to live. He'd crawled through those ten years. Only the knowledge that one day he'd free his mistress and feel her reward again had kept him focused.

"Sir!" The urgency in the soldier's voice made him get to his feet and turn. The heat vanished, leaving only a memory to tantalise. He strode forwards, pushing past soldiers at the doorway and onto the skywalk, fighting rising panic: the children weren't in sight. "Where are they?" he demanded.

His captain turned and saluted. "Sir. They jumped."

Hell and damnation. He shouldered his way to the parapet and looked down, relaxing when he didn't see two sprawled bodies. His Lady's legacy was not lost; the thought of telling her such a thing sent cold fear through him. He squinted against the darkness. The moat looked still but flowed fast; the children could surface anywhere along the channel. He turned to the soldiers, ready to give the order to begin a search, but caught Shanisa's eyes.

She held her hands out, pleading, he knew, to give the boy a chance. A few extra minutes to get a head start. Phelps swallowed the lump in his throat. Baelan reminded him of himself: trapped and helpless and angered by it. He remembered the boy on his naming ceremony, how proud he'd been that Phelps had chosen him, how straight he'd stood when Taluthna had placed his ankhar. Remembered, too, the trembling wreck the Empress had reduced the child to. He set his shoulders, wanting with all that remained of his will to stand with Shanisa and claim tribal sanctuary for the boy.

A bolt, white and angry, made his back arch in sharp agony. His Lady knew his thoughts; she always did. She held him, reminding him of his place and how little his will mattered. Pain ran through his head, pinning his spine, along his arms and legs. His hands clawed, his muscles cramped, but he fought against crying out in front of his men. He turned from Shanisa, putting the thought of her soft eyes from his mind, and pointed at the captain.

"Find the children," he said, every word wrenched through gritted teeth. "And when you do, bring them to me."

The pain eased. Soft footsteps sounded and he turned to face his Lady, standing at the entrance to the palace. He bowed his head. He had no right to stand against her. Pain pounded through him, so it was only force of will keeping him on his feet.

His men left the skywalk to join the search in the gardens. The parapet was empty of all but his Lady, her personal guard and the watching tribes-people.

The Empress let him go. He slumped to the ground, grasping for the last touch of her, trying to hold it as a drowning man might hold the rope to safety. Pain, yes, but it was preferable to the nothing that waited. The stone was hard under his cheek. She walked to him and stopped, the tip of her boot just inches from him.

"Never again," she said. "Or it ends. Understand me, Taran?"

He nodded, scraping his cheek along the ground.
"My Lady," he whispered.
"You may stand."
He forced himself to his feet and stood to attention, shoulders back, hands clasped to stop them shaking.
"Find the children," said the Empress. "Or you will face me for your failure."
He nodded, throat dry. He knew the price of failure – he'd seen too many others pay it.
"Come." The Empress beckoned to Shanisa and her brothers, who followed her into the palace. As they left, Shanisa looked back once and her eyes showed no censure, only pity.

***

Kerra ducked through an arch, into the wild garden's tangle of roots and weeds and hidden corners planted against the outside wall of the palace.
"Where to?" Baelan, beside her, asked.
She didn't know for sure. It had been years since she had managed to get away from her minders and make it out of the palace, squeezing through a gap in the brickwork. She'd been about five, at most, and the trouble it had brought onto her – her mother in a panic, her father gravely telling her why, even if she hated it, she must stay with her guards – had scared her enough to stop another attempt.
Even so, she hadn't told anyone how she'd escaped. She'd refused to, holding firm against her mother's demands, her dad's reasoning, and the whispered confidences of her nurse trying to wrestle out the information. In a life as full of constraint as hers, the secret had been a precious thing, one she'd hugged to herself: that somewhere in the wild part of the garden, there was a way out. She'd never used it again, but the knowledge of it had been hers and hers alone.
She paused, casting her mind back. Tall grasses

had closed over her as she'd run – that was how she'd lost her security team. This part of the garden was different from any other. It was truly wild, full of animals making use of an area so filled with life on the dry planet. Ground squirrels and nerados, the desert mice, inhabited it, drawn to the water that seeped, artfully, down a narrow rill from the moat.

She pushed forwards, her eyes adjusting to the darkness, and there, behind a fallen tree, the wild grass grew as tall as she remembered. She ran to it, jumping the tree, and Baelan followed.

A voice sounded, from behind her, loud and commanding. "Check through the arch!"

"Down!" she said. Baelan dove to the ground beside her, and they lay flat. The grass closed over them, just as she remembered.

A light swept back and forth, making each blade sharp and defined. She barely dared to breathe. Baelan tensed, and she knew he must be fighting the urge to get up and tackle the soldier, to hold on to his temper and good sense.

Footsteps came closer. The light swept around again. Another set of footsteps joined the first.

"It's a mess in here," said one of the soldiers, his voice gravelly. "We need to send in a full squad."

"I'll order it." The commander, this time, she thought.

Their footsteps drew away. Silence fell, but she lay, unmoving, imagining one of them inside the arch, waiting to see if anything moved. A small squeak took her attention and a mouse forced its way through the grass.

"Let's go," she whispered. If the wildlife was moving, it must be okay. She hoped. "But stay down."

They slithered through the grass, snake-like. It remained closed over them and she hoped it was enough to mask their movements. At last they reached the wall, and she felt along its brickwork, rustic to complement the garden and rough under her touch. She ran her fingers along, tingling in fear.

Her hand sank into a space between two bricks. She pulled the grass in front, tugging it out in tufts. A glance over her shoulder showed only the tips of grass and the sky above. If anyone was watching, they'd be on her before she could react.

"There," she said.

"Let's see." Baelan pulled a strand of grass out of the way. "You're joking."

"What?" Had the gap been filled?

"We'll never fit."

She squeezed a breath. It hadn't been tight in her memory, but she'd been five then. She joined Baelan and saw that he was right, there was no way he'd get his wiry form through, let alone her, a year older and a little heavier. She drew back, cold with the realisation that she didn't have any other answers.

"But, look," he said. He tugged at one of the bricks adjacent. "The cement has loosened." He pulled a chunk of it out, crumbling it to the ground, and then another. He grinned at her. "We can take out a few more bricks."

They'd be lucky not to bring the wall down on themselves. She didn't voice it, though, but scrabbled at the brickwork. Her nails bent back, but she didn't care. She pulled and pulled, her skin raw, and another of the bricks came away. Baelan, too, was making progress.

The wall creaked. Rubble fell, showering her hand. Baelan, ignoring it, freed another brick.

"In there. Spread out, do a full search." The commander's voice carried to them. "I don't want to have to go back over ground like this."

It had to be now. They didn't dare pull out any more bricks – the sound would carry. Baelan's eyes met hers. He nodded. He lay flat and wriggled forwards, into the gap. His body vanished, and then his legs. A small scraping followed by an *oof* warned her it was tight.

Footsteps crunched closer. The mouse scampered along the wall, camouflaging itself with the grass. She wished she could.

She got down, face flat. She didn't think of the wall giving way. She didn't think of being too big, or getting stuck until someone grabbed her ankles and pulled her out. She scraped along the ground, dust in her nose. The weight of the wall pressed above her. She wriggled, and the bricks creaked.

"You're nearly there." Baelan's voice, close by. "Keep going."

She did. Her shirt caught. Her hair got tangled in the brickwork, but she wrenched forwards. She had no room to move. She had to turn her head to keep going forwards. Panic was all around, that she'd get stuck here and no one would be able to get her out. Her breath seemed to go nowhere – it was a struggle to take each one.

Baelan's wrists seized hers, encircling them. He pulled, giving her something to purchase on.

"Harder," she hissed.

He gave a yank and she slid forwards, face scraping along the rock. She bit back a yell, but broke through and scrambled to her feet, stifling a cough.

Baelan was filthy, only his eyes and teeth visible in the darkness. She must look as bad. She found herself doubling over in a laugh, fist in her mouth to muffle it. They'd done it. They were free.

Her smile fell away. Free of the palace, only.

"What now?" she asked.

Baelan rolled his shoulders. "Now I get to show you the secrets of my city." He stayed in the shadow of the wall and made his way along.

"This way," he said, taking her down a narrow alley, and then another. "We need to get to the tribal area."

"Why?" That would take them deeper into the city.

"Just trust me." He led her down another street, skirting the back of the tribal area, and around the side of a house and into a yard. A creeper, one of the native plants, hardy to the heat and tough, covered much of the opposite wall. He pushed it to the side, revealing a steep passageway. Stairs led down, into darkness.

"I know a way out." He grinned, looking smug. "It takes us right into the desert. They'll never find us."

He stepped into the darkness. She paused, but the palace was only a couple of streets away – soon the search would spill out onto these streets and she'd be found.

She stepped up to the passageway. Baelan was waiting for her, almost out of sight. She took a last glance around and drew in a quick breath. She had no choice but to trust him again. She climbed down the stairs, hoping this plan was a lot better than his last one.

CHAPTER THIRTY-FOUR

Kare paced the bedroom of the safe house, having called rank and shut himself away. He stopped at the stacked laser-pulsors, turned, reached the blasters at the other end of the room and turned again, ticking options off on his fingers.

He could go into the mesh and try to sense the children. One moment's concentration would do what he needed, but it would be dangerous. His mother's presence sang across the city to him, so strong were the ties of hate between them. He'd be lucky if she didn't already know he was here, creeping through her streets, breathing the same air. If he joined the mesh and used the power, there would be a good chance she'd sense him.

He could call the Roamers to the planet and have them find the kids and lift them. He had comms cleared with Farran and the other drop-ships. Temptation bit, deep, and hard to resist, but to involve the Roamers before his mission would advertise he was here just as loudly as his powers would. It would also expose the pilots.

Which left the final option – he could undertake the assault on his mother. He'd lost the advantage of the rest-day, and the opportunity to enter the palace as planned, but if she wasn't aware he was on-planet he still had the element of surprise. Either the kids would be retaken – in which case winning the palace won them, too – or they'd still be on the run and, hopefully, lucky enough to have survived.

He sat on the bed, and laced his hands together, barely aware of the sharp pain from his fingers. The kids did have a chance – Kerra knew the palace as well as anyone. If they got out, and reached the desert, Baelan knew enough to keep them safe.

But it wasn't only that. He couldn't just take this decision as a father – too many others relied on him. He had to take this as a soldier, and the only person who could take his mother out. He had to think beyond his personal loss and worries, however hard it felt. Once he did that, there was only one way forwards. Although, his feelings as a father *did* matter. His children had escaped, for now. If he took his mother out before they could be found and returned to her, she could not hurt them.

His decision made, he stood. Taking his mother out was the only way to win. And he had to win.

***

Baelan led the way through the passageway. It stretched longer than he imagined, sloping downwards, below the depths of the city. The only noises were the sound of his and Kerra's steps and the occasional scurrying in the darkness. Fair dues to her, though, she hadn't flinched or hesitated – he'd been afraid she'd be scared of the night creatures.

His own chest hurt, tight with tension, his ears alert for any movement coming in the opposite direction. The tunnels weren't used a lot – too much traffic and their entrances would be discovered – but it was possible a tribes-person would pass. If so, he'd be found. He hadn't forgotten his mother's conversation with Phelps on the ship: at best, the tribes would hand him over to the Empress. At worst, they'd keep him to themselves.

A flicker of light appeared, and he slowed until Kerra caught up. He pointed at the light.

"That's the central square of the tribal quarter," he whispered. Voices carried farther in these passageways than it seemed they might. "We're going to come out opposite our temple."

She nodded. He had to remember she might never

have seen the inside of the quarter and, even if she had, honoured personage that she was, she wouldn't know it like a tribes-person did. Although he'd only been there a handful of times, the layout was similar to the lost cities in the desert, familiar and predictable.

"We need to get into that temple." He swallowed, about to come clean. "And we can't be seen."

"Why not? Aren't you one of them?"

"They won't like that I sided with you and our..." The name caught in his throat. His confusion had been less since hearing his mother and Phelps on the ship. Some of what he'd believed, at least, was true - the Empress had been unkind, and the tribes had treated him badly. Phelps had proved he wasn't a real father to him - and that he didn't want to be. Even so, accepting himself as his father's son was hard. "Our father. Until I have time to explain, it's best they don't see us."

She didn't ask any more questions, but walked beside him to the end of the passageway. He drew against the wall, giving his eyes time to adjust to the lighter courtyard. He pointed across, at the temple, and she nodded.

"Will it be open?" she asked.

"Of course." A temple to the Lady was never closed - supposedly symbolising her closeness to the tribes. Having met her, he felt it was to symbolise how she never relented.

"Will there be guards?"

"No." Not here, where the only people who entered were from the tribes, or the occasional foray by soldiers. "But there may be some who have come to ask their Lady's blessing."

Kerra gave him a sharp look and he shrugged. She couldn't expect him to forget everything he'd grown up with.

"So what do we do?"

"Wait." He tried to work out the longest he'd ever seen anyone seeking penitence or blessing. Half an hour, perhaps. Or, to be safe, an hour – some of the elders could stay in reverence to her a long time. He hunkered down in the shadows, and watched across the square. Bats flittered through the courtyard, chasing moths drawn to the light. All was still, otherwise.

At last, Baelan got to his feet and Kerra followed. He waited for the pins and needles to stop, and gave her a sharp nod.

"When I go, follow," he said. "Keep your head down." He wished he had a hood for her – the lantern-light would catch her blonde hair. "Keep going, no matter what. Don't stop."

She nodded and crept to the mouth of the passageway. He stood beside her, his spine straight, so tense it looked like it might break. Nothing moved in the courtyard. The temple seemed an age away.

He stepped out, resisting the urge to look at the buildings surrounding the square, their windows faceless and dark. He started across, his steps quick, but not at a run. Kerra stayed beside him and he winced at the shine of her hair. They crossed to the centre of the square, utterly exposed.

"Keep going," he muttered. She did, but he could sense her need to speed up matching his.

They were only feet from the temple when the sound of footsteps broke the quiet. A shout carried to them, followed by another.

He grabbed Kerra's arm. "Run!"

She didn't need telling a second time. They ran into the temple. He darted past the icon of his Lady, for the first time in his life failing to stop at the statue, and into the bathhouse. Moist air hit him, making him aware how dry his lips were, how his skin was parched. It would be good to take water with them. There would be little night left when – if – they made it into the desert, and the heat would build quickly.

Footsteps, close behind, kept him moving. He

would deal with the water later, if he got out of the temple. He led Kerra to the back chamber, to where the spring emanated from the rock. He ducked through the arch and hit the keystone with the flat of his palm.

"Push it in!" he yelled. The followers would not look here first - they wouldn't expect a child to know of this chamber.

She pressed her hand to it, and he put his back to the wall, pushing with all his might. His uncles had made this look easy. It gave, with less noise than he feared, well enough used to keep the mechanism smooth.

"Get in!" he told Kerra, and guided her into the passageway. He followed, and the two of them swivelled the door back to.

"Can you lock it?" she asked.

"Not from this side." He grabbed her hand. "There will be no light and it's a long way."

"Better get going, then." Her voice quavered, just a little, but her hand didn't pull away.

He led her along the corridor. Best not to tell her how deep it ran, or how many tonnes of sand rested above them. It was bad enough that one of them knew. Sand shifted under his feet, but they ran.

A grinding noise came, far in the distance.

"What was that?" asked Kerra, out of breath.

"The entrance," he said.

"Will they know we're here?"

He thought of the sand underfoot, how their feet would be moist from the temple. It would leave enough of a trail for any competent desert-dweller to follow.

"Just keep going," he said, hands in front of him to know the turn in the corridor. Getting lost didn't bear thinking about. They took the turn his mother had selected, last time in the passageway, but not until he scuffed their footprints, meddling with the story they told. It wouldn't stop their pursuers, but it might slow them.

He ran again. He didn't dare look behind, for fear

of seeing light. Noises came in the darkness, the sound of feet. He ran, blind in the darkness, until something stopped him, taking his feet from beneath him. A scrabbling noise told him Kerra, too, had fallen.

He put his hands out and felt stairs ahead of him. His heart jumped with hope. He grabbed the back of her shirt and threw her forwards.

"Climb," he said. He looked back and was sure the passageway was lighter, that someone was carrying a torch and gaining. He climbed after Kerra. His chest burned but he still managed to climb. They emerged into the village where he'd met Taluthna, and Phelps had claimed him as his son. It felt very long ago. He leaned over, hands on knees, getting his breath.

The sky had a long streak of red in the black. Morning - and daylight, when tracking would be easier - was coming. He slapped Kerra's back.

"Run," he said, hating that he had to, his body screaming for rest. He led her to the edge of the desert and pointed at the first of the dunes. "And don't stop."

CHAPTER THIRTY-FIVE

She only asked with a hard edge in her voice. "What do you think? You know the desert better than I do. Does Baelan know it well enough? He's only a child." She couldn't help herself. If it hadn't been for the boy, Kerra would never have run in the fire forest, she was sure of it.

Lichio frowned. "I know the desert mostly from the perspective of stopping people attacking from it, not trying to hide in it myself." He shrugged. "My desert training is no more extensive than yours."

She never thought she'd thank Kare for insisting on the training, and for putting in place a biannual refresher. She'd hated hers. But if Kerra *had* gone to the desert, at least she'd know some of the survival skills needed. It didn't allay the fear that gnawed at her, however – it only gave more detail to the things she dreaded.

Enough. She didn't even know if the kids had made it to the desert. She pushed her hair behind her ears and leaned forwards, ready to work; fretting wasn't going to help anyone. She blew out a breath. "What do you have for me?"

"Three former senators have been approached who are willing to stand for you."

"Who?"

"Elenda, Tomj, and Christophe," he said.

She made a mark at each of their names, but stopped at Christophe's. He had been part of the conservative faction who had hated her reforms on Abendau. "Christophe's reasons?"

"He's no fan of yours, he told the agent that, but

he doesn't want the Empress. Plus, he doesn't believe the Senate was dissolved legally."

"Because it wasn't!" It was, she understood, a standoff in Abendau, with the Senate broken up but refusing to recognise the legitimacy of the Empress' regime.

"Quite. Imprisoning the president without trial isn't in any statute book I've seen." Lichio gave a wicked grin. "Simply put, that's annoyed his sense of propriety more than you coming back. You're the president in his eyes and, therefore, the Empress has no basis to deny you safe passage into the city you're elected to govern. He was always a bit anal about legislature, as I recall."

She half-choked on a laugh. Anal wasn't the word; he practically had the constitution rammed up his butt. Lichio gave a smile, pleased, she guessed, at raising a laugh. She returned a nod of acknowledgement. "What about Harald?"

"As we suspected: he's the Empress' man now." He flipped his data pad shut. "I hate to say this, but there's nothing more you can do from here. You have three senators who will be bringing holo-reporters with them. That's it."

It saddened her, about Harald. He'd been instrumental in bringing in the reforms in Bendau, the first of the humanitarian projects she had managed for the Senate. He had taken Kare's original Imperial decree and advised on the rework needed to meet the Senate's approval. To see a man who'd been so focused on doing the right thing being used to do the wrong hurt her. But it wasn't the first time she'd seen it happen – the slow reduction of Eevan had carried more pain than anything Harald could do – and she knew Lichio was right, and there was no going back.

"You don't think there is enough support to get me into the city?" Damn, what was the point of this if she was to just sit on a ship and wait for news in orbit? She might as well have stayed on Ferran.

"You know it's not. If it had just been the affair, I'd say yes, you could ride it out. In fact, in some areas of Abendau that might even have helped your reputation. It would have made you human and fallible. But unless you can disprove the leaks, I can't see you having anywhere near the support needed. But if you take your time getting removed back to the ship and don't get yourself arrested, I should be able to get into the city. Just make sure you don't cross from the arrivals-side of the port, and they cannot take you." He grinned, like a child given a new toy. "I've sort of missed being on the rebelling side - authority isn't all it's cracked up to be." He got up and stretched, almost touching the low ceiling. "I'm going to kip."

She watched him leave, and pursed her lips. He thought she was going to give him cover so he could play at being a rebel soldier? If he were ten years older she'd blame a mid-life crisis. As if she was going to settle for being a diversion while Kare was at risk, and her daughter faced who knew what in the desert. Abendau was her city, it had been for a decade, and no one was going to stop her taking it back. A diversion? Lichio had said she was the politician. He'd told her to work out how to play this, and that's exactly what she'd do. And not one of her plans involved sitting on a ship and waiting.

She opened her data pad and started to read through the documents she had downloaded on Ferran - the ones she had been purported to leak. They had, undoubtedly, not come from her. She was many things, but not careless around data.

She opened the document about Bendau and read through it. She hadn't had the chance to read each clause before leaving - she'd been too busy fighting the fire-storm it had caused - but now she took her time, going through each line in detail, hoping that some way to refute the charges might occur to her. After all, a later form of the document, ratified by the Senate, had been available by rights-request.

Could she argue that its leak hadn't mattered? That it had given away nothing of import? But she knew that wouldn't work – in admitting being careless with a single piece of information, she was finishing her political career.

She would change some of the document now, given the chance – specifically the timescales set. If she'd had another five years, she would have done so much more in the neglected second city.

She frowned at one clause. It was a requirement for the Senate to formally take command of the city's policing outreach program. She had never asked for that in any policy – nor would she. Security, policing and the military were the areas that Kare had made clear to her – privately, when they had first talked about their vision for an Abendau freed from Imperial control – he would not rescind. Their safety and that of Kerra lay with the military and police. He would retain control. She had known never to put any reference to those structures in any document: she never wasted time on battles she could not win.

A slow smile spread over her face. This was not her document. This was the work of someone who had consistently challenged Kare on the subject, who'd tried to erode his hold on the military time and again. Harald. He had first mooted the policy – but it had taken her position to force it through. This was the early document, before she'd redrawn it.

She tapped her finger on the screen, thinking quickly. It was one thing to know the document was not hers, but she had to be able to prove it – at least to the Senate and republic. She brought up her files, searching for the document she had finally presented to the Senate. All her documents had been subject to version control, each change slavishly recorded. There was a full audit trail of her involvement.

She scrolled through the list, searching for the specific clause. There was no record of it. She hadn't written the document circulating the news-holos. This was Harald's document, not hers. All she had to do was provide the audit trail to support her.

***

Baelan scanned the desert. Kerra hadn't slowed him down greatly, but where he'd planted his bare feet without leaving a mark, she'd left clear footprints in the sand. He thought about trying to cover them but, for now, keeping ahead of the search was the most important thing.

"Will they find us?" she asked.

"They might," he said. He glanced over and saw she was holding her hand to her side. He'd pushed them hard to get this far so quickly. "Sorry. We need to keep moving."

She nodded and straightened. Kudos to her, she hadn't complained. "Let's go."

He set off, towards the ridge of dunes that marked the start of the Great Desert. It would take another hour to reach at their current rate. He looked back over his shoulder, not able to stop himself. *Oh, shit.* A line of scoots stretched across the desert.

"Can we hide?" Kerra's voice was terse, not panicked.

Not with the steps in the sand she'd left. "It depends."

"On what?"

"If they're using tribal hunters or soldiers." He squinted, but the searchers were too far away for him to make out if they were riding the light scoots the tribes used, or heavier, military-grade, ones. He didn't have time to find out. "Let's keep going. If we get a bit more distance behind us, we could burrow in for the day. Keep out of the heat."

"We'll need water," she said.

He knew. And he didn't have a knife with him for cutting the buck-cactus. "I'll sort it out." He started across the sand, feet slipping as he hurried. "You know our father's in Abendau? If we could get word to him…"

"There's no way to. Not with him not in the mesh." Kerra looked at him sharply, but he didn't have time for working out what it meant, not with the scoots getting closer.

He broke into a run, and she matched his pace. With his power, he could have shifted the sand over her footprints. Hell, with his power he could have dealt with the scoots and made sure they never got close. Without it... he'd be lucky if they had an hour left.

A noise invaded the clear air: the low rumble of engines. Over the dune-ridges ahead, more scoots appeared. Kerra stopped, and backed away. The pursuers behind them had fanned out. There was nowhere to run. Nothing he could do would hide them from a full desert search, not digging into the sand, not finding a cave-ridge. The scoots started forwards, in their direction. He grabbed her arm.

"Run!" he shouted, but the roaring noise of the scoots grew. He zigzagged across the sand. Kerra half-fell and wrenched her arm free.

"Keep going!" she yelled.

He slowed and stumbled as he looked to see where she was. The scoots were close now, but she was on her feet, facing them. Her hands were spread, and he felt her now, a tug at the back of his mind. She was in the mesh.

"Go!" she yelled. The engine noises were louder, coming from every direction. The mesh couldn't match their number, even with someone more experienced using it. Even their father would struggle to get out of this.

"Head into the dunes!" he shouted. "It will slow them!" He added an extra burst of speed.

Someone grabbed him and swung him onto a scoot. The familiar spiced scent of a tribesman surrounded him. He tried to see if they had Kerra, but was held too tightly. The scoot turned in a tight circle, its engine idling, quieter than when it had roared its chase. On the scoot alongside, Kerra was held against another tribesman, her eyes closed. Beside her, a scoot lay on its side, smoking. She'd managed that much, at least.

"Take them to the village," shouted the tribesman holding Kerra. "And inform Phelps."

They left, Baelan craning to see if Kerra was all right. She still had her eyes closed, ignoring everything around her.

CHAPTER THIRTY-SIX

The prosthesis sat along the inside of Kare's jaw, hard against his teeth. He leaned over the sink, close to the mirror, and carefully inserted lenses so his eyes turned a deep brown to match the wig he pulled on and adjusted. He blinked, unused to the lenses, but couldn't help smiling. He looked nothing like himself.

Good. He felt nothing like himself, either. Without the mesh, he'd returned to the person he'd been for ten years, powerless, relying on his own instincts. It felt oddly right: no expectations on him beyond that of any man; no need to be the magician who did the impossible.

That was now, though. Later he'd take every scrap of power in the mesh and turn it to his bidding. He'd use it against his mother and make sure she knew that in hurting him and those he loved, she had made the biggest mistake of her life. He hadn't been strong enough to finish the job last time, but maybe this stranger in the mirror was. He nodded at his reflection: let this man do what had to be done. Let him be focused, not distracted. Let Kare give himself to this stranger, this he who he'd never been, and find a way out for all of them.

He squared his shoulders, as ready as he'd ever be, and left the room. His squad were lined up the hallway, prepared for the attack. Weapons were being checked, muted voices were going over plans one more time, uniforms of the palace servants were being checked and adjusted. He found Kym and gave her a firm nod: he'd promised he'd stop his mother. It was time to do exactly that.

***

The tent was dark on the inside and, whilst cooler than the full heat of a Belaudii day, sultry. Kerra curled in one corner, her head pounding. She'd been given only tribal food to eat: spiced packets of thin pastry and vegetables, and some sort of meat she'd been about to eat when Baelan said it was lizard. Then they'd served a clutterback's leg, all bowed and black, and she'd been sure she was going to be sick. She half-wondered if they'd done it to make her, the outsider, look silly – but Baelan had taken it like a delicacy, peeling the skin, with its charred hairs, and biting into the pale meat beneath.

She glanced at Baelan, sitting on the other side of the tent, equally as silent as she was. The two tribesmen standing either side of the entrance flap had been watching him as closely as her – what he'd said in the city, about the tribes not trusting him, seemed to be true.

Had his powers started to come back? She wasn't sure if she'd know when hers did – the mesh was dominating that part of her, growing and extending to fill parts of her mind she'd never noticed before. Did Baelan know she was in the mesh? She couldn't sense him in it, but would he try to use it if he knew he could?

The mesh swirled at that thought, angry. It didn't want Baelan. It was bigger now, a seething collection of people and images and thoughts, but she still had no real idea how to control it. Nothing had made it easier to work with: not focusing on it, not calling for Laurena to reach her.

She curled up tighter and fought the shivering that wracked her, but the sound of steps made her sit up. Baelan shot to his feet, and his eyes met hers, wary, watchful. A moment later, the flap of the tent was pushed aside. Baelan's mother ducked in, her face bland and impossible to read. She glanced, briefly, at Kerra and then away, dismissing her.

"Mother!" Baelan ran to her and looked like he was going to throw his arms around her, but stopped short when his uncle walked in, back straight, eyes cold.

Phelps followed, his dark uniform contrasting with the sunlight behind. He stooped inside and dropped the flap, casting the interior back into semi-darkness.

"I see it's our escapees," he said. He gave a smile that would have befitted a shark. "Time to return to Abendau."

Heart pounding, so scared she might be sick, Kerra got to her feet before she could be forced, and flicked her hair back. She kept her steps steady – let her not show how frightened she was – and walked up to Phelps, close enough to smell the mix of cigaros and sweat from his uniform. She glared at him.

"Quite the little le Payne." He grabbed her chin, tipping her head towards him. His fingers were hard, and she wanted to wrench away from his grasp but wouldn't give him the pleasure. He lifted his other hand and brushed it on her cheek. "But with the Varnon eyes. What will your parents give to get you back? Themselves? Each other? Or will they let you rot?"

"Nothing," she spat. She clenched her fists, refusing to let her control slip. She had something he didn't know about, but she had to choose her moment. "They'll destroy you instead."

"Of course they will." He gave a harsh laugh and let go of her. "Get them loaded up. I'll escort them to our Lady myself. But first."

He clicked his fingers and the two guards stepped forwards, smartly grabbing her and Baelan. The doctor entered the tent, the same one as from the ship, carrying a small case. He opened it and took out two syringes, handing one to Phelps. With the other he approached Baelan, who twisted, kicking out. It made no difference – the doctor grabbed his arm and injected him.

He approached Kerra. She wanted to draw away, but instead faced the doctor. She stole a glance at Phelps. Let him think he was winning. The prick of the needle stung, but she didn't care anymore. She could face worse than that.

"We don't want to go back." Baelan squirmed free and planted himself in front of Phelps.

Baelan's mother took a step forwards, throwing off her brother's arm when he tried to pull her back. "I claim my son, Taran Phelps. All you have to do is give your bond to the elders and he will be kept with the tribe. He'll face their justice, but he'll be safer." She held out a hand, palm open in a silent plea.

"I can't." Phelps met her eyes. His mouth twisted in what may have been sympathy. "But I will do what I can for him."

"If you meant that, you wouldn't take him!"

"At least he'll have a voice for him in the palace."

"Then let me come back, too," said his mother. "I will speak to my Lady Empress myself, and beg for clemency. *Please.*"

"The Empress has already decided," he said. "You know this. You must stay with the tribes. The council agrees." He lowered his voice and Kerra had to strain to hear. "Don't push further, Shanisa, or you will be left in the position where you have no voice at all. Bide your time, and our Lady may soften. I swear to you, when – if – that happens, I will inform you."

"And Kerra?" Baelan's voice was shaking. "Will you help her, too?"

"That," said Phelps, "is out of my hands." He clicked his fingers, and two soldiers entered the tent. "Let's go." He opened the flap and pointed Kerra out.

"It might not be as bad as you think." Phelps grabbed her wrists as she passed. "You have some value, after all, as long as your parents are prepared to deal."

He pulled her forwards, and she staggered beside him. A scoot idled just ahead, bigger than the ones from the earlier search. She recognised its model from the compound: military grade, shielded and armoured, capable of carrying four people. Once they were on and the shield activated, there'd be no way off.

Baelan's uncle lifted him, ignoring the kicking legs, and forced him into one of the two back seats. He drew the restraints across, holding the squirming Baelan with one hand, and tightened the strapping so it dug into Baelan's skin.

"You son of a desert whore!" yelled Baelan. "I hope your eyeballs burn out!"

His own eyes were wide and wild; if Baelan had access to his powers, his uncle would know by now. She thought of the water in the rock pool boiling. Everyone would know. He fought, scrabbling at his uncle's face, still cursing, his language more inventive than Kerra had ever imagined, but his uncle gave a short laugh and turned away.

His mother approached. She bent over Baelan, whispering something, and he calmed, sitting easier in the seat. He gave a sharp nod at something she said, and sent a glare at Phelps before resting his head against his mother's shoulder.

A wave of loss swept through Kerra. She hadn't had the chance to say goodbye to her mum. Their last words had been angry. If she was here, Kerra would tell her she was proud of her, no matter what she'd done, and that she loved her. The sand blurred as tears threatened.

"Get on, girl," said Phelps, dropping her wrists. "Unless you want to be forced as well."

She rubbed her wrists where he'd held her; she never wanted his filth to touch her again. She climbed onto the seat beside Baelan and pulled her own straps on. She touched the mesh. It pulsed, forming into something new and hungry, and she pulled back, angry at herself. She was useless; she had access to enough power to stop Phelps and was too stupid, or scared, to work out how to use it. If her dad was here, he'd blow Phelps into space.

Phelps climbed onto the scoot's nav-seat and keyed their course into its small control panel. In a moment he'd bring the shield up and secure her and Baelan in place.

"Child." Shanisa leaned over and touched Kerra's arm. She smelt of spices and perfume, a heady mix that made Kerra dizzy. "May our desert gods go with you, and see you returned to your parents." She glanced at Phelps under hooded lids. "Your father has been more to my son than his named one. I wish for you to be returned to him."

Kerra didn't know what to say. The tribes prayed to the Empress now, not their lost gods; Shanisa must understand Kerra could accept no prayers to her grandmother, so had fallen back on a religion banned to her. She risked much from the elders, even Kerra knew that. The gesture touched her more deeply than she'd expected. She nodded dumbly, and the woman backed away.

The shield came up, muffling the sound of the engine and casting her into a world apart from the real one. Baelan was tense, coiled like a snake, his anger clear.

Two scoots took up flanking positions around theirs, and Phelps turned their scoot in a wide sweep away from the camp, towards Abendau. Its Old Quarter with its red buildings was framed in the light of the desert sun. It was getting late; the sun had dropped behind the palace, giving the roof tiles a sheen of gold. By nightfall, when the evening dew had formed on the metal tiles, she'd be back there.

She hunched forwards, as far as her restraints would let her, and tried not to look ahead, but inward. Somehow, she had to gain control. And she had to do it now.

CHAPTER THIRTY-SEVEN

Sonly's stomach did a familiar lurch as the grav-reg adjusted for landing, and distracted herself with her data pad. Still only three senators were prepared to meet her, and, frankly, none of them high-profile enough. She'd struggle to be the distraction Lichio needed, let alone anything more. She tapped away, connecting, connecting, connecting. At least there had been some media response to her release of the amended document and challenge of the allegations.

Lichio shifted in his seat, for once looking less than elegant in a battered pilot's suit stripped of any insignia.

"Remember the drill," he said. "Delay as long as you can but don't leave the port. As long as you remain space-side, they can't invoke any arrest warrant on Belaudii." He paused and gave a slight shrug. "Not quickly, anyway, so make your show and get back to the ship. Get into orbit if you have to. Wait until you hear from me or Kare. I don't intend to do anything other than get in, give support, and get out."

He honestly expected her to run? She stifled hot words.

"And, Sonly." He raised a finger. "No heroics. We're going to have enough trouble getting off planet without having to dig you out, too."

"I don't know what you're talking about." She sniffed and turned her attention from him. Sometimes she hated Lich, he was so hard to fool.

"Sonly...?" She didn't answer, and he cursed softly. "Remember the last time the Empress had you, that's all. She was prepared to hold you then, as president. She'll have even less compunctions now."

She remembered it: the cell they'd put her in, how they'd used Kare to break her resolve. Fear edged her thoughts, a slight shivering of her shoulders, but she pushed it away. There was no time for fear. "Thank you for the reminder."

"You could lose more than just a political career in Abendau." He sounded frustrated. "Make the Empress wonder what you're playing at, that's all I need. It's what you're good at, and it'll give her no time to worry about what Kare might be doing. Or me."

No doubt he was right. She crossed her hands in her lap. Her stomach was in knots, and it was hard to tell if it was from the flight, or nerves. A distraction in the port, some publicity against the Empress, would be something to achieve in the circumstances. She gave a careful nod. "I know my role, Lich."

"Thank you." A soft alarm sounded, and he made a twisted face of horror. "Let's see if this bucket lands better than it took off." At a shuddering lurch, he raised an eyebrow. "Not holding out much hope, though."

There was no chance to reply: the ship banked unevenly and an alarm sounded. The thrusters roared. Flung back in her seat, she started to count. By three hundred they'd have landed.

She'd reached only one-fifty when the shuddering stopped with a thud. The engines closed down, leaving a heavy silence.

"Well, that was fun." Lichio unstrapped his restraints, unruffled as ever. She hated good flyers: they made her feel inadequate.

She got up from her own seat. Her stomach was still jumping, and she couldn't blame the grav-reg now; it was nothing other than pure nerves. She was about to walk into Abendau port, where her name must be on every detention list, with nothing behind her but a battered reputation. If she called this wrong she could find herself whisked over to the palace cells. A chill tracked her spine.

She took a breath and followed Lichio down the access-way. They waited together as the hatch opened. A set of steps concertinaed from the undercarriage. They looked rickety, here in the expanse of a mostly-empty commercial hangar.

"Ready?" asked Lichio. His mouth quirked into a half-smile but he was pale, as if he, too, was just realising what he was doing. If he was recognised, he'd be arrested. If he wasn't, he'd be joining a raid he claimed had little chance of success.

What would she do if Lich never reported back? How long would she wait, hoping? She wanted to say something – anything – to support him, but could think of nothing. Instead, she smiled and hoped it looked more convincing than it felt. "I'm ready, I just hope Abendau is for us."

A soft beep sounded. "Cleared for disembarkation."

"Let's go," said Lichio. He gave an ironic bow and ushered her out of the hatch.

They disembarked into the vast hangar and left through the passenger exit, down a long, faceless corridor towards the security-hub of the port. As they walked, low sounds ahead – voices, announcements of flights – took precedence over those of the docking bays. The smell of engine fumes faded, replaced by the aroma of the spiced food Abendau was famed for, coming from the commercial sector behind a bank of security scanners.

Lichio squeezed her elbow. "This is where I'm leaving you." He nodded at the door leading to the port's passenger-security hall. "Keep your head up, don't look back, and knock 'em dead." He paused, and then added, "But not literally. We don't need any more scandal."

That made her laugh, even though she was tight with nerves and her fingers tingled with adrenaline. He pulled on an old, battered cap and tilted it over his eyes.

"Lichio," she said, her voice halting. She touched his arm. When he was a kid he'd been army-mad, running around the base with sticks in place of a rifle, determined to beat the bad guys. All of them. He'd no idea what would be asked of him. Her throat tightened. "Take care of yourself. I couldn't bear it if anything happened to you."

"You too." He gave a quick grin. "Love you, sis."

It was so casual, so unforced, so Lichio. She smiled. "Love you too."

He gave a mock-salute and made his way through the commercial travellers milling around the concourse. He blended in perfectly; even his walk was different, less graceful, somehow, the rolling gait of one who'd spent a lot of time on ships and not always ones with grav-regs.

He vanished into the crowd, and she faced the door to the security hall. From beyond she could hear voices and the sound of security-scanners.

This was it: time to not just face the music, but to make it sing her tune. She thought of Abendau's city streets, where Lichio would weave his way through, keeping to the shadows. Had he really believed she'd let him walk into danger and not do what she could to support him?

Abendau was her city, its people had voted for her: let the Empress try to stop her claiming it back. This fight was what Sonly had been born to, what she'd trained for years to face, and she was more than ready for it.

CHAPTER THIRTY-EIGHT

The lights of Abendau came closer, sharp pins against the now-dark sky. The sand was lit up by the scoot's lights, reminding Kerra of the night she'd been taken from the compound, the night she'd learned what it really meant to be a Varnon.

She had to do something: anything. She closed her eyes and reached inside. No matter how strange it felt or how uncomfortable it made her, she had to find a way to make the mesh work. She glanced at the two scoots flanking theirs: she'd have to deal with them, too.

She gritted her teeth, and the mesh responded to her, faster than the last time, switching its broken shape into something more orderly; a circle of minds, a linked hive of power, formed around her. She let it settle into shape. She'd tried shaping it, she'd tried controlling it, she'd tried coming out of it. None of it had worked. Maybe she should just let it have its own way.

She focused on the stream of power, endlessly circling. It had formed into a deep pool that wouldn't drain, its shape smoother than the one her father had governed. Slowly she let the knowledge of the power grow. She breathed deeply, relaxing. Colours bloomed and vanished behind her eyes, in tandem with the power – a red for a sudden surge, purple holding it steady, a blue for when the mesh was quiet and still. She let it go where it wanted, take what it needed of her. The hive-mind oozed into every corner of her, but she stayed calm.

It stilled to a steady, warm purple. She no longer knew where the mesh ended and she began. Slowly, she concentrated on the scoot. She reached out, steady and careful, and the power came with her. It was working.

Stop the scoot. The response was a cascade of power; a flower opening to its full potential. She focused on the engine.

The scoot slammed to a halt. The shielding fell away. Phelps cursed, loud in still air. Baelan looked over, his eyes alert, questioning. She smiled. Yes, she'd done it. She, who could barely shift a cup across a room, had stopped the scoot. She felt for her seat-bindings, and they were loose. Quickly she undid the clasps. Baelan did the same, looking between Phelps and her, eyes shifting and restless.

Phelps, night creature that he was, turned at the soft clicks. "Stop."

She'd had enough of him. She jumped from her seat onto the packed desert sand and glared up at him. "Get down." She held her hand out, palm open. The mesh hummed with anticipation and she smiled at the sensation of being so right, and so complete. "I'm warning you."

"A nice bluff." His face grew colder. "Get back on the scoot." He raised his hand to the other scoots. "Take her."

Bluffing, was she? Baelan jumped down, giving a soft thud as he hit the sand. She advanced on Phelps. The stream of power was still there, waiting, and she blasted it at him, knocking him from the scoot, hard onto his back.

"Hey!" Booted footsteps ran across the hardened sand. The other scoots were idling a few feet away, their soldiers on the ground, hoping to take her.

She raised a hand. The power waited. This must have been how Baelan felt in the forest. Like he couldn't be stopped. She hit out, hard. The lead soldier's head snapped back, hit by something, and he fell, yelling. She hit the others, one after the other, and none of them got back up.

"Way to go, sis!" shouted Baelan. "Watch Phelps! Hit the backstabbing bastard again!"

She spun and Phelps was struggling to his knees, one hand reaching for his blaster, the other across his chest as if protecting it. She had hurt Phelps, the way he'd hurt her father. He freed his blaster, and brought it up but, with a quick close of her fingers, it fell from his hand. She advanced, slow and steady. His eyes were wild, staring. He was frightened of her. She opened her hand, letting the power build again. He was right to be frightened. She could do anything she wanted. It felt amazing.

"I'm not bluffing." She smiled, ready to use it. She wouldn't just stun him, she'd finish him.

"Kerra!" Baelan's shout broke her attention. She swung to him, furious, but he held up Phelps' blaster. "I can take him."

"No need," she said. Phelps was on his feet, his eyes desperate and dangerous. "I can deal with him." He'd killed Sam, who'd protected her at the compound. He'd taken her father to the Empress, not once but twice. And he'd taken her. She opened her palm. "I want to."

"Kerra...?" Baelan's voice was small. "What are you doing?"

"I'm enjoying myself." She was, too. "It's incredible. You must know – you've had power like this all your life."

She turned back to Phelps, ready to hurt him like he'd hurt others. The general had left, sprinting across the sand, kicking it up with his heels, small puffs against the dark sky. No matter; she could reach him for miles.

Baelan grabbed her hand. "Let him go," he said.

She shook her head. She could finish it right now.

"Trust me." He was grinning, the way he had in the forest when he'd known something she didn't, and the light in his eyes was similar to when he'd told her about the sprites. "Let him go. It'll be better this way."

She lowered her hand. Baelan knew the desert better than she did, and he hated Phelps at least as much as she did. More, perhaps – the man had never pretended to be her friend and then abandoned her. Phelps disappeared from sight.

"Did you do all that?" Baelan asked, taking in the scene: the scoot on the sand and the soldiers lying in a tangled heap.

"Yeah." She found herself smiling. "I've fixed the mesh." A part of her, deep-buried, tried to protest, but she pushed it away. Her dad had been the wrong person; she was doing him a favour by making the mesh stronger.

"Kerra." Baelan looked more than worried, almost frightened. "I don't think that's a good thing. We don't really understand how it works."

Details, details. She looked at her brother with pity. To know only his single-stranded power, and not this... this... magnificence. She was never going to let this go. She couldn't remember why she'd been fighting something so right.

She turned her head to Abendau, her eyes narrowed, thinking. "Can you drive a scoot?"

"Of course," he said. "Why?"

Why? Wasn't it obvious? Their father wasn't the right person to face the Empress, not when he had to force and twist the mesh to his command. She was; he needed her with him. She jumped into one of the two front seats, leaving the control seat free for Baelan.

"Good," she said. "Take me to Abendau."

***

The transporter reached the palace and pulled into one of the service entries. Kare swallowed against a dry, tight throat. The palace operatives had confirmed the Empress had returned to her personal quarters.

Cold terror gripped him at the thought of going into the building, of feeling its walls imbued with the sense of his mother. He climbed out, drawing the cold desert air into his lungs, and held out his security documents with a hand as steady as it needed to be. He stared at his feet; he was a cleaner entering the palace, in thrall to the Empress. He should know his place.

A soldier stopped in front of him, and his nerves grew. His disguise should be enough, but the palace garrison knew him well. Assuming some of them had survived the change in regime, a mannerism, or the way he walked, his crooked fingers perhaps, could be picked up. If he was picked up, the rest of the squad would be, too. He could feel their tension, as if the air was cracking with it.

"You're new," said the soldier.

Kare nodded his head. "Yes, sir." He took the voice of Kerra's old tutor, desert-reared, and matched the cadence. It might not be the perfect match his powers allowed him, but it was close enough that they wouldn't pick him out by his voice. "I was based in the compound until now."

"Your clearance documents."

Kare handed them over and the soldier went into the palace, out of sight, leaving Kare to wait and will himself to stay calm. His docs were top-notch; there was nothing to worry about. Long moments stretched. The rest of the squad had theirs handed back, one by one. They got into the transport and their muted voices reached him, talking about the rally planned in the city later, their plans, anything except their colleague.

Kare stared forwards, not allowing himself to glance at the transporter. Damn, there was something wrong; this was taking too long. He itched to know the man's thoughts. Sweat broke under the heavy cleaner's uniform; to have come this far and not even make it inside couldn't be thought of.

Footsteps rang out. The soldier returned. His blaster was loosened in its holster and Kare couldn't remember if it had been like that before. He stopped in front of Kare, running his eyes up and down him, contemptuous of the ragged hair and old uniform. "You're clear."

Kare let his shoulders sag – a cleaner undergoing a

palace security sweep was always nervous, in his experience – and took back his documents. "Thank you, sir."

He climbed into the back of the transporter. His colleagues gave a few jeers about being checked out but fell into silence once the door closed. The transport passed smoothly under a long arch and stopped in a service courtyard, one of many in the palace.

The doors opened, light from the floodlit courtyard spilling in. Kare got out first, jumping onto the cobbles, and the team followed. They unpacked the cleaning equipment from the back of the transporter, working in near silence, the perfect model of palace efficiency.

Soldiers manned the courtyard: two on the arched entranceway, two at the door into the palace, others patrolling the ramparts, but no one approached to check his squad's work. Cleaning crews filled the palace at night, invisible in hierarchy-obsessed Abendau. He half-smiled; good, let his mother's blinkered vision, her focus on a person's status and not their worth, be her downfall.

The back doors of the transporter closed with a dull thud. Kare straightened, fighting to keep his nerves under control. He stepped towards the entrance to the palace and the security hall beyond, on the balls of his feet. A familiar surge of pre-battle adrenaline filled him, and it wasn't unwelcome. He stooped through the door into the entrance hall, carrying a floor cleaner in one hand, a vermin-sensor in the other. It was appropriate: tonight, the palace was going to get the cleaning it had long deserved. One that removed all the vermin. Especially the spider at the centre.

He cracked his knuckles, the familiar pain keeping things real, and walked into a future he had never foretold.

CHAPTER THIRTY-NINE

The double doors slid open in front of Sonly and she passed into the port's security hall, filtering through with the other new arrivals. Just below ceiling height a pair of personnel-scanners worked at full speed, sending constant beeps through the air to accompany the buzz of voices. Body after body flashed as they scanned the crowd. Any possible contraband or weapon brought the scanner's attention onto the person, showing them in a red colour, easily picked out by the roving security teams. No wonder Lichio hadn't come through here – with the sort of equipment he routinely carried, he'd light the whole hall up. He'd have to bypass the cargo-security bays, too, but he had been privy to the port's security procedures over the years and should have the knowledge to work with.

Beyond the scanners a second line of security waited, this one human. She'd have to get past that and out into the main concourse, full of luxury shops and eateries. Therein lay the problem, and the one Lichio had felt insurmountable. She was the president. She was known – even if she had tried to get through on false documents, she'd have been picked up, not to mention how it would look, trying to sneak into her own city. Once that happened, she would not be allowed to pass – and if she forced it, she would be arrested.

Her hand went to her waist, without thinking, to where the holster for her pistol would normally be strapped. Despite its being legally held and within ordinary parameters for a personal citizen, it would have brought her to the early attention of the security guards.

Without it, she felt bare, which was silly – the pistol would make no difference to her plans. In fact, if she got to the point where she needed one, things would have gone badly wrong.

She stepped past two security guards, their batons by their sides, shock-tensors full. She kept her head down, not wanting to be recognised so soon. Not here, where there were too few people to notice her. Already Abendau was reverting to what it had once been: brutal, cruel, the Empress' city. It further strengthened the knowledge that, once recognised, she'd be dealt with robustly. Her only defence lay in who she was.

She swerved to avoid a pilot undergoing a full search at a security bay well back from the main line of bays. He held his arms out, his face resigned, and she noticed there were others waiting in a cordoned-off line. Normally, she wouldn't come through a security hall such as this, but be whisked through the VIP channels. The fresh eyes allowed her to pick up the disparity between the back of the hall and the section closest to the concourse, where there were no shabby pilots, but passengers in stylish clothes much like her own. Their luggage was richly embellished with great family insignias to indicate the planet they were from. Some, like her, would have landed in private ships; most would have flown first class in shuttles. However they'd got there, that was the company she needed to be in.

She joined a line for the security barriers, choosing one in the centre, and scanned the concourse beyond. There was no sign of any of the senators. A brief tickle of worry started as the queue moved forwards quicker than she'd expected. Without support, this was going to be brief. She gulped past a hard knot in her throat. Without support, it could be a visit to the city and the Empress: Sonly under arrest was undoubtedly what the regime would prefer.

She reached the head of the queue, and the guard on the main desk held his hand out. "Your pass."

"Certainly." She handed over the documents proclaiming her President of Abendau. Her face, one of the stills she used for publicity, stared out of the security holo.

The guard's eyes widened in recognition. She savoured that moment, and the pause he gave before turning away and beckoning another guard over. It felt good to be doing something instead of waiting and worrying.

"I wish to pass into the city," she said.

He grabbed her arm, his fingers hard. "We have orders to detain you on sight, Ms le Payne."

"You have no right to anything until I clear security," she said. "I'm under intergalactic administration until then." A small crowd had gathered. She held her head up and let her voice ring out. "If you arrest, detain, or do anything to me, these people will know."

She cast her gaze around the crowd, who appeared more inquisitive than militant, and fought the urge to stand on tiptoe to get a better look at the concourse. She needed the senators, right about now.

"Got your clothes on?" asked a man in the crowd. A ripple of laughter spilled out, but she ignored it. If nothing else, at least she'd make a different news story today.

The crowd parted, their laughter dying away as a news-crew passed through their midst. The security guard tightened his grip for a moment and then loosened it. More people joined the watchers, drawn by the cameras.

"Sonly le Payne." The voice was professional and known to Sonly. Sinead Solento, one of the leading news broadcasters on Belaudii, and always up for a scoop. "Can you give us a smile?"

She could, of course, but she didn't. Instead, she stared at the camera, allowing her anger to build just enough that it would show. This was her city, that she'd been voted to lead, and she was having to turn somersaults just to get in.

Sinead beckoned four holo-recorders forwards. She had been one of the journalists tipped off that the story they'd been covering for the last day might not be the accurate one. As she was never one to miss a scoop, Sonly had been sure she could be relied on. The recorders fanned out so they captured each angle of the incident. Sonly's stomach rippled with an excitement familiar from her early days in Abendau when every success had been fought for. She'd missed this when she'd led the Senate.

More security reached her, one talking into an earpiece. He gave a firm nod and approached her. "Ms le Payne, we have a directive issued for your ar—"

She pulled herself up to her full height. Yes, she'd definitely missed this.

"On what grounds?" she asked. She waited, and no answer was forthcoming. She spread her hands, taking in the three cameras. "Any action you take will be on the news-holos as soon as you do it." She lowered her voice and leaned in to the security chief. "I'll make sure it's one hell of a show. Arresting the elected president for returning, unarmed and openly, to the city? *That's* the sort of headlines I would like to see."

A clamour of voices rose in agreement, building all the time. Let the people know, if she made it into the city, that their voice had helped to get her past security. She faced the guard. "Let me past. I wish to speak to the people in my city."

He looked around the growing crowd, tight against the barrier, and seemed a little less sure of himself. Sonly hid a smile: Abendau might be the Empress' again, but something had to be left of the years of peace and democracy and the hope she'd carried.

The crowd grew bigger by the moment, joined by more press, their holo-recorders zooming in on her.

"You heard the president. Let her past." Christophe emerged from the crowd, his voice holding the calmness of a statesman used to being obeyed. He gave Sonly a nod, his face impossible to read. Not welcoming, as such, but not cold, either. Proud, perhaps.

That took her aback. Christophe, who'd hated her reforms and opposed her at every juncture, proud of her? For what? Coming back to the city, presumably, instead of running from the shattered remains of her career.

She found herself smiling at him. He wasn't hiding like most of the Senate. Three had promised their support, and only he had the courage to see it through. He must know, just as well as she did, that if this gamble failed, the Empress would make him pay. His career, at the very best, would be over; the cells of Abendau palace were entirely possible, too.

The security chief looked from Christophe to the holo-recorders, to the crowd, to Sonly, unsure what to do. The crowd picked up on the chink of opportunity. They started to chant. Her smile widened. She ducked through the security gate, and no hands stopped her. The crowd gathered around her.

A diversion, was she? If so, she'd be the best damn diversion anyone had ever seen in Abendau.

CHAPTER FORTY

Michio bypassed the main cafeteria and doubled back towards the docking bays, mentally going over the plan of the port. Getting to where he needed wasn't straightforward, but there was no direct way without passing through security. Whilst Sonly might be able to delay and bluster, he'd be under military arrest within minutes of being identified.

He put his hand inside his uniform, checking his blaster, and then picked his way down the line of concealed pockets. He was probably carrying too much equipment, but in ten years as an intelligence chief he'd learned it never paid to be under-equipped. Besides, he'd need every advantage he could get: a decade behind a desk blunted anyone's edge. He'd forgotten what it felt like when every decision could be your last one. How exhilarating it was to be on such high alert that the world took on a sharp edge of clarity, reminding you why life, even when it was shit, was worth holding on to.

He kept his movements casual as he slipped through an access door to the docking bays and stopped at a security door beyond. It wasn't manned, not in this obscure corridor, but it was locked with both a code lock and a security-override alarm. And a camera, fixed on the door.

He cracked his knuckles and reached inside his jacket, pulling out a decoder. Normally, he wouldn't try this – a decoder would never work through the parameters of coding quickly enough. But here, in his own port, he'd narrowed the parameters by locking in the first three of ten digits – the identifier for the port itself. He bit his lip, remembering the plans and making sure he had identified the section correctly, and inputted the next two. Quickly slapping his hand back, he attached the decoder to the lock.

He pulled out a direction-finder and leaned over it: just another pilot turned around in the maze of corridors and cargo bays. He'd learned over many years in security – those who skulked were caught. The more brazen and open were less likely to get stopped. He fought the urge to glance at the lock.

A soft buzz sounded, making him jump in sharp hope. He pushed the door and it opened. *Excellent.* He slipped into the empty service corridor beyond, ensuring the security door closed after him, and forced himself to a casual saunter. He wouldn't be the first pilot to bribe the access-codes from a broke staff member; if discovered, he'd be sent back to the public areas with little more than a slap on the wrist. Provided, of course, he wasn't recognised. He sped up.

He made his way down the corridor, keeping the layout of the port in the front of his mind. Once, he'd known it well – but as the focus of Kare's military strength had moved to the compound, the port had grown, becoming more commercial, and Lichio had focused less on it. He'd needed the couple of days' flight-time to refresh his memory. He passed into the next sector, through a little-known firewall space, and down a stairwell to street level.

He was getting close now. His hands started to sweat. He pulled the hat farther over his eyes; he might have a lower profile than Kare, but he was hardly unknown. He turned a final corner and there, at the very far end of the corridor, was Exit 7: the back access-way from the port, and the least monitored. The same exit he'd secured during Kare's slave revolt, when the port had been a simpler building with much less traffic. He'd led a squad down this corridor and had given orders for the door to be stormed. He wished he had a squad right now.

He took his time, scanning the corridor's security coverage. Pretty standard: wall-mounted camera coverage with section-controls to seal the corridor in an emergency. Presumably a standard team of four soldiers in the guard-room beside the exit. None of it was going to make taking the exit any easier. He slipped his hand into his uniform's pocket. The four soldiers would need to be taken out at the same time. He tightened his fingers around a neutron grenade; it felt very flimsy for the job at hand.

He made his way up the corridor, making sure not to break his stride. Confidence would get him further than subterfuge, he reminded himself. He passed a series of doors on either side, secured entries to the docking bays, and hummed to himself.

A soldier stepped out of the guard-room and advanced, hands ready on his rifle, eyes sharp. "This is a restricted section."

Lichio's throat tightened, but he managed a smile. "My ship's allocated to Bay 13." His voice came out reasonably strong, all things considered. "I thought this was the right section?"

The soldier glanced back, presumably at his colleagues. Lichio's hand tightened on the grenade. He fought the urge to charge; he needed to be close enough to take all four soldiers. There'd be no second chance.

"No." The soldier's voice was flat, but his stance was relaxed; Lichio obviously wasn't the first pilot to turn up lost. "That's in sector four."

Another soldier stepped out of the guard-room. *Come on, come on, where are the other two?*

"So." Lichio stopped about six feet away, beside a short access-way leading to one of the secured doors. "Back up this corridor and then where? This place is a maze."

"Back that way, round to the right and follow the corridor. You'll reach the commercial hub. Cross it to reach your bay."

The soldier turned away. His partner watched Lichio, covering with his rifle. Maybe there were only two; Lichio's plans predated the change of administration. He primed the grenade, counted three, and tossed it.

"Back!" yelled the second soldier. He sent off a shot, but it was wild, and pulled his partner towards the guard-room.

Lichio dove to the right, into the niche. A dull explosion sounded; shrieks filled the air. He winced. It was a dirty way to fight. He lifted his head and scrambled to his feet. He snatched his blaster out.

A hand grabbed his shoulder, spinning him around to face a huge soldier, at least as big as Silom had been. The access-door stood open, revealing an observation room beyond. *Crap.*

The soldier's fist came at him, too quick to dodge. His head crashed against the wall, but he held on to his blaster – somehow – and brought it up in a low arc.

"It's le Payne!" The soldier grabbed for Lichio but he kicked out, taking the soldier in the knee. It gave with a crunch, bringing the bigger man down, but a second soldier barrelled out of the room, blaster raised.

Now or never. Lichio squeezed off three shots, glad of every close-combat course he'd taken. He took the first man cleanly, but the second had crouched in the shelter of the doorway, and shot at him.

Lichio dived, yelling as the beam brushed his arm. He rolled into a crouch and brought his blaster up. One chance to get out before the corridor was sealed. He fired. The soldier gave a strangled yell and lay still.

Alarms blared from the corridor. So much for subtle. Lichio ran. He hit the shattered security door and crashed through it into the night air. He sprinted away from the port, towards the tribal quarter, where he could get lost in the maze of streets.

Damn, he'd made a meal of that. There was no

chance the coverage wouldn't have picked up who he was, not with the soldier recognising him. Someone would be sure to put two and two together and came up with Kare. *Not good.*

He slowed and wove through the old section, refusing to give in to the urge to run, or hide. Head up, open and brazen, all the time. He skirted the tribal quarter's red-stone walls, choosing alleys seemingly at random, but each cycle took him closer to the palace.

Finally, he reached a square, well-lit and full of restaurants, and stopped to catch his breath. There was no sign of any pursuit. He took out his comms unit, all the while watching the square. It connected a moment later and his shoulders sagged with relief at the familiar voice.

"Simone," he said. "It's me. Where are you?"

CHAPTER FORTY-ONE

The palace administration had shut down for the night. The only teams working were security and cleaning teams, making their way to their allocated zones. Kare passed a team dressed like himself and his squad. They had their heads down, thoroughly cowed, careful not to meet the eyes of any security. Under the Empress' regime people knew their place. He remembered *that* from inheriting the palace from her.

His squad climbed the back staircase, their steps echoing. This was the side of Abendau palace rarely viewed; the dimly-lit access-ways that lay behind the façade of opulence. The air was cooler here, carried on a slight breeze from the desert, and he shivered. The stairwell reminded him of the medical wing attached to Omendegon – it had the same sense of hidden secrets, a lost place no one cared to acknowledge.

The squad reached the second floor. Hickson pushed through the security door and stopped to clear the squad's work schedule with two security guards. They allowed the team to pass, but their eyes were sharp, their hold on their weapons professional, and it was all Kare could do not to hurry, for fear they'd recognise him even through the disguise. He slumped his shoulders and ducked his head instead.

They entered the Empress' private section of the palace, and the hard flooring was replaced by soft, thick carpets. These outer chambers were mostly anterooms for private meetings, designed to impress, screaming wealth. He remembered his own refurbishments; the discussions with his finance chief had been long and drawn out, exhaustingly so, even though his décor was nowhere near as opulent as what he'd inherited.

He padded down the corridor. It seemed impossible he'd owned this place, that he'd lived here until his nightmares convinced him to build the compound and get out. Time shifted, bringing memories. He'd been born here, had suffered in its cells as nowhere else, had ruled from its throne room. Now, he was back to clean the place. A harsh laugh threatened to come, and he choked it away. He was going to clean this place like it had never been cleaned before.

The squad reached the last security door before the Empress' private quarters. Security here would be tighter than the checks in the courtyard. He waited in line as each of the team had their IDs checked, their retinas recorded, their DNA confirmed against records. The lights were hot and it was easy to blame them for the sweat breaking on the back of his neck. If his records hadn't been updated, this would be where his attack ended.

Gods, it must work; he'd checked it and checked it, going over parameter after parameter in the system.

He had the sudden urge to use the mesh to scan for his mother. He held it in check, imagining her turning on him the minute he did. He could face his mother, but not the guards as well. Despite temptation, he needed to bide his time. Even without the mesh, he could feel her, a coldness in the air, a sense of heaviness in his chest. He was damned if she'd get a chance to call the shots on him ever again.

He shuffled forwards, head down. He was a servant, in the palace of the Empress. He *should* be scared. He wondered if the servants who'd cleaned his chambers had been scared. He hoped not, but fear was a hard thing to unlearn, and Abendau had years of it to overcome.

"Hand." The security guard didn't look bored, as many of the palace staff did, but sharp. Only the best would be on duty at these doors, and it was impossible to tell if he was a real guard or one of the planted operatives. Kare held his hand out and waited as the DNA sequencer's needle stabbed him, leaving a tiny red mark. The machine ran the results through the system, numbers on the screen falling as it searched for a match to his DNA. He found himself barely breathing.

"Look straight ahead."

He stared at the retinal-scanner. Beyond, in the first room, those already cleared from his squad were splitting into their work teams. His mouth was dry. He willed the green light of the DNA sequencer to come up.

What if some last remnant of his old record remained? What if there was something added to the system since he'd been ousted, and his reprogramming had been discovered? He had to resist the urge to lift his hand and pull at his collar; his scar was too recognisable to take that chance.

A bleep. He tensed, sure the light would turn to red, but it changed to green.

"You're clear." The soldier gave him a hard push towards the rest of the squad. "Now get on with your work."

Charming: manners were already deteriorating. He met Kym Woods' eyes, hard and unflinching, and held back a smile.

The cleaning equipment with its concealed weaponry was being scanned, a task certainly being carried out by an operative – the equipment would never have passed otherwise. The agent took his time, occasionally going back to check an item before giving it the all-clear. His face was bland, unreadable; Simone had done a good job getting someone in this close, and the operative was doing a better one.

"They're clear," said the operative at last. "They can go through."

The gilded doors at the top of the room opened.

Gods, he knew those doors. He'd closed them behind him each night for years, before going to his room and facing his history, nightmare after nightmare, until morning came.

He forced himself to breathe, slow and steady, and calm himself. Tonight was different. He wasn't here to sleep, or to relive Taluthna's hellish playground. He was here to free himself, to move past what was done to him.

The doors had opened fully. Beyond, the final corridor stretched. Its walls were flocked in deep crimson, the colour of blood. The carpet was woven of gold thread.

At the end of the corridor, a final set of doors, grander than the ones he had just passed through, waited. Gods, he was close.

The brief sound of a scuffle made him turn back to the security room. The guard who'd carried out his DNA checks lay dead on the floor. The operative who'd scanned the equipment stood over the body. He met Kare's eyes and gave a sharp nod. "Sir."

Kare took a deep breath; this was it, the point of no return. He pulled off the wig and removed the prosthetic cheeks; the lenses could wait until later. Feeling more like himself, he stepped into the middle of the room. The second operative had sealed the section, and the rest of the squad were already dismantling the cleaning equipment to remove the weaponry from within.

Kare took a blaster and a phaser, and set both in hip-holsters. Two stun grenades were handed to him. He immediately felt better; powers were one thing, and he'd feel even better when he was back in the mesh, but nothing beat a blaster on your hip. He straightened and faced the squad; in minutes they'd transformed from a beaten-down cleaning crew to the hard-eyed soldiers they were, professional and deadly.

"Team B," Kare said. "As planned."

Their corporal gave a sharp salute. This order, the confirmation that the attack would be carried out with his mother in situ, was the decision point. There would be no turning back, now. If the alarm was raised, this team would hold the door to this hall as long as possible. Already, the operative was running observations through the security holos; the door could be held as long as Kare needed it to be.

"Team A," said Hickson. "Room-clearance."

Four soldiers set off down the corridor, entering each room in turn, checking it, and moving on. They moved with practiced ease, one opening the door, another covering the two entering each room, flash-grenades at the ready. They worked their way down the corridor but, as expected, the anterooms were deserted.

Kare smiled, slightly smug: he'd known his mother wouldn't want lackeys in her personal space. She wouldn't trust anyone close to her except Phelps and her inner council. The thought of the bonus of Phelps as well as his mother cheered him.

He jerked his head at Kym. "Let's go."

She joined him and he had to smile. He might feel better armed, but for Kym it was a religion; she bristled with weaponry. The rifle she held appeared moulded against her, she held it so tightly. They walked to the gilded door at the far end of the corridor, past the open anterooms, Hickson's team taking point.

Kare paused outside the door. From here, there were three rooms – a living area, a boardroom and her bedroom, with its huge window overlooking the city. A window he'd stood at, night after night, trying to know her city and palace and understand why she'd done what she had. He'd never found an answer.

"Just the security team beyond the door," said Hickson to the squad.

Team A stepped up to the door and silently carried out a weapons check. At Hickson's nod, they burst through, a flash grenade thrown by the first disorientating anyone in the room.

A yell came and then the sound of return fire. Kare moved up to the door, crouching, his blaster out and ready, a grenade tight in his left hand, his thumb on the trigger.

One of the Empress' soldiers snatched up the comms unit, ignoring the gunfire around him, his only focus on his job. Kare brought his blaster up, moving on instinct, but a shot aimed at him made him duck back, and his own shot went wild. Hell, they were screwed if a comms got out.

Kym straightened, fluid, paying no heed to the gunfire around her. She took the soldier with a casual grace, barely seeming to aim. He reeled back, hit the wall, and slumped to the ground.

"Nice," said Kare. He ducked his head around the door, but Hickson's men had the last of the guards in hand.

"I told you. I don't miss."

He nodded and stepped into the room with its three closed doors. He pointed Team A to the boardroom, Hickson to the sleeping quarters, and Kym to the living area. He could feel his mother's presence, close, awakening; this was how she felt to others, a persuasive hum of awareness, always working her influence on those in the palace. If she had time, she'd work through the squad until all she had to do was open the door and ask for their weapons.

Not this time. He closed his eyes, feeling for the mesh, and reached, drawing into himself, the technique already automatic after only such a short time.

The mesh repelled him. He opened his eyes and blinked. Farran had said it might take a bit of effort to open the centre he'd closed so tightly two days ago, but he hadn't said anything about being forced back.

"What is it?" asked Kym.

He shook his head. "Nothing. I just need a minute." He concentrated on the sense of his grandmother's chamber, its Seer's prism defining the heritage he needed today, and found the mesh again.

Relieved, he tried to snatch it, but was forced back. "What the hell?" Fighting panic, he took a deep breath, and reorientated himself. Once more, he dove into the mesh, the Roamers' King, the living centre they needed to maintain their unity, and demanded it yield to him. Again, it repelled him. He felt around it, sensing the shape of it; the mesh was definitely keeping him out and away from what – who – was in its centre. He tried again, gentler, feeling for the centre instead of demanding to be it.

The shape of the person's mind came to him, and he gasped – he'd know her anywhere. He pushed again, calling Kerra, telling her to let go, but she didn't respond.

"What's wrong?" asked Woods, her voice sharp. "We need to finish this job."

"I know." He met her eyes. "The mesh – my powers. I can't get to them."

"Can't get to them? Why not?"

He shook his head, not able to answer. He was the Roamers' King; the mesh should bend to him. A tickle of uncertainty came. On his last day on Syllte, he'd stood in the chamber the Roamers wanted him to take for his own as the final gesture he was one of them. He'd turned away, not ready to give up Kare Varnon, with his own heritage and background. Not ready to give up Ealyn and Karia, the outcasts, or forgive what had happened.

He thought of Kerra, piloting the Roamer ship. Her pleading eyes as Sonly had explained the pilot had offered to teach her Control, how she'd told Kerra she carried Ealyn's blood and skills. He thought of his own sister, more like Ealyn than their mother, with the same skills as Kerra – the healing, the Control.

And he thought of Baelan, the cuckoo Kare didn't fully understand, the lost boy with power seeping out of him. Baelan was his son, born of the mixed powers, and had more than his share of the Empress running through him. As did Kare; it was no coincidence he was the one facing his mother and seeking to end it. Of his family, only he had enough of her blood in him to do it.

Kerra was a Roamer, more than either he or Baelan ever would be. She could hold the mesh in a way Kare could never do, embracing it as he'd refused to. The mesh, it seemed, wanted that.

Coldness washed through him. It would use her as it had used the Queen, his grandmother. She'd abandoned her child for the mesh - what would it demand of Kerra?

He stared at the door, helpless to regain his powers. If he called off the assault, he'd never get another chance, but if he went ahead he'd be going in powerless, stripped of the reason he'd come himself to do this. The irony wasn't lost on him - fate had known it had to be him, however he did it.

Kym hefted her rifle. "Well," she said, "we'll have to do it the hard way."

He blinked; that was what Silom had said when he'd led the palace raid without the wounded Kare. He'd managed without his powers for ten years. He touched his blaster - he wasn't helpless.

Taking a deep breath, he faced the door to the living quarters. He could feel hatred in the air and had no doubt his mother had found him. It gave a perverse pleasure to know he matched that hatred and more.

"Now!" he snarled. To hell with it, he'd still take the bitch down. The hard way, if he had to.

CHAPTER FORTY-TWO

Phelps ran, feet pounding over hard sand. The Varnon girl's eyes had shone with an intention he knew well from years of working for a psycher. She'd turn on him if he stayed, and no blaster would make a difference. His only hope was to get back to the tribes and track the children down with their strength of numbers.

He ran along the top of a ridge, looking back once, but there was no pursuit. He slowed to catch his breath. When this piece of work was finished, he'd have to find a way to free himself. Being the Empress' henchman was destroying him, piece by piece.

Surely he was strong enough to leave. He could go back to Hiactol, take residence near the wooded vales of the northern territory, and stay there until he forgot the Empress' hold and became something of the man he'd once been.

A gentle drumming sounded beneath him. He straightened, mouth dry. There were pockets in the sand below. He tapped the ground with his toe-capped boot, trying to find a solid way forwards. A soft cracking came from beneath him and he jumped back, looking wildly around for softer sand, a dune, anything he could jump to. The cracking sounds grew louder, more deadly than any bullet. Around his feet, the cracks widened. A clutterback nest.

The ground gave way with a sickening hiss. The sand sucked him into the cavern below.

He fell, landing hard on his shoulder, but rolled to his feet. The dark was quiet, waiting. He strained his eyes. It could be an abandoned nest, one already farmed for its pearls. After a few moments of silence he drew a deep breath; it *was* empty. He looked up at the hole he'd fallen through. It was at least four feet above his head; he'd have to find another way out. He walked forwards, hands out.

A scuffling sound stopped him. *An echo, it had to be an echo.* He went to move again, but the unmistakable click of a clutterback's legs stopped him. He couldn't tell if it was ahead or to the side. It grew louder, more than one spider, coming from the sides of the nest, the roof, all around.

The spiders came into view, each as high as his knee, legs bowed into great arches. One climbed across the hole in the roof, and the dim light dropped to a single crack in the darkness. He backed away, fumbling for his pistol, and pulled it loose. Stopped by the wall, he stood, breathing heavily. Scrapes and whispers came from the darkness.

The wall moved. He jumped forwards, but a leg draped over his shoulder, almost embracing him. A sharp sting impaled his spine, and he yelled at the pain. Wetness spread from his crotch. His hands went numb, making his weapon drop with a clatter. His legs gave way, the warmth of his piss vanishing into cold emptiness. Another sting, this one in his neck, and he arched. Another pierce, below his ear. He tried to scream, but cold was spreading across his face. He knew he was being pulled into the nest only because the crack of light in the ceiling faded. They descended on him. His paralysed eyes watched as they began to feast.

CHAPTER FORTY-THREE

Baelan kept his head down and concentrated on the control panel. He'd told Kerra he could drive scoots, but he'd never driven one this size, and it was straining his arms to hold the steering column steady. His eyes flicked between the speed information, the navcom data and the fast-approaching city.

"How are we going to get into Abendau?" he shouted. "I can't take this through the tunnels."

Kerra didn't respond. He slowed the scoot and glanced over at her – she was staring ahead, eyes sharp and unreadable. He tapped her leg. "Hey! Belaudii to Kerra!" The scoot skidded and he had to grab the steering column to keep it on target. "How are we going to get into the city?"

"Through the main gate," she said, as if he was stupid.

He brought the scoot to a halt, fighting its weight. "No way." Didn't she know what it was like getting into Abendau? Maybe, as a VIP, she didn't understand how secure it was. Or how fond of their weaponry the gate guards were. "They'll take us."

"They'll try." A little smile danced on her lips. "They won't get past me."

She sounded nothing like herself. She was so sure of herself. Confident. He took in her stance, hunched forwards, her focus on the city. She looked older. He reached for her. "Kerra...?"

Shadows danced across her face, but she didn't answer. He squeezed her hand, very gently. Perhaps she was in the mesh again. Perhaps he'd reach her more easily through it. He gritted his teeth and looked for the mesh inside him, and he could see it, zoned away where it was easy for him to ignore. Half-wincing, he took hold of it. He'd never liked the idea of all those minds, so close to his. It was the Empath in him, maybe – it was too much, to be so close. Still, needs must.

The mesh pushed him away. He nearly tipped off the seat. It had never done that before. He tried again and the rebuff came even quicker.

"Kerra," he said. He raised his voice, and her eyes met his. "What's going on?"

She was like a stranger, not the sister he'd spent the last couple of weeks with. "It doesn't want you," she said. She gave a little shrug. "It wants me." She leaned forwards, her hair swinging over her face, and stared at Abendau. "It wants me to go to the city. It wants rid of the Empress. It will give me the power to do it."

That was nuts. He had to stop her. She might think she was strong enough to take on the Empress; so had he, once.

"Kerra," he said, picking his words. He was scared of her, he realised, and it wasn't just because his own powers hadn't come back yet. Even facing her with everything he had, he'd be frightened of her. "I've had the sort of power you have."

He needed to get through to her, scared or not; there was no one else to do it. Somehow, reaching out to her made him more sure of what he wanted, less mixed-up and confused. Kerra was good fun; it was nice to have someone his own age to talk to, especially one who didn't treat him like an outcast for being different. He wanted to find a way to be like she had been – relaxed and accepted, not twisted and confused. He'd thought, since hearing his mother and Phelps talking on the ship and realising more about where he stood and who he meant what to, that he might be getting closer to that place. To come close and then lose Kerra to her own mixed-up thoughts wasn't something he wanted. He laid a hand on her arm. "If you give me a couple of hours, I'll have my power again. It's not enough. Not to take on the Empress."

She laughed: high, almost mocking. Fear crept up his spine. Phelps had run from her, and he'd never seen Phelps frightened of anything. He'd stood up to the Empress and he'd never backed away from Baelan.

"You have never had power like this," said Kerra. She picked out every word. "I can do anything. Don't you understand?" She stretched her arms wide, as if taking in the expanse of stars above her. "The mesh, all of it, is the centre of me. It's so much more than it ever was in our father."

"But he's the centre," Baelan said. Realisation started to come, and it wasn't good. "Kerra, where is our father? Is he in the mesh?"

"He can't be. Like you, he doesn't fit."

Oh, shit. If he'd guessed his father's plans correctly, he was relying on the mesh when he met the Empress - that was the only thing that made sense of the questions he'd asked Baelan.

"He didn't want it." She smiled, and it wasn't a nice smile. "But I do, and I'm right for it."

"But he needs it. To face the Empress." And Baelan needed him to face her, if he had any hope of being free. He felt a tug of guilt at his selfish thought and blinked, surprised. Guilt wasn't something he normally did.

"Not the way he used it." She pushed her hair back from her face. "I'm going to him. I'm going to bring the power of the mesh to him."

He let his hand drop from her arm. What should he do? He could refuse to drive, but what if she decided to go into the city on her own? He couldn't face her down, not with the medicine still in him, and he wasn't going to help anyone if he was fried in the desert.

"Why force the gate?" Maybe he could talk some sense into her, the way his mother used to when he lost control. "If we get into the city quietly, you could keep your power under wraps until we reach the palace." She cocked her head, as if thinking about it. "Although I really don't think you should go anywhere near the palace."

"And leave Dad to face the Empress alone?" That, at least, sounded like Kerra. "She'd destroy him."

"Then you should give him the power. The way it's supposed to be." He frowned and leaned closer. "How do you know he's in the palace?"

"He tried to take the mesh back," she said. A light danced in her eyes. "But it was wrong. That's why I need to keep the shape the way it is, so the power lasts; he'd drain it, forcing it to his will."

She was cracked in the head – right up there with the Empress, as far as he could tell.

"Our father needs the power, and you've blocked him?" He took a deep breath. Hopefully if she fried him, she'd do it quickly. "Are you crazy?"

She didn't look angry. She didn't look anything other than smugly right. "I know exactly what I'm doing." Her eyes narrowed. "And if you'd done as you'd been told, we'd already be at the gate."

Do as he'd been told. He was surrounded by megalomaniacs, between his grandmother and father, and now his sister. Let alone Sonly-the-supposedly-magnificent. It was beyond annoying. He crossed his arms. "Give Father the mesh. Now."

"Drive."

"Give it back to him. Think about it, Kerra. You'll still have power, you'll be in the mesh, it's not like you're losing anything."

"And give up this?" Her eyes shone in the moonlight. "Would you give up your power?"

That stopped him. "I wouldn't leave him in danger." Was that the truth? If his father was in front of him, now, needing help, would he give him the power? Or would his oath come rushing back and force him to obey it? He hoped not. He met her eyes; he'd work out the truth later. What mattered is the Kerra he knew wouldn't. "Yeah, I'd give him it."

"You lie." There was no doubt in her voice. "Now, drive."

An impulse hit him, so strong that he took hold of the steering column, not able to stop himself. He wanted to wrench the scoot to the side, to refuse, but she was holding him, giving him no will of his own. This wasn't Kerra, this was something else, something—

"Oh, it's me, all right," she said, laughing. "It was what I was born for."

He drove, fighting her all the way, twisting to escape, but it made no difference. She might well be mad; he had no way to stop her.

They reached the gate. The scoot surged forwards. The guards yelled, shooting. Something exploded to his left, rocking the scoot, but he kept going, driven, as if a toy, by Kerra.

CHAPTER FORTY-FOUR

Sonly left the port by the main exit, head up and unbowed. Kare had been right. He'd said, the night in the cells, that the people of Abendau would not forget her. No matter that the Empress was back, spreading back through the city – ten years had changed things. Sonly had left her mark.

The security team from the port, faced with the media and a growing crowd, had been forced to let her pass and hand the problem to city security. By the time they'd arrived, she'd been deep in a crowd intent on safeguarding her. Short of inciting a riot – and the city's security was thin during the changeover after the coup – there was no way to stop her. And certainly, given the number of news-drones now surrounding her, no way to do it quietly.

She made her way along Grand Boulevard towards the palace. Soldiers waited at the gate, but they showed no signs of being prepared to open fire. Emboldened, she put her shoulders back and marched to the head of the crowd, no longer bothering to hide in their mass. Ahead, a larger crowd had gathered in the centre of the boulevard, pennants waving, so vigorously that their tails snapped, snarling in the air.

The protestors' faces were lit by small fires in braziers along each pavement; a traditional Abendauii protest march, then, with fire and voice and wind. To see it in the city the Empress held gave Sonly hope. When Kare had first taken the empire, such a protest would never have been dared. It seemed the Empress hadn't yet dampened the people's voice.

"That's the main crowd. The best I could do on such short notice," said Christophe.

"You did well." He had, too; she counted several hundred protestors to join the hundreds, perhaps close to a thousand, already gathered around her. The people of Abendau didn't want to go back to the old ways, it seemed. She remembered that Lichio had mentioned a protest planned, too – if it was another like this, the city's authorities would definitely be kept busy.

Christophe cleared his throat. "The pictures of you..." His cheeks flamed red, contrasting with his greying beard, and it was hard to tell who was more embarrassed.

She bit back an apology. She was done apologising for who she was. "They were taken without my knowledge," she said.

"Quite." He gave a quick nod. "I will abide many things in politics, but I won't stand over smear campaigns." He nodded, almost absently. "I'm glad you were able to explain about the leaks. I found it hard to reconcile that with you."

Sonly nearly stopped – only someone behind catching her heel reminded her to keep walking. Christophe's stoicism was famous. It was rumoured he'd last cracked a smile about two decades ago, and *that* may have just been a cough. And as for voicing a clear opinion....

"I'm grateful for the support," she said. She paused, wondering if she dared push further, and then decided she must. Too much was hanging on tonight. "Why have you supported me, if I may ask? You've never liked my politics."

"I never liked your approach," he said, his voice prim. "You rely too much on the people and not enough on policy." They were speeding up, carried by the crowd. "If you must know, my father was Bendau's mayor when the Empress came to power. She removed him by blackening his name to the city."

"The allegations were false?" she asked. She knew about the scandal, of course. That it had involved a tribal girl ensured it had a notoriety mentioned in most histories of the town. But she'd never known what lay behind it.

"That's not what matters." He looked deeply uncomfortable.

The rumours were true, then. But so were the pictures of her and Jake, and they still told a lie. She nodded her understanding, closing the matter.

"What matters is you have my full support. Whatever happens tonight, the Senate will stand firm: that I will see to." He gave a sly smile. "Harald was voted off this evening by the interior council, as were other members of the Empress' faction – your return gave the council the faith to do so. I hope you don't disappoint."

No pressure, then. "I won't."

They stopped in front of the palace gates, both crowds merging into one. Her own picture was on many of the pennants, she realised. That sort of thing used to happen to Kare, his face being used in places he hadn't authorised. He'd hated it, but she'd always envied him for being in position to be used. Now she understood how he felt – it wasn't the notoriety, but the expectation. She wanted to tell the crowd they had it wrong, that it was the whole Senate they needed to promote, not just her. She stopped herself, remembering her advice to Kare over the years: that people needed a person to trust, not a legislature. This time she was that person. It was up to her to meet it as well as he had, day after hated day.

She held her hands up, waiting for the holo-recorders to come closer. When they had, she called out, her voice ringing, "The Senate has returned." A yell grew, from those closest and those at the back, giving her more confidence. "Tell your friends! We'll take our protest to the gates of the palace. To the Empress herself. The time has come to return our city to where it should be."

She faced the palace. At any moment, surely the gates would open and her rebellion would be cut down. The bitch knew what she could do with the Senate behind her, and not to underestimate her: it was why she'd tried to silence Sonly. But the soldiers behind the gates stood firm. They knew the crowd couldn't breach the great gates and take the palace. No crowd ever had, not since the Empress had taken the city with her tribal army.

The soldiers manning the protest were edgier, though, their hands on their weapon butts, their shields raised and ready. They could feel the passion of the crowd. They were beginning to see this wasn't a normal political rally that could be held back by the daunting prospect of what lay beyond the gates. More people joined her crowd, coming from the old quarter, the merchants' village, rich and the poor alike, come to reclaim what they'd voted for - freedom, equality, a voice. Her.

***

Lichio stood in the shadows at the bottom of Josef's embassy's garden, Simone beside him. The conservatory where he and Josef had sat, night after night in a private world of their own, was dark and silent.

The sound of cheers came from the boulevard: Sonly's name was chanted over and over again. He met Simone's eyes and managed not to swear. Instead, he grimaced. "I told her not to overstretch herself."

Simone smiled. She seemed to be thoroughly enjoying herself, back in the thick of things. "She doesn't appear overstretched. You should be pleased."

"You think so?" He gave a short laugh. It was good to see Sonly with the fire back in her. He'd been afraid, seeing her on Ferran, that it was quashed forever. "You aren't the one who'll have to listen to this being recounted for the rest of your days." He turned his attention away from Sonly; she did seem to have things in hand. And, if she didn't, there was nothing he could do. "I want every operative you have to meet me at the tribal graveyard by the moat."

"Yes, sir." She was the only person he knew who could put a smile in her voice. "We're going in, then?"

Lichio looked at the palace's white walls looming over him. Had Kare reached his mother yet? Was he already fighting for his life, or still searching? He gave a firm nod. "Yes. We're going in."

CHAPTER FORTY-FIVE

K are hit the door with his shoulder and crashed into the bedroom, Kym behind him. The time for subtlety, for hiding, was over. His mother was there, as he'd known she would be, framed against the bay window. Her back was turned to them. Kym brought her rifle up and aimed; he unholstered his blaster, kneeling. Neither could miss.

Heavy boots sounded. Her guards were coming. He set a smoke-grenade off. It wreathed, surrounding him and Kym. Kym's shot rang out, his next, and then Kym again, shot after shot. Her scope stayed fixed on his mother; the smoke would make no difference. There was a crash as the window shattered.

Their shots ended, leaving only silence. He barely dared breathe as the quiet stretched on. The window his mother had been standing at was gone. They must have found their target.

No movement came from her end of the room. His shoulders went down, and he got to his feet. He'd actually done it: taken his mother before she was ready.

He started to cross the room. Sounds came from outside, dulled by the smoke, but the name was unmistakable. Voices, calling over and over for Sonly, and that made no sense – she was on Ferran. A thought began to occur – that Sonly had never been good at doing nothing – and he hurried towards the window, alert for any movement.

A familiar touch at the edge of his senses made him stop. It stroked him, gloating. Strong and unbroken. His breathing turned harsh and a chill washed through him, one of terror, made stronger by her knowledge of it. Of him. Behind, Kym gave a strangled choke.

"You came," said his mother, her voice smooth. "Your wife landed an hour ago, and her brother." Lichio and Sonly? He wanted it not to be true, for her to be lying, but he'd heard the crowd. If Sonly was here, Lich would have come. "It stood to reason you were in the city."

She stepped through the smoke, untouched by the gunfire, a smile on her face. Damn her, she'd been ready for him, already shielded. He'd been a fool to think otherwise. He knew, without looking, that her personal escort would be behind him, blocking any escape.

He composed his face, refusing to give in to his fear. There was nowhere to go, nothing to do but face her.

***

If Lichio never saw the culvert of the moat at Abendau palace again, it'd be too soon. Only weeks before, he'd clambered through it to escape, now he was crawling under the old arch, past the grille he'd forced, and back into the freezing water. He heard a splash and sharp intake of breath behind him – when this was over, he really needed to get Simone a nice desk job. She deserved it after all the crap he'd thrown at her over the years.

He splashed out of the moat before it entered the main channel, and leaned down, letting Simone take his arm to pull herself out. He led the way through the gardens, keeping to the shadows. He was sick of shadows, too.

The tribal burial ground was ahead, an ancient church-land that preceded the palace by generations, part of the now-flooded original building. It lay in the most secret part of the garden, not open to the public or visitors.

He stepped through an arch, set into the red-stone wall, and stopped in a small square of cleared ground. No plants or false water here, just tombs of red stone surrounding him in the darkness.

The night was utterly silent. Anytime he'd been here – not often, as even in the daylight the place was eerie and old –

it had been quiet. No birds, no wind, nothing but the unshaded sun beating down on its dead people.

"Where's your team?" His whisper seemed to carry, unmuffled by trees or the running water.

"At the west wall." Simone went to move past him, but he caught her arm.

"Wait." The silence held. No desert-mice moved. No bats swooped. "Don't rush into anything."

He strained his eyes, but there was nothing out of place. Satisfied, he moved through the burial ground. If his team were here, that would be enough to send the mice into their hiding places.

He reached the west wall of the square. The wall had a small cairn inset within it; Ankshara, the first of the elders to be buried in Abendau. His operatives – a group of five – stood alongside it, lined along the wall. He sent a silent thanks and strode up to them.

"Sir," said one. His eyes flashed a warning, and Lichio slowed. "Ru–"

A squad of palace guards emerged from the dark shadows of the tombs. Lichio's hand was already on his blaster even as his eyes took in the number emerging.

"Step forward, General," said their captain.

Mouth dry, Lichio moved away from Simone. There were too many for him, a whole squad. He dropped his hand from his blaster, brought it up to his pocket, seeking a grenade, a proton-burst, a star-bomb, anything.

He was grabbed and twisted, his legs kicked from under him so that he fell, sprawling. A soldier landed on his back, knocking the air from his lungs. He tried to kick, but his legs were taken, sharp shig-wire digging into his skin and tightening as he fought. His hands were pulled back and cuffs put on. Hard hands pulled him to his feet and gave nowhere for him to go.

"Take him to the cells," the captain spat. "We'll deal with him after."

After what, he wanted to ask, but was marched away too quickly.

***

"I came, Mother." Kare forced himself to step forwards, but she held a hand up and he stopped. He tried to force himself towards her again, teeth gritted, but couldn't move. Kym fell to her knees beside the door with a low groan. She cradled her rifle against her, her tight fingers the only defiance.

"No further." The Empress was calm, unruffled, holding him with no effort. He closed his eyes and sought inwards. There was no response from either the mesh or Kerra. He squeezed his hands into fists, letting pain sharpen his thoughts. *Kerra: I need the mesh.*

Nothing. He opened his eyes and faced his mother. It wasn't just his power she could sense: it was the shape of his mind, his focus on her. How long had she known he was coming for her?

A line of soldiers pushed past him. He held his head high, calculating. If he grabbed his mother, set his weapon to her, they wouldn't shoot. His muscles tensed, ready, but he held where he was. Damn, she was strong.

"It won't be clean," the Empress said. The chill in him turned to ice. His breath was harsh in the room, driven by barely held panic. "It won't be quick, either." She gave a soft laugh. "Nor for le Payne, making his way through the grounds. Or your wife, who thinks bringing a rabble will be enough to stop me."

His mother was going to take everyone he loved and hurt them, and he could do nothing. Useless again. He should never have tried this. She knew it; she was enjoying his thoughts. He could see it in her face, feel it in her touch. He glared at her, trying to free himself, but she gave him no chance. Instead, she increased her hold.

"Take him," said the Empress.

It wouldn't be quick. Her words came back. This time, if he lost himself, there'd be no return. He'd die not enough of a man to care. "No." His voice was a whisper, squeezed from his tight throat. He'd promised himself he would die first, not be anyone's dog again. He thought of Beck, and the memory of the sadistic bastard – dead, but stalking his dreams – moved him, where nothing else could; he *had* to fight.

"Woods!" he said, the word squeezed past his mother's hold. Sweat broke along his brow, but he'd done this before, resisted her without his power. "You said you never missed." She tried to stir, but fell back.

"She never took Silom's mind," he said. The Empress increased her hold on him. His throat clogged with effort. "She stole everyone else's, but not Silom's. Fight. Like he did."

A soldier grabbed his arm. His other wrist was pulled behind his back. He wrenched forwards. "Come on! Fight, Woods!"

A light came into her eyes, something of the determined look he was used to. His arm was twisted, the blaster taken from him. He was pulled back. He dug his heels in. "Fight her!"

Somehow, Kym climbed to her feet, her rifle held high. The Empress' power flexed – focused and deadly. Her soldiers raised their weapons.

"Bitch!" Kare yelled, staggering forwards, taking the attention from Kym. "Look at me, you bitch! Look what you've left." Gods, it was hard, fighting her. He wanted to drop to his knees and give up. "One son, who'll die standing for everything you abhor." His father hadn't given in to her. "No Empire, not with Sonly down there." Sonly, too – she'd always resisted. The thought of her strengthened him. "No heir to carry it forward – the children hate you as much as I do."

Kym made a gagging noise. It wasn't working. His

mother knew him in the way only they understood each other. She wouldn't be diverted. She raised her hand, eyes on Kym. "Take her."

A laser beam passed in front of Kare, a deadly needle, and Kym cried out.

"No!" Hands held him. He tried to dive for her. Kym fell, her tunic burned through. Her hand clutched her rifle. They'd have to prise it from her.

The Empress turned to the window, her hand going to her throat. Kare felt it too, a new presence, something as strong as his mother, as determined as her, as cold as her. Something familiar. *Gods.* He fell back against his captor, stunned.

A shot blasted. Kym was on her knees, face screwed in pain. The Empress' guard responded, the gunfire deafening. Kare broke free and stumbled forwards into the line of fire; he'd go down, here and now, and give Kym another few seconds to finish the job. She rolled to the side, firing all the time. A soldier yelled and fell, and then another.

Pain ripped through Kare's chest. The shot hit with enough force to tear him from his captor's grasp and send him sprawling. He hit hard against the wall, his arm under him. It gave with a crack. Numbness spread as he slid down the wall. He heard Kym's yells, saw shots criss-crossing the room. She'd take the Empress for sure.

His breath bubbled and he smiled. He'd cheated his mother; he'd die before she could hurt him. He closed his eyes, accepting the blackness, accepting there was nothing more he could do. Let it end. Let it all end.

Someone joined him in the numbness: his father and sister, sitting either side of him. Silom, too, and Sam. The dead gathered, waiting for him to join them.

"Kill her," he whispered. "Don't miss."

CHAPTER FORTY-SIX

The scoot lay on its back, crashed just in front of the gate. Its engine whined and its wheels turned, fruitless. Kerra staggered away and took in the wreck of the gate and the bodies of the soldiers scattered. They'd tried to prevent her getting into the city, she remembered, but everything else was a blurred half-memory of power and screams and shots going wild. The scoot crashing had scattered the last few soldiers, leaving her free to get off and push her way past the rubble.

A soft groan and some clattering stones proved to be Baelan crawling out from under the scoot. He had a red mark on his cheek, and his hair was sticking up in every direction, but otherwise he looked fine. He brushed red dust off himself and looked at her, his eyes wary. He looked around the gateway, slowly, taking in the bodies strewn like dolls, the rocks that had been brought down.

"Wow." He blinked, as if dazed. "Remind me to stay on your good side."

A part of her, hidden deep within, tried to smile, recognising his words as a joke, but the mesh swirled, quicker and stronger, and the recognition of what his words meant fell away. There were no minds in the mesh with her now, just a consciousness. It had a sense of age to it, and a coldness far from the Roamer minds she'd known. What that meant for the Roamers, or if it was only she who'd lost perspective, she didn't know. Somewhere, a faint part of the old Kerra wanted to get out, but she was buried and tired: the mind was louder, and vengeful. It wanted the Empress. She'd stolen its children.

Soon, she needed to get there soon. Urgency ran through her, making every limb tingle with the need to run.

She ran down the street, the city a blur as she powered forwards. Baelan barely kept up. She held her hands out by her sides, wider and wider, as if that would give the power room to move, to be, and the mesh kept growing.

She reached the Grand Boulevard, not caring who saw her. She was untouchable. Ahead, a crowd had gathered, but she didn't care about that either. She sprinted up the avenue. The palace was just ahead.

A new power met hers and clashed, focused on her. Her grandmother. For a moment fear filtered past the mesh and Kerra slowed, but the mesh surged, sweeping her doubts away. Kerra would show the Empress who was stronger. She'd force the gates of the palace and do what her father had failed to do, what Ealyn hadn't managed, and take her down.

"Kerra!" The voice came from far away, from her childhood. She ignored it. "Kerra!" Louder this time, and insistent: her mum had always been insistent.

Her steps faltered. *Mum?* She turned, seeking through the crowd, and there in the centre – always in the centre – stood Mum, her blonde hair shining under the street-lights, her eyes filled with tears. What was she doing here? She was supposed to be on Ferran. Mum ran, pushing past those around her, until she reached Kerra and pulled her into a hug, so tight it was like she'd never let go.

"You're alive," Mum said. "I thought you were dead."

Kerra tried to pull away. She had a job to do. She had to keep going – to stop would be to face the wrongness inside her.

Her mum stepped back. "Kerra?" She pushed Kerra's hair from her face, as if she was five and just in from the garden. "What's wrong?"

Nothing. Everything. There was no way to explain things, not to someone who hadn't had this sort of power. Kerra turned to go, compelled by the urgency of the mesh, but one part of her wanted to sink into her mum's arms and not leave.

"She's taken the mesh!" shouted Baelan. He was breathing heavily, his face red, but somehow he'd kept up. "And she's gone completely off her head with it."

The little sod. She faced him, furious, and he backed away, fear dancing in his eyes. There was no smug superiority now, no sure knowledge that he had more power than she'd ever had. Baelan was scared. She could see it in his thoughts, as clearly as if he'd spoken it.

"Kerra!" Her mum's voice was sharp, pulling at the part of her that had listened to that voice all her life. "Is it true?" She grabbed Kerra's wrists, holding them tight, and looked closely at her. "Why?"

Why? Couldn't she feel the power?

"It's mine," said Kerra, and her voice sounded surly. It wasn't the right explanation; it didn't even start to explain about the power. Her father would never defeat the Empress himself, but her mum would never understand that; she thought he was some sort of god.

"Your father needs the mesh," said Mum, her voice shocked. "Kerra, he's up there with nothing between him and the Empress. You have to let it go."

She sounded so sure. Mum always sounded sure and, what's more, she was usually right. Kerra looked into her eyes, trying to tell what was true: her mum's words or the driving knowledge within her. She wished she could ask herself, the buried girl, but she'd no idea how to find her.

"I can't." Even the words didn't sound like herself, but older, deeper in tone. She met her mum's eyes, wanting her to know that it wasn't anyone's fault, that it was just the way it was.

"Kerra Varnon," said her mum, as if she was a child, "you give the mesh back to your father now. It's not yours."

It is, it is, it is. The mesh swirled, insistent. *It was meant for you, it's your gift.*

It's not. The voice came from within, faint and barely there. *Laurena.* Kerra nearly sagged at the relief of someone else being in the mesh. She'd been sure she'd broken everything. Laurena spoke again: *You're not the Queen. You're not ready yet.*

That's what she'd told her dad as he was leaving. That she wasn't ready. Something woke inside her, the person who'd been proud of him going to the palace to face the Empress. That Kerra wouldn't leave him in there, powerless. And he was – she'd felt his attempts to take the mesh, had known his terrible fear. The mesh had tried to hide it, and she'd been happy to ignore it, but she couldn't anymore; not when she thought about him leaving Ferran, a plan in place, so brave and ready. A plan she'd ruined. Her breath was coming in gasps.

"Kerra." Her mum wasn't going to let up – she never let up, ever. She crouched down, where she couldn't be ignored. She radiated authority.

"Now," she said.

"She's right, Kerra." Baelan, the little snitch. She could feel him touching the edges of the mesh, seeking to find her. It pushed him back and he stumbled, but came forwards again, reaching for her. She brought her hands up to her ears, closing out her mum, but Laurena was still there, and Baelan, and the mesh, each shouting the old presence down. She didn't know what to do.

"I'll help." Baelan gazed at her, unblinking, his eyes so like their father's. It felt like he could be trusted even though he called the Empress his Lady and wore the ankhar of the tribes. He'd also hunted crabs with her on Syllte. He shared her blood. "What can I do?"

Let it go, said Laurena. *Ealyn never needed the mesh. Your father didn't want it. Don't let it steal you.*

Kerra reached for Baelan, her hands shaking, and he took it. She was scared; scared if she let go she'd never get this back; scared it might hurt. Her mother grabbed her other hand, holding it tightly.

"It's okay," Baelan said. "You'll still have your own

power." He didn't look away, not once. He felt like her real brother. "You'll be a healer again. That's something incredible."

A healer, not someone who would kill people to get her own way.

"I know you'll do the right thing," said Mum, and her voice was soft. "Now send the mesh to your father. He needs it."

He did, too. Kerra could feel him now, a tiny presence, distant and fading. He'd been hurt, he had nothing to use, no way to help himself. It was already too late. She turned all her focus on him and he responded, a touch of his love, a sense of the security he'd always offered. The new Kerra was swept away. She couldn't remember why she'd been keeping the mesh from him.

The mesh fought her. It tried to burrow deeper. It didn't want to lose her, it wanted her in its centre, to give it strength and feed it. She clenched her fists. Her great-grandmother had held the mesh and controlled it, and her father; there had to be a way. But it wasn't the way she'd been doing it.

"How do I let it go?" she yelled. "Laurena, what do I do!?"

"Stop wanting it. Like when you Control – don't force it."

Kerra focused on Laurena. She'd go to her. Slowly, she moved from the centre. It was like fighting through mud. She started to fall, knees buckling, but Baelan and her mother held her up.

"You can do it," Mum said. "You're not just a Varnon, love, you're a le Payne, too. We don't let anything stop us."

Kerra nodded. That was the way of it; keep moving until it ended one way or another. Because she was either coming out of this, or she'd die trying. She concentrated on Laurena, nothing but Laurena, and found her way through the eddies of the mesh, past other Roamers supporting each movement she made away from the centre.

She reached Laurena. The Roamer enveloped Kerra in her own awareness. With a snap, the mesh slipped from where it had sat. It faded into the background. She took a deep breath of the sweet air of Abendau, and another, and opened her eyes. She'd done it. Everything was okay. It was really okay.

Except Dad; he wasn't okay. She could barely feel him. The Empress was alive: the fight was over, and she'd won.

"It's my fault," Kerra said. Baelan hugged her, practically holding her up, and he, at least, seemed to understand.

CHAPTER FORTY-SEVEN

The door slammed behind Lichio and Simone, and the footsteps of their escort faded away. Lichio took a deep breath, collecting himself. The soldiers had taken his jacket, damn them, with his equipment, but there must be something going down in the palace – there'd been no body scan, only a cursory search. He winced; cursory maybe, but it had been thorough enough to find his hidden firearms and a few other surprises as well.

No point panicking until he knew what he was up against. The room was in darkness, but when he felt the wall behind, his hand slipped on cool tiles. Carefully, he tapped his foot on the floor and was rewarded with a gentle knocking noise.

"The cells," he said. *Where else?*

"It would seem so, sir."

"You okay?" he asked.

"Fine." Her voice wasn't as calm as usual. Damn, but he shouldn't have risked her. The only good to come of it was that her cover was blown. She'd have no excuse not to take a nice, comfy desk job when she got out. *If* she got out.

To hell with that. He'd get out – he had to. Kare was in the palace, facing who-knew-what. He went to the cell's door and knelt by the sealed lock. The fools hadn't considered the skills an intelligence chief might have, or the information he might have at his disposal. They'd taken him like a lamb and hadn't considered that in his sullen obedience he might not have used up all his tricks. That even as he'd shifted his hip to let them find his second pistol, it might have been to hide other, more important, things.

He wriggled his fingers. In the past ten years there had been three attempts to break out from the cells – and only one had been even halfway successful. There was no point trying to bore out, or set off alarms and rush the guards who'd come running. Those were inelegant.

He hummed to himself. If there'd been a key-pad, the code Kare had given him – the sneaky bastard, keeping something like that to himself – would have overridden security, but it was on the outside. He ran his hands over the wall until he found the dimpled cover of an access panel.

He pulled off his right boot, lifted the insole, and fiddled for a moment to open a cover over the shallow heel, his fingers feeling too thick for the delicate job. Inside lay a small toolkit, one with a sonic pulsor. He set to working around the panelling – the thin, shell-like cover would allow the pulse to reach the lock mechanism.

It took a few minutes. Simone's breath was soft, tickling the back of his neck as she leaned over to watch. A soft click made him smile, but he touched the door to be sure. It slid under his fingers. Carefully, he pulled his boot back on and got to his feet. Kare mightn't mind prancing around the palace in bare feet; he had somewhat higher standards.

He stopped and felt through his hair, searching for the thicker strand. He snagged it, pulled it out with a slight wince and heard the soft whirl of the mechanism starting. Careful to hold it by the end of the strand, he set his other hand against the door. Standard operating put one soldier directly outside the cell and one at the end of the cell-corridor. He assumed that hadn't changed – common sense dictated that both guards didn't stay where a clever prisoner could grab them.

He ran his finger the length of his thumbnail on his left hand, depressing the implanted chip as he did, and winced as the circuit cut in. No alarms would sound from the cells tonight. He slid the door open.

"What the—?"

He grabbed the soldier, pushed his chin back, and lifted the garrotte. This wasn't going to be pretty. But he needed effective, not pretty. He set the wire against the soldier's skin. The soldier fought, twisting in Lichio's grasp. A soft whirr came from the garrotte and then it cut, the wire scissoring into the skin. Warm blood spurted, covering Lichio's hand. The man kicked and gave a strangled cry, but Lichio held him, head turned away. It was some moments before the kicking stopped and he was able to lay the man down. He wrapped the wire into a coil, replacing it into his shirt pocket, and red blossoms of the dead man's blood spread. He reached for the guard's blaster and unholstered it with hands that barely shook.

He pulled the sleeve of his shirt back, exposing the graft on his arm. A frisson-patch, expensive and top of the range. And as deadly to him as the garotte had been, if he got its application wrong.

"Hey!" The second soldier was approaching. He'd have already called in, but would not know his alarm had been silenced. Lichio ducked into the doorway of his cell and turned his wrist over. He grabbed the edge of the rough patch of skin, and pulled.

The graft came away. He counted down from five, and slammed his hand into the corridor, facing the soldier, depositing the powder it had contained on the wall, allowing extra time for the dry desert air to ignite the powder. A brief flash of light made him cover his eyes; a strangled yell confirmed his estimate.

He stepped out. The man had his weapon up, but his other hand was covering his eyes. Lichio raised his own blaster. He'd told his own people time and time again that no one should be left in the cells without a full body scan. It was shoddy work. He took his time, making sure of his aim, and shot. Especially not an intelligence chief.

The man fell. Even without the alarm, he had little time – the cameras in this corridor were monitored from a guard station above. He stopped at the code-lock for the block and punched Kare's code in. He set off at a run, his hand hitting the beacon on his belt, calling his people in the palace to him.

***

It was over. Kare watched through slitted eyes as the captain of the Empress' guard turned Hickson over. The major gave a low growl and the captain gave him the coup de grace of a single shot to the forehead, before moving on to Hickson's second.

His mother stood by the window, looking over the city, her eyes flashing as if seeking something. Soon, reinforcements would overcome his squad in the anteroom, if they hadn't already. Pain wrenched through him, coming from the wounds in his chest and stomach, from his arm, bent and broken, from his aching head. He tried to look to the side where Kym lay, but the movement brought sharper pain. Instead he concentrated on breathing, taking shallow breaths, noting from a distance how each was weaker than the last. Something bubbled on his lips each time; he thought it might be blood. Good. Perhaps by the time they tried to take him, he'd be dead.

***

Sonly watched as the troops forced their way through the crowd, using batons to quiet the rowdier protestors. Screams sounded. The thuds of aural-flares split the air, sending the crowd reeling back, hands to ears. Gas-shells followed, bringing tears and burning throats. Sirens started, adding to the confusion of the change of tactic from the palace soldiers. A change of tactics that told Sonly everything about what was happening in the palace, and who was winning – Kare would not have ordered this.

Her eyes streamed, but she managed to draw a breath. Kerra, stunned, stood against her. Baelan also had his arm around his sister, saving her from the hard gates of the palace, making Sonly revise her opinion of the boy.

Another barrage of sound and gas came down, and the last of the crowd scattered, leaving the less fortunate to lie like litter along the length of the Grand Boulevard. Only a few stood with her, the core of the protestors.

Sonly faced the palace and its soldiers, refusing to be cowed. She choked back gas-tears but kept her head up. The Empress could defeat her, and Kare; she could claim this day a victory, but she'd never get Sonly to back down from what was right.

A soldier broke away from the fighting on the Grand Boulevard and made to grab her arm, but she pulled it away. "*Don't* touch me."

"You're to be detained," he said.

One holo-recorder was still in place, its operator pale-faced in his defiance, tears washing two rivers of clean skin through grime. Christophe was by her side, jaw tight with fury. His eyes met hers and she couldn't betray his belief in her. She squared her shoulders and tightened her arms around Kerra.

"I wish an audience with the so-called Empress," she said, making sure the holo was capturing her words. "The Senate hold the legal authority in Abendau. I lead the Senate and I expect to be admitted to the palace, the centre of my own government."

The soldier took her arm again, his grip firmer. "You'll accompany me."

"Wow." Baelan's voice was out of place - not stunned, or shocked, but awed. "Look. Above the port."

Dark ships descended from orbit, a fleet of them. Freighters, judging by the line of their lights and their size. They filled the skies.

"They came." Kerra's voice was sluggish. She

tugged Sonly's arms. "I told the Roamers to come for me, and they did."

Sonly smiled – the Roamers, here to claim their own; the Roamers with a fleet of ships big enough to take the skywalk and cut the palace off from the port. Big enough for her to force Abendau to its knees? Possibly. Not hers to command, of course, but who was here to tell the soldiers that?

"Open the gates, or I'll have them attack the palace." She raised her voice, so the holo-recorder would capture her words. She hoped it was broadcasting live – she doubted the footage would survive the day if her bluff didn't work. "I am the elected representative of Abendau; I am" —was, but what hadn't been officially released didn't count— "the leader of the Free Republic, the legal galactic entity." She faced the recorder. "The people of Abendau voted me to lead them. They know your mistress cares nothing for her people."

She waited, breath held, and stared at the captain, daring him to arrest her. If he did, she'd make sure it was worth it. The holo-recorder remained, the Roamers held their position, the remaining crowd didn't disperse, and still the moment drew out and the guard didn't give way.

***

Karlyn! The voice came to Kare from far away, through the mesh's familiar hive. Farran. He'd said he'd stay in orbit. *Karlyn, take the mesh.*

He tried, reaching, but it was too far away, too hard for him to grasp. His eyes closed. It was too late, as well. The fight was over, his mother had won. She had Lichio, and Sonly. She knew where the kids were. He'd lost everything, and taking the mesh wouldn't change anything. He'd gambled and failed.

Take it. The mesh started to fill him one last time and he didn't fight against it. He was done fighting; let what would be, be. He'd die King of the Roamers. At least he'd end things as his father's son and not his mother's.

He reached out with his good arm, his hand crabbing until he found Kym. He wouldn't die alone, and neither should she. He tried to pat her, to comfort her, but she didn't respond. He thought she might be dead. She'd said she didn't miss, and she had. Or maybe his mother had cheated.

It didn't matter. He closed his eyes, exhausted. The mesh settled within him. He could still feel Kerra's shape in it, the sense of her powers, not his, and that comforted him. He supposed when he died it would go back to her.

It had been destroying her. The mesh was greedy. He knew that from holding it - it had sucked at him, always asking him to take more of it. His grandmother, when he'd met her at the end of her days, had been a husk given entirely to the mesh. She'd given up a son for it.

Kerra was too young to take it; she'd never keep it in its place. And the boy needed guidance from someone who understood him. With a groan, Kare opened his eyes. He looked at Kym. He was sorry - he'd lost her Silom. Now he'd taken her life.

Except he hadn't. She grew stronger under his hand. Her eyes opened. Her hand tightened on her rifle. She tried to say something, but the words didn't come. He patted her, clumsily. He knew. She never missed.

He made himself move. His arm, broken and useless, jarred and he bit back a scream. Beck had made him get to his feet with a broken ankle. He'd beaten him senseless and forced him back up to be beaten again. If the Empress thought pain would finish him, she hadn't understood the lesson she'd taught. He got to his knees and took every bit of the Roamer power, full of Kerra's healing skills, and focused it on Kym. He held his good arm out for her, keeping it strong and straight as she gripped it and levered onto her knees.

The Empress sensed them. Kare straightened to his feet, sweat breaking, and pulled Kym with him. He braced, ready for the Empress' onslaught. Bodies lay around him: his squad, dead at his feet.

The Empress hit out, hard. She wasn't tired. He stumbled, and threatened to pull Kym with him, but she twisted free. Another hit from his mother sent him onto one knee. He sucked at the mesh, pulling Kerra's power.

"My empire," said the Empress, a parody of his words a decade ago. "My people. Nothing has changed."

The sound of yelling came from the corridor. The Empress turned her head to it, distracted, and Kare drew his thoughts together. He pulled himself to his feet, using the wall for support, and faced his mother.

The door burst open. Lichio was there, a plasma-rifle in hand. He took down the first of the guards, and yelled, "Someone do something about that bitch!"

A squad followed him, some from Kare's palace guard. They opened fire on the Empress' soldiers, driving them back. The Empress tried to move against them but Kare blocked her, holding on grimly.

"Do it," he told Kym. "I can't hold on long."

She took aim. "Gladly. And this time I won't fucking miss."

The shot echoed. His mother reeled back, into the frame of the empty bay window. Another shot. Kym charged the plasma-chamber, a small smile in place, and fired again, sending the Empress hard against the sill. She yelled, teetering, arms wheeling, but steadied herself.

To hell with this. Kare sent everything he had ripping across the room, hitting her square-on. She crashed backwards, over the sill and through the open window. She dropped, her screams whipping through the air.

She tried to pull her power around her. He drained the Roamer mesh, refusing to let her; as long as she was dead, he had nothing else to achieve. The room went dark around him, he was swaying, and someone – Lichio, he thought – grabbed his elbow, keeping him upright. He felt his mother's fear, felt her hatred of him. He felt the pain that took her as she hit the ground, the agony that shot through her as she died.

Her presence left and he fell to his knees, too shattered to stand, in too much pain to care, and everything went dark.

CHAPTER FORTY-EIGHT

Sonly's eyes tracked up the wall to the huge window she knew so well, the Empress' chambers. Gunfire came from it. A figure was silhouetted in the window and her throat closed, tight with fear. She needed her diversion to have worked, to have given Kare the opportunity to blindside the Empress. She needed to get past the palace guard, inside, and see what had happened.

A shriek filled the air. The figure at the window fell, tumbling limbs and a long scream.

Kerra grabbed her arm. "Dad...?" Her voice carried more than fear: a cold certainty.

"It's not." Baelan, at the other side of Sonly, sounded sure. "Look."

The shriek was long and high-pitched. The figure fell, a flash against white walls. Two of the gate guards ran towards the palace. A sick thud came, and a soft *ooh* from the crowd. Kerra buried her face against Sonly. Behind her, Baelan muttered, "By my Lady," and it was hard to tell if he was sorry or glad.

"Let me through," Sonly said, pushing at the gates. Baelan gave her a quick grin and touched the gate, and it swung to. She could warm to him, she decided.

She started to run. She should be glad the Empress was dead, but took no satisfaction in it. She'd take no pleasure in anything until she knew Kare was alive. She reached the entrance to the palace and slowed at the sight of more soldiers.

"Let me into my palace," she said. She drew herself up to her full height – not impressive, admittedly, but it made her feel better. "Now."

They did, stepping aside, their leadership unclear.

She pushed past them and ran up the main staircase, heading for the heart of the palace.

***

Kerra turned to Baelan. "It's too late, isn't it?" She should go with her mum, but she didn't know how she would face her when she reached her father, knowing that she'd done it to him, taken the mesh and all his hope.

He frowned, staring up at the palace. "I can't feel him. Can you?"

"A little." Her father *was* there, but it was only the smallest pulse. He'd drained the mesh, as she'd known he would, and now he had nothing to pull on, nothing to help him. She focused on him, sending what power she had, but it was too small.

She turned to Baelan. "Come on." She didn't have enough power on her own, but between them they might. "We need to help him."

"I can't." Baelan looked at the ground. She didn't think she'd ever seen anyone look sadder. "I swore to my people I'd kill him."

She took a step back. "But he came for you. He stood by you." The flicker at the back of her mind was going. "Please, help him."

Baelan looked older than the boy who'd left the palace with them, shivering and shocked, as if he'd grown during their escape. Shadows from the palace gates criss-crossed his face, dark and light, making his expression impossible to read. But he didn't move.

Disgusted, she turned away. She ran along the driveway to the palace.

"Kerra." The sound of metal clattering on stone made her stop and turn. Baelan stood. At his feet lay his ankhar. His fists were clenched, as if fighting something, but he stepped towards her. "Let's go."

***

Lichio dropped to the ground beside Kare. He lifted his wrist and found a weak pulse.

"Kare," he pleaded. "Can you hear me?"

Nothing. Once, Kare could have recovered from this, but the power he must have expended to carry him and Kym through those last minutes would have left the mesh empty. His eyes fluttered and he murmured something that might have been *Lich*, but then lay still, his chest barely moving.

Something ran down Lichio's cheek, surprising him. He squeezed his eyes shut, clearing the blurred room from his vision, but it made no difference; still the tears fell. He sat, surrounded by the mess of battle, oblivious to the squad watching him, and held his friend. At least Kare would have someone he knew. That, at least, had to be something.

He heard the clatter of footsteps from the anteroom, and Sonly's thin voice asking where Kare was. She came through the door at a run, her face streaked with tears, breathing hard; she must have run through the whole palace. She stopped, and he imagined what she was taking in: the amount of blood, Kym Woods slumped, blood dripping through her fingers; the unmoving Kare.

"Lich...?" Her voice was dull. She knew. He gave the tiniest shake of his head.

She dropped to his side and took Kare's hand. It lay, pale and still, in hers. She reached for Kare, took him from Lichio's arms and held him against her. Her long, low sound of sorrow filled the room, and he was transported back a decade to another death in the palace, to another friend bleeding out after an attack by the Empress.

***

"Stop!" said Kerra. The Empress' rooms were at the very top of the palace – they didn't have time to reach their father. "Can you feel it?"

The mesh was coming back. It circled her, seeking

her to take it, but she shook her head. It was her dad's. Taking it would mean he was dead.

"Fight it; stay with us," she whispered, sending the mesh to where his presence had been. "I'm not taking it. Fight. You can do it."

The mesh remained within her. She squeezed her eyes shut, searching, searching for the last spark that was her father, but it was weak, just at the edge of the mesh, fading away. She grasped it, gave all her strength, but still it faded.

"No," she whispered. This couldn't be happening, there had to be something she could do.

"Fight." Kerra focused on the wound, focused on closing it. It was hard, it took so much effort. She glanced at Baelan. "Hold my hand. Give up your power."

He could make the difference. He was the strongest of them all. But he didn't understand the mesh, or what to do. He took her hand. Her father was still there, the smallest of a million pricks of light. She dived back into the mesh, ignoring its demands, carrying Baelan with her, and focused everything she had on their father.

***

"Kare. Stay with me." Sonly's voice was harsh, demanding, undeniable. Kare tried to tell her to give him a minute, that it hurt, but he couldn't hear his voice. His eyes wouldn't open, either.

"Come on, you've made it this far." Lichio, even further away. Too far away to be reached. A distant squeeze on his hand and Lichio went on, "You've made it. Now live to enjoy it. You should have died years ago. Don't do it now."

Yes. He should have died on the ship with Karia, not stood and watched, safe on the planet below. He should have been with her. He could sense her beside him, and his father, their presence strong. He'd missed her. She held her hand out and he tried to lift his own to take it, but it was heavy, too heavy, and someone was holding it and not letting him go. He sagged back.

"Kare, please!" The voice was from another world. Sonly would have to find her way to him later; he couldn't get back to her now.

Karia raised her hand to her mouth, a smile dancing. His father was behind her, in his familiar pilot's suit, hair falling over his eyes.

"Not yet, son," he said. "We don't need you yet." His hand tightened on Karia's shoulder. "Do we?"

She shook her head. She had a light cradled in her hand, a tiny one. She blew on it, her lips pursing into a secret smile. It drifted across the space between them, staying small, taking its time.

He'd taken a light from Karia once before, he remembered. All it had done was bring him more pain. He wanted to refuse it, but his father took a step forwards. He smiled, a smile Kare remembered well.

"Go back, son. It won't be the same this time." His father had never come to him, in all the years since he'd been lost. "Trust me." He'd always known what lay ahead. He vanished, and Kare lay, his breaths shallow, sharp pain growing with each.

He looked at the light. It grew and he recognised it: the mesh, seeking to heal him, to give him strength. He drew in a harsh breath. Gods, he hurt everywhere. Someone - his father, he thought - held him.

Slowly he opened his eyes and saw it wasn't his father, or Karia. They were gone, replaced by Lichio, his face pale, and Sonly. He felt son and daughter's presence holding him. He took another breath, deeper, embracing the pain. He chose to live.

EPILOGUE

The chamber echoed with the endless sound of waves. The incense hadn't quite faded, making the sense of place as strong now as it ever had been. Kare sat on the edge of the bed, remembering the first day he'd come here, how he'd taken his grandmother's hands in his and discovered he was more than the Empress' son. It had been the day he'd realised there was a different future, one that didn't force him to continue an empire he hated. The day he'd been freed.

Except he wasn't the King the Roamers needed. He had no power of his own. He didn't Control. He was nothing but a shell for them to fill, where his grandmother had been the living centre of them. Regardless, he was the King they had for now. Kerra had been so shaken when she'd left Abendau. It had taken weeks to get to the point where she'd talk about what had happened, and longer to start to put it behind her. Perhaps one day she would inherit the mesh – she appeared Ealyn's heir more than he'd ever been. At his death, at the very least – and he still had more enemies than he cared to think about. She had to be ready for it and understand how to control it. More than that, she had to want it.

And Baelan? He'd never be happy in this chamber – he didn't understand the Roamers. He was of the tribes, of Belaudii. That's where he belonged, once he learned to control his power and found his way back to the boy he might have been without being twisted to Phelps' agenda.

Kare looked at the ceiling, at the hook for the prism, at the light reflected from the ocean. "All right," he said. "I accept."

For now. For as long as he was needed. The mesh pulsed its acknowledgement. He stepped out of the room and down the corridor, his boots clicking against the stone floor. He wouldn't be back here, not for a long time. Or on Belaudii. He needed his own place, not one forced on him. He needed time to find out who Kare Varnon really was.

He reached the main cavern, where Farran waited. He crossed to the ship, touching hands with the Roamers who lined the port. Once on board, he paused at the top of the gangway. Familiar voices carried along the ship's access-way, half-raised in argument: the le Paynes, fighting over some political point only they cared about.

He smiled, and ducked into the main cabin. Lichio stood, talking with Sonly. Josef watched with his dark eyes and his quiet way of taking everything in. He acknowledged Kare with a quickly raised eyebrow.

"Well, you're the president. I'll leave you to decide," said Lichio. "We're taking a ship to Mersor."

They left, Sonly taking a last hug from her brother – and giving one to the slightly bemused Josef. Kare sank onto the couch and patted it. She came over. She was wearing the blue he liked. It made her eyes shine.

"So," he said. "Where to, Lady President?" He stretched; he felt weightless, like he could touch the sky if he wanted. "I have nothing pressing to do."

"You'll get bored."

She knew him too well. He looked down at his hands. "The role – the outer zone development minister?"

"You're going to take it?"

He paused, remembering a dead girl from years ago, lying under a poisoned sky. The outer zone had so many half-terraformed planets. There were accidents all the time – domes breaking from age, colonies wiped out and never missed. Without the money of the richer systems, everything was run on a budget, and that budget was costing lives. It had been for years.

"I thought I might. I can base myself on Ferran and travel as needed." Space travel, after all, had once been his life. "My name might bring in some additional funding." It was nice to have the shoe on the other foot. "In fact, I thought I might tap your budget for some of it. You owe me a few social projects."

Baelan could stay with him; he'd teach him as his own father had taught him. Shanisa, too, already with Baelan and eying Kare warily each time they met. And Kerra – travelling would give her a chance to learn the Control she'd lost, and give her some freedom from Sonly's world of expectation.

"We'll see." Her comms unit buzzed and she left, answering it as she did. He leaned his head back and closed his eyes, relishing the quiet. He could feel his father and Karia with him, he was sure of it. He'd done it for all of them – killed his mother and destroyed her empire. Let it be enough. Let him pass into a future he'd never seen but wanted to embrace.

THE END

Printed in Great Britain
by Amazon